INTRODU

The Rescue by Kathleen Y'Barbo
With less than two months to go u~~ntil the challenge,~~ the last person Adam needs to cozy up to is the one woman he'd been willing to risk his stake in the Bachelor Club fund to marry. Actress Amy Foreman is in trouble, and no Hollywood blockbuster can save her this time. Will Adam's penchant for rescuing lost strays put an end to his membership in the Bachelor Club?

Stealing Home by Rhonda Gibson
Will Lovelace is determined to complete the Bachelor Club pledge. Broken hearts of the past lead him to leave the dating game. He figures the baseball field offers a safe haven from all things feminine until he meets Joey Diner and his sister, Charisma. Will soon has to ask himself if he wants to remain in the Bachelor Club or steal home in Charisma Diner's heart.

Right for Each Other by Bev Huston
For cartoonist Isaac Brooks, being afraid to leave his home is no laughing matter. Until recently, it was something he felt he could live with. But when he meets a pretty British game show hostess, Isaac struggles with his growing attraction and the need to deal with his problem. Will he be able to overcome his fears in time to win her heart or will she return to England never to see him again?

Joyful Noise by Janet Spaeth
Joseph Montoya has no musical ability, but when Rosa Cruz fills in as the choir director at Blessed Family Church, he finds his heart filling with song. Impulsively he signs up for voice lessons from her. He tries—unsuccessfully—to hide his lack of talent, while she worries about his role in the upcoming recital. How can he possibly perform? As a teacher—and a Christian—she knows what she should do, but love has entered the picture. . . .

The Bachelor Club

ISBN 1-59310-558-4

Cover image © Thinkstock

Illustrations by Mari Goering

Published by Barbour Publishing, Inc., P.O. Box 719, Uhrichsville, Ohio 44683, www.barbourbooks.com

Our mission is to publish and distribute inspirational products offering exceptional value and biblical encouragement to the masses.

 Member of the
Evangelical Christian
Publishers Association

Printed in the United States of America.
5 4 3 2 1

The Bachelor Club

A Childhood Game Sets the Tone for Four Romantic Novellas

Rhonda Gibson

Bev Huston

Janet Spaeth

Kathleen Y'Barbo

BARBOUR
PUBLISHING

Prologue

by Rhonda Gibson

Dedication

To the memory of Willard McConnell,
my dad and own
Mr. Fix-It.

Prologue

"Ask him."

Willard Lovelace looked up from the toaster he was working on. "What can I do for you boys?" His features softened when he saw the determined look on his six-year-old son's face.

Little Will tossed a baseball from one hand to the other gloved hand. "Dad, would you do something for us?"

Willard set the toaster to the side. "Depends on what you fellows want me to do. I'm not good at robbing banks or lying to mamas," he teased them.

Each boy stretched up to his tallest height and puffed out his chest. Their young eyes snapped with excitement.

"This is not funny, Mr. Lovelace. We're serious," Joseph Montoya announced for the group.

Willard forced himself not to smile at Joseph. The boy was very mature for his seven years, or at least he liked to act like it. Willard's gaze surveyed the other boys. Isaac Brooks stood beside Joseph. Isaac was the prankster of the group. He held a worn joke book in his hands, and a smile brightened his face.

Then there was seven-year-old Adam, the animal lover of the group. His mother always complained that Adam brought home every stray he found. The boy hung on to a kitten at the moment. Since Adam's mother was Willard's sister, Willard heard about it all the time. Last was little Will. He was actually Willard Junior, but everyone had taken to calling him Will. Little Will's full bottom lip was clenched between his teeth again. A sure sign the six-year-old wasn't too happy about this meeting. Will slapped the ball into the glove once more.

"I see. Sit down, boys, and we'll talk about this." Willard motioned for them to take a seat on the grass in front of him. He watched as each of them wiggled around to face him.

When they were settled, he asked, "Okay, what is this something you want me to do?"

Joseph nudged Will with his elbow.

Will frowned at his friend and then proceeded. "We want to start a club," he blurted.

Willard rubbed his chin as if in deep thought. "I see. What kind of club did you have in mind?"

Again, Joseph elbowed Will.

"We don't like girls, so we decided we want to start a club for guys who won't never get married," Will answered while frowning at Joseph.

It was all Willard could do not to laugh, but the serious nods from the boys kept him from doing so. "I don't know. Never's a long time! Don't you want little boys of your own someday?" he asked.

The children looked at each other.

Adam was the first to answer. "I do." He stroked the small

yellow kitten. The little fur ball tried to get loose.

Both Will and Isaac answered at the same time, "Me, too."

Joseph relented. "Okay, we can get married someday but not until we're real old." He scrunched up his face for a moment and then added, "Like thirty."

The other three boys nodded.

"I still don't know what I can do to help," Willard said, feeling old himself. To the boys he must seem ancient since he was thirty-five.

Joseph looked at Will meaningfully. Will moved out of range and continued playing with the ball and glove.

"We need someone to take care of our money," Joseph finally said after several failed attempts to get Will to talk.

"I'm confused." Willard tried to sort it all out but decided that six- and seven-year-old boys were a puzzle he didn't have all the pieces to. "Joseph, you seem to know what's going on. Why don't you just tell me the whole thing?"

Joseph stood up and squared his small shoulders. He spoke with an air of importance. "Well, it's like this. The club rule says we can't get married 'til we're thirty. And we gotta give you our allowance to be in the club. You know, kinda like dues for Boy Scouts 'cept we get it back when we get old. You can keep it for us 'til then." He searched Willard's face to see if he was following along.

When Willard nodded, Joseph continued. "We said if somebody broke the rule, he didn't get no money back." Joseph dropped back to the ground.

"I see." Willard rubbed his chin. "All of you agreed to this?"

Each boy nodded. Willard noticed that Will was the last to

consent. He chewed his lip with a fury as the ball flew from one hand to the other. "Will, is this what you really want to do?" he asked in what he hoped was his gentle parent voice.

"Except the part about losing all my money." Will moved even farther from Joseph.

"I have to agree with Will. When you get older, you'll get jobs and houses and you're going to need some of your money to live on. What do you think of only giving up half your allowance? Would that be better?" He watched as the boys all huddled close together. Even Will moved back into their circle.

Willard really didn't think the boys would play this game for long. They'd want their money back in a few days, and it would all be over. But he wanted to let them make decisions for themselves and see what became of this newest venture. He picked up the toaster and continued working on it while they talked.

"We think that's a good idea, Mr. Lovelace," Joseph finally announced.

"Have you boys thought of a name for your club?" Willard heard the screw click into place and set the screwdriver down.

"How about the We Hate Girls Club?" Joseph asked.

Willard rubbed his chin. "I don't know. What if the girls heard it and it made them cry?"

Isaac's head shot up. "That wouldn't be nice." Sure he had their attention, he added with a grin, "Knock, knock."

Will threw his ball glove at Isaac, and the other boys groaned.

"No, I don't think so, either," Willard agreed, ignoring Isaac's attempt to tell the knock, knock joke.

"How about the Never Get Married Club?" Will offered. He caught the ball glove Isaac threw back at him.

Joseph answered, "No, we can get married when we're old, remember?"

Willard waited several more minutes while the boys tossed out and rejected one name after the other. Finally he'd had enough. He really needed to get back inside the shop and get another appliance to work on.

"Boys?"

They all looked back up at him.

"What do you think of calling it the Bachelor Club?" Willard waited, wondering which of them would ask him what *bachelor* meant.

It was Will.

He smiled at his son. "A bachelor is a man who isn't married."

The boys all smiled their agreement.

"Well, if that's all. . ." Willard stood to go back inside the Mr. Fix-It Shop.

Joseph jumped to his feet. "Wait. You have to take our money."

Willard accepted the sock full of coins. "Don't you want to take some of this back? You're only giving half, remember?"

Isaac, Will, and Adam stood up, too.

Adam answered for them all. "We already spent most of our allowance, so that's okay." He set the kitten on the ground and watched with a smile as it scampered away.

Willard rolled the top of the sock up and stuck it in his pocket. "Okay, boys. I guess that takes care of everything."

Once more Joseph stopped him. "Don't forget: Don't give

the money back until we're thirty, okay?"

"Okay, I won't forget." Willard turned to enter his store.

The boys started to walk away. "Hey, guys, how do you make a tissue dance?" Isaac asked. When the others ignored him, he answered himself. "You put a little boogie in it." The boys groaned.

Willard laughed. He set the toaster on the counter, his thoughts on the boys. They sure were cute, but he'd give it a week and they'd be back asking for their money.

The Rescue

by Kathleen Y'Barbo

Dedication

This one's for my sisters: to Sue Ellen,
whose love and patience rescued me more than once,
and to Robin, who is still taking in strays and loving me.
"Thank you" doesn't cover it. I love you forever and a day.

The righteous cry, and the LORD heareth,
and delivereth them out of all their troubles.
PSALM 34:17 KJV

Chapter 1

Adam Chambers backed into the kitchen and set his coffee cup on the counter, never once taking his eyes off the female trespasser on his deck. At least she sat with her back to him, buying him some time to think.

Zeke nuzzled his hand. Adam reached absently for the black Lab's morning treat and tossed it to the other side of the kitchen. He did the same for Rufus, the aging, deaf springer spaniel who pranced in circles around his more sedate counterpart. For good measure, he threw several more into the hall beyond them. Neither dog needed to catch sight of the visitor. The last thing he wanted was to let the noisy canines announce his presence before he figured out what to do.

What to say.

Whether to say anything at all or just head for the hills.

He drummed his fingers on the tile and watched her shift positions. Honey blond hair, gathered into a ponytail and caught up with a simple white ribbon, framed a face whose features he could recite from memory. Brows a shade darker than her hair, eyes the color of a gray winter's sky, and a nose so straight you'd never know it had been broken in junior high at the last basketball game of the year when she'd dropped her pom-pom and. . .

He shook off the stupid memory and reached for his coffee. *Think, Chambers. Think!*

Lifting the cup to his lips, Adam took a sip and let the strong brew slide down his throat before he realized he hadn't added his customary three spoonfuls of sugar. He made a grab for the spoon and stabbed it into the sugar bowl. Where had things gone wrong?

The day had started just like any other. He rolled past each detail of his comfortable routine in his mind: Every morning, he awoke at precisely four forty-five and had his half hour of one-on-one time with the Lord. At a quarter past five, he threw on his shorts, sweatshirt, and sneakers to run the three-mile perimeter of his property with his dogs then poured a cup of black coffee and went to sit on his eastward-facing deck to watch the sun rise over the pines. By seven on the dot, he'd showered, shaved, and begun the three-mile drive to town. The only variation to his day came on Sundays, when he would turn his well-loved Ford pickup toward Tierra Verde's Blessed Family Church on Main instead of his clinic at Park and Elm.

This morning, the first day of October, the alarm sounded as usual, the Bible's words touched him as they always did, the air felt crisp with the promise of an early winter, his run was invigorating, and the coffee tasted fine as he'd headed for the deck. Unfortunately, that is where his familiar routine fell apart, for right there in *his* rocker, the very one he'd sat in until the outline of his posterior could be seen in the sagging seat, sat a woman.

And this wasn't just any woman. No, of all the females who'd ever arrived at his doorstep—not that the number was high, by any means—this one was the least welcome of all.

Why, after all these years, would Amy Foreman plant herself in *his* rocker on *his* porch? Better yet, why was the woman of his dreams—lately the female of his nightmares as she seemed to be smiling back at him from every movie billboard, television show, and women's magazine in existence—sitting here at all? Shouldn't she be in Malibu deciding which script to turn into her next blockbuster hit? After all, it was practically the middle of the night back in her state of choice.

With the first rays of light sliding over purple mountains to peek through the pines, Adam watched Amy take in the view. She snuggled into the oversized hooded sweatshirt, tucked over knees bent to her chest, and Adam realized she must be freezing. From what he recalled from world geography class, California never quite reached the depths of temperature that an early fall here reached.

How'd she get here? He'd certainly seen no unusual vehicles on his run around the property, although had she driven, her car probably sat outside the locked gate. Parked along the road, it would have been hidden by the stand of pines and underbrush that shielded his home from the street.

He checked his watch. Half past six. She must have slept there. No wonder she looked cold. A gentleman would ask her inside, offer her a cup of coffee, maybe even build a fire and offer to let her warm up before she went on her way—and she would definitely be on her way just as quickly as she'd arrived.

Adam heaved a sigh and took another sip. No, there would be no worries of having Amy Foreman wear out her welcome. She had a track record of leaving even when he begged her not to.

You should thank her for that, you know.

Placing the cup on the counter, Adam crossed his arms over his chest and watched a breeze kick up the end of Amy's pony-tail. Thank her? He'd never thought of things quite that way.

Somehow he'd never managed to convince himself that Amy had done him a favor by choosing Hollywood over a quiet life as the wife of a veterinarian, even though his buddies had tried. After all, they reminded him regularly that she'd practically assured him certain victory in gaining his part of the sum that had grown under Uncle Willard's supervision since childhood.

What his friends couldn't know is that she'd all but assured his permanent membership in the Bachelor Club since not a single woman alive could compare to Amy Foreman. He paused to chuckle. Hadn't Oprah said as much the last time Amy had been interviewed on her show?

The subject of his thoughts snuggled deeper into the dark blue sweatshirt and adjusted the hood so that all Adam could see was the top of her head. Another niggling stab of guilt almost sent him outside with a blanket and a smile, but something stopped him. Was it the money? No, while the sum wasn't any-thing to sneeze at, he certainly managed nicely as the owner of the only veterinary practice in town.

It was the principle of the thing. Yes, that's it. He'd waited this long, gone along with the terms of the club for more than two decades. Why jeopardize his membership now with the end so close in sight?

That's it. You're no quitter, Chambers. You can't possibly take a chance on losing what you've come so close to winning.

Indeed, with less than two months to go until his thirtieth birthday on New Year's Day, the last person he needed to cozy up to was the one woman he'd ever been willing to risk his stake in the Bachelor Club fund to marry. And yet, there she sat.

Rufus saw her initially, although Zeke was the first one to bark. Before Adam could step away from the door and quiet the dogs, she turned around and spied him.

He froze.

She smiled.

Later she would probably wonder why she smiled, or rather how she managed it, given the direction her thoughts had turned in those cold hours before the dawn and Adam Chambers arrived. The insincere smile, she decided, was a habit gleaned long ago from one too many boring Hollywood premieres or perhaps learned earlier as a girl who wanted everyone to think life was perfect in her little corner of the world. No matter how you felt, whatever the situation, you plastered on a smile and waited for the cameras to flash.

When had her life been reduced to *this*? Worse, when had she decided *this* was her life?

People in Hollywood smiled because it was expected of

them. Here, in Tierra Verde, they smiled because they meant it.

So why wasn't Adam smiling? Hadn't he wished her well the day she left? Surely he'd forgotten all about their near miss with the altar by now. No matter that Amy hadn't been able to accomplish the feat.

"What are you doing here?"

The same words, expressed by someone else, might have sounded harsh and unwelcoming, but Adam spoke them with something akin to wonder. She realized her artificial smile had been replaced with a real one.

Welcome home, Amy Foreman.

"Hi, Adam."

Not the great soliloquy of introduction she'd planned in the wee hours of the morning, but a good beginning, nonetheless. She tried to rise but found her legs stiff and uncooperative. Leaning forward in the rocker to massage her calves, Amy let her attention wander back to Adam.

He wore gray shorts, running shoes, and a green sweatshirt with his alma mater, Colorado State, emblazoned on the front in block letters. He also wore a frown. As Adam leaned against the door with his arms crossed over his chest, Amy searched for traces of the old Adam, the love of her life she so stupidly left behind.

Somewhere under the frown and matching furrowed eyebrows was the man who could always make her laugh and whose memory always made her cry. Today, however, he'd buried that man under layers of irritation, or so it seemed.

A mismatched pair of dogs complained at the door, and he took a step forward to release the latch and allow the screen to fly open. The animals, one a sleek black Lab and the other a fluffy black and white springer spaniel, made a beeline for her. The Lab stuck a warm but wet nose in Amy's hand while the springer danced around her and barked. Amy tried in vain to pet them both, but the springer's hyperactive pacing wouldn't allow it.

Adam retrieved a stick from the deck and threw it into the shadowy trees. The yelping pair took off in pursuit, leaving Amy to wipe her hands on her sweatshirt. She took a deep breath of fresh air, scented with nothing more than pine and the slight tinge of acrid smoke from someone's fireplace.

Fall in New Mexico. She'd almost forgotten how it felt.

"What are you doing here?" This time the words held less wonder and more worry.

She swung her gaze to meet his. "I suppose that's a fair question." *But how to answer it?* Nothing but the truth would do. Still, there had to be a way of phrasing the truth where all of it didn't come spilling out at once.

"I came to see you," she finally said.

Her answer seemed to take all the fire out of him. Rather than lean, he now stood and then began to pace, finally stopping to place both hands on the deck rail and stare across the pines to the purple mountains beyond.

"Why now, Amy?" He turned to face her, eyes narrowed. "Why'd you have to show up now?"

Another opportunity to tell the whole truth; another chance to parcel it out in pieces. "I've been asking myself the same question all morning."

One of the dogs barked off in the distance, a temporary

distraction at best. Too soon, silence fell between them, rising thick as the morning fog clinging to the ground beyond the deck.

Clearing his throat, Adam shook his head then ran both hands through his close-cropped dark hair. "You got any answers to go with that question?"

She'd freeze before she could finish a story as long as the one that led her to Adam's front door—or rather to his deck—but pride kept her from saying so. Instead, she gathered the borrowed sweatshirt around her middle and stuffed her fists into the warmth of its pockets.

The Lord got me this far. He'll do the rest.

"Why don't I start at the beginning, then?"

Adam checked his watch and exhaled a long breath. "How long's this going to take?"

"Awhile," she answered. "Depends on whether you want the whole story or just the abbreviated version."

"I have a morning of surgery ahead of me, starting in less than an hour. Give me whatever version gets me to the clinic on time."

"All right."

This time when she attempted to rise, her legs obliged. She squared her shoulders and prepared for the biggest performance of her career. With more preparation, she might have pulled off a much grander performance. Instead, she winged it.

"Adam, I need a job."

Chapter 2

A job?" Adam shook his head. "Are you kidding me? You came all the way up here, stole my favorite chair, and ruined my morning just to ask me to help you get some movie part? Since when do *you* play veterinarians?"

This was *not* going as she had planned. Time to clarify, to explain her predicament in such a way that the kinder, gentler Adam she remembered would see he was her only hope.

"No, Adam." If only he weren't looking at her like that. "See, what I need is to—"

"To what, Amy?" Adam took a step forward and stuffed his hands into the pockets of his shorts. "What is it you *need* from me after almost five years of total silence?" He paused. "And remember, you promised to give me the *short* version."

She gathered herself up to her full height and squared her shoulders. A girl couldn't make it in the movies without learning how to take care of herself. Adam Chambers might look intimidating at this moment, but Amy had stood toe-to-toe with some real heavy hitters in Hollywood and come out the winner.

What was one New Mexico veterinarian compared to that?

Again she braved a look directly into his eyes. She gulped. Who was she kidding?

Amy sank back into the rocker and stared at the brilliant oranges and purples of the October sunrise without interest. "I need a job. That's the short version." She looked up at him and waited for some sign of what was going on inside his head then added, "Please."

To her surprise, he sank down beside her and stretched his long legs out in front of him. "*Is* this about a movie?"

Another tempting opportunity to spill her guts. Doing so might make her feel better, but she dare not implicate Adam in a mess he had no hand in creating.

"Actually it's about more than just a movie," she said carefully. *There. Enough of the truth to keep things honest and shield Adam from the fray.*

He seemed to be considering her request. Amy's hope took flight. If she could just lie low awhile, perhaps the Lord or the authorities in California would intervene and the nightmare that had become her life would be over. In the meantime, all she could do was pray that Adam Chambers would give her the chance she didn't really deserve.

Adam rose and called his dogs. She watched the playful pair race toward the deck then turned to stare at their owner.

"I know you didn't want me to leave, Adam," she said softly. "Please don't hold that against me now. I *really* need this job."

His laugh rang hollow. "*You* need a job? You, the next Grace Kelly? Oh, that's funny."

Amy cringed at the reference. Some reporter for a British

tabloid coined the phrase in Cannes last year, and the American press had jumped on the comparison. Oprah did an entire show on the premise, even polling the audience to ask which Grace Kelly movie should be remade with Amy as its star.

Thanks to Oprah, talk of several remakes of Kelly's classic films with her in the lead had begun to make the columns in *Variety*. Script treatments were rumored to be in the works at several studios. Amy sighed. She'd never get a chance to play the sheriff's new bride in *High Noon* now.

Not after what Ed did. Her heart jolted at the thought of her business manager. How could she have been so stupid?

"No."

"What?" Amy looked up to see Adam's broad back disappear inside the house. The dogs were gone as well, leaving her in the same state she'd started—cold and alone.

No? She climbed to her feet and leaned against the rail to steady herself. Had he really said no?

"Hey! Come back here, Adam!"

Before she realized what she'd done, Amy found herself standing in a rather austere yet homey kitchen—a man's kitchen—heavy on the wood and tile and totally devoid of anything the least bit feminine. A lone picture decorated the counter beside the phone—a colorful photograph of snow-peaked mountains in winter. Dwarfed by the mountains were four men dressed in hiking attire and surrounded by a coterie of dogs and camping equipment. They all wore smiles—and familiar faces.

The Bachelor Club.

The sound of a door slamming in a distant part of the

house echoed around her. "Adam?"

She headed toward the sound, but running water stopped her in her tracks and silenced any further attempts at conversation. Backtracking to the kitchen, she found the dogs sharing the mat beside the back door.

Amy leaned against the tile counter and shook her head. The Lab ambled over to stick his cold nose in her hand, and she knelt to pet him. As the spaniel danced in circles around her, the Lab rolled onto his back and offered his belly.

At least someone in this house was glad to see her—not that she blamed Adam in the least. It was her ambition that led her away from Adam and from Tierra Verde, but it was her foolish pride that kept her gone.

Pride that prevented her from calling Adam when he didn't call her.

Pride again when she begged the Lord to send Adam to her.

Pride and worse, disobedience, when she ignored His leading to go to Adam.

What a mess she'd created with her stubborn pride.

The Lab whimpered and touched her hand with his oversized paw, indicating she'd been lax in her attention. "I have all the time in the world," she whispered. "Which one of you wants to hear my sad tale?"

The springer stopped his dancing and inched toward her, nudging the hand that scratched his canine companion. "All right," she said, "I'll tell both of you, but you have to promise not to tell your boss."

A short while later, the water stopped. By that time, Amy had a plan—and pancakes—ready.

No matter how many pancakes she plied him with, Adam would never allow Amy Foreman to turn his clinic into some Hollywood spectacle. Oh, it would start innocently enough. Local folks who'd heard the news would start lining up to catch a glimpse of her. Next thing you know, there'd be reporters crawling out of the woodwork and creating a scene. He'd have paparazzi snapping cameras when he came in to work and helicopters buzzing the building every time she took out the trash.

And if that weren't enough, there would certainly be the—

"Dr. Chambers?"

Adam jumped at the sound of his assistant Judy's voice. He motioned for her to come in then wondered what was up when she closed the door behind her. As she settled into the seat across the desk from him, Adam noticed the normally unflappable redhead looked a bit flustered.

Considering her hobby was racing motorcycles and her household contained one husband, seven assorted indoor pets, and eight kids, this situation was a definite point of concern. "Everything all right, Judy?"

All three earrings on her right ear and the seven decorating her left shook as she nodded then broke into a broad smile. "I just wanted to thank you for taking my suggestion seriously."

"Suggestion?"

Once again she nodded. "The one I put in the suggestion box last week."

Aah, the suggestion box. His mother's idea. Give the woman one week of substituting for the receptionist and she acted like she owned the place. After the second week, Adam stopped interviewing temps because Mom kept scaring them away with baby pictures and talk of potential grandchildren. By the time she mentioned Adam was her only son, most candidates were already out the door. Only the thought that Wilma, his receptionist for the past decade, would soon return kept him from losing his mind faster than he lost his temps.

When Wilma announced she'd decided to quit to get married to a Marine over at Camp Pendleton rather than return, Mom settled into the job and would probably go home to Jesus before leaving the post to someone else.

At least the suggestion box idea had worked out better than the "free cat bath with checkup" promotion that Mom decided to implement as a back-to-school special last month. That harebrained idea had caused him to nearly lose the best pet groomer in the county. Only a promise not to require her to groom reluctant felines—plus Fridays off—had kept the groomer working for him.

He still had scars from bathing those unhappy cats.

Adam kind of suspected Dad was behind the scheme to keep Mom working—and for reasons that were not financial. After all, it was a well-known fact that Chambers men valued their peace and quiet.

If only Adam could find some. Maybe later he'd slip over to his folks' house and see Dad.

"Dr. Chambers, did you hear what I said?"

"I'm sorry." He trained his attention on Judy. "What were you saying?"

"Just that I never expected you to go for the idea of job

sharing, but your mother said you would—"

Job sharing? What was she talking about? Adam ran his hand over the network of faded cat scratches on his arm. "My mother said I would what?"

A light knock interrupted her answer. "Adam dear, it's Mom." His mother peeked in and offered a smile. "I'm sorry to interrupt. I thought you were alone."

"That's all right, Mrs. C.," Judy said. "I was just thanking the doc here for taking my suggestion about job sharing and making it happen. I'm really going to be able to use the off time now that Junior's going on the racing circuit with his daddy and me." Judy rose and slipped past his mother to disappear into the waiting room. "See you next Friday, boss," followed in her wake.

"Job sharing? But I have an afternoon of surgeries scheduled and my best—and only—surgical assistant just walked out of the building." He gave his mother the sternest look he could muster. "She's coming back next *Friday?*"

Mom returned his look with a sweet smile. "Yes, dear, that's what she said."

Adam gripped the arms of his chair and closed his eyes. "Mom," he said slowly, "what have you done this time?"

"It's not what *I've* done, Adam," she said coyly. "It's what *you've* done—at least as far as the staff knows." She put up her hand to silence him before he could even protest. "Don't you want to be thought of as the best boss in the county?"

"Actually, I—"

"Well, I thought so." Mom looked as smug as a cat with a fresh lizard. "Now, do you honestly think I'd leave you without any help? Myrna can take over Judy's job assisting you in surgery. She's done it before."

"True," he said slowly. "But then who will help you at the front desk?"

"Come on out here and see."

Adam rose, eyes narrowed. Nagging suspicion gave way to outright dread. "You didn't."

Her smile broadened. "You'll never believe who I just hired."

Chapter 3

It was obviously going to take Amy much less time to learn the filing system and the proper way to rinse a canine than to earn Adam Chambers's respect as an employee. He'd said one word when he walked into the waiting area to find her already standing behind the reception desk.

That word was *no*.

It had been the only word exchanged between them for the past two days. Mrs. Chambers said to give him time and he'd come around, but Amy had begun to wonder. Thankfully, she had little time to be concerned over the mental state of her employer. Who knew that being a veterinarian's receptionist and part-time groomer's assistant would be so time-consuming?

As she expected, word had leaked out in the community that Amy Foreman had returned to Tierra Verde. More than a few pet owners had made appointments for their animals; some just showed up and stared then left with autographs and pictures, claiming their animal felt better.

Thankfully, these were the minority. Most of the citizens of Tierra Verde still thought of her as just plain Amy, the kid who grew up in a little three-bedroom ranch over on Third Street and worked at the Quick Cluck after school and on weekends.

Mrs. Chambers turned the lock on the front door and switched off the lights. Silhouetted against the window and the mountains beyond, her trim figure gave her a youthful appearance that belied the fact she was the mother of the vet.

The vet. Amy suppressed a groan as she stacked the last of the bags of dog food on the display shelf and rose on creaking knees. Adam had already gone home for the day, slipping out the back door like she used to slip away from premieres to avoid the paparazzi. While he hadn't spoken to her again today, at least his silence meant he hadn't fired her yet.

There was always tomorrow, though. Her tenure as a veterinary receptionist and part-time groomer could be over as quickly as it began. She pushed away the thought and checked off the next chore on the list—taking out the trash.

"Dear," Mrs. Chambers said slowly, "I know I said I wouldn't pry, but do you mind if I ask you just one little question?"

"Of course."

Betty Chambers had been asking "just one little question" off and on since she commenced the interview for the job back on Tuesday afternoon. So far the questions had been fairly easy to answer—standard stuff about Hollywood, the movie business, and the like.

Amy reached beneath the desk to snag the garbage bag. When Adam's mother did not reply right away, Amy stopped midway through the process. She found the older woman still standing silhouetted against the large glass window. Her attention seemed to be focused somewhere beyond the busy street outside, perhaps on the mountains in the distance or the dark thunderhead looming above the distant peaks.

"Mrs. C., are you all right?"

Slowly, she pivoted to face Amy. "I'm just fine, dear. I was about to ask you something important." She paused. "What was it? Oh, yes, do you suppose you could do me a wee little favor?"

Wee little favor? "Sure," Amy said as she went about the job of tying the strings on the garbage bag. "What can I do for you?"

"You can tell me what a man—Detective Miller—from the Los Angeles Police Department is doing calling your cellular phone." As soon as the words were out, Adam's mom frowned. "Forgive me, Amy, but I am terribly nosy. Your phone rang while you were counting inventory in the supply room. I thought you might want me to take a message." She paused. "Truthfully, I'd hoped it was some big star calling to check on you."

Sheepishly, she handed Amy a note written on clinic stationery. Amy sank onto the nearest chair and gripped the paper.

Adam's mom knelt beside her, dark eyes full of concern. "Are you in trouble, Amy?"

How many opportunities had she been given to answer such a question since she arrived in Tierra Verde? Did the Lord want her to share her burden with someone? She smiled. As dear as Betty Chambers was, she couldn't be the confidante Amy needed.

Times like now were when she missed Mama the most.

She placed her hand on Mrs. Chambers's sleeve. "There's been a theft," she said, choosing her words carefully.

That much was true. Her business manager had, in effect, robbed her blind then told her he would go to the press and claim a hidden drug habit had caused her to drain her own fortunes. If only she could prove the truth.

Well, it was his word against hers, and in Hollywood, highly functioning, award-winning drug addicts were a dime a dozen. Ed Moore, however, was a respected businessman with connections in all the right places and a client roster that read like an Academy Awards after-party invitation list. Why he chose her bank accounts to drain was a mystery—a mystery she'd retreated to Tierra Verde to try to solve.

Amy rearranged her smile. "I'm sure the detective called to update me. Please don't worry."

"Wasted words, young lady," she said as she patted Amy's hand. "You know I always thought of you as the daughter I never had."

"I know, but I'm fine. Really." She held Mrs. Chambers's gaze until she felt certain the older woman's concerns had been answered. "I suppose I ought to finish up here so I can give the detective a call." Gathering her purse along with the trash, Amy rushed out the back door before she risked spilling her secrets.

"You let me know if you need anything, you hear?" followed her into the evening air.

"Yes, ma'am," Amy called just before the door slammed shut, even though she knew she wouldn't—wouldn't need anything and wouldn't let anyone know even if she did.

It was a habit learned from childhood, this self-sufficiency, and one that currently served her well. The other habit was holding on to sentimental things—in this case, her girlhood home. As she tossed the garbage bag toward the Dumpster, she gave thanks that she'd managed to rescue the little house on Third Street from a last-minute sale to satisfy the tax man not so many years ago.

If only she could find someone to swoop in and rescue her the same way.

"Hey!"

Amy jumped back and dropped her purse then tripped over it and landed on her posterior on the pavement. Adam Chambers's head rose above the rim of the Dumpster—fortunately, it was still attached to his body.

"You scared me to death." Amy clambered to her feet and wiped the dirt off the back of her jeans.

Throwing his leg over the side, Adam stuffed a folded piece of paper into his shirt pocket and leaped from the Dumpster. "Yeah, well, you didn't do any good for my heart, either."

Their gazes met, and Amy's heart thudded to a sudden stop at the double meaning of his words. In an instant, as he took a step toward her, her own heart raced. So did she—in the direction of Third Street.

"Hold on a minute. I need to talk to you."

You mean you need to fire me.

Amy ignored Adam to pick up her pace. She had bigger problems than allowing Adam Chambers to terminate her employment, but none of which she could solve so easily as outrunning them. Passing Uncle Willard's Fix-It Shop, Amy turned at the corner and headed for the little white house with green shutters and its sadly bent mailbox.

"Amy, wait," Adam called.

"Can't. I have a call to make."

"Big Hollywood movie to accept?" he shouted. "No. It's Oprah, and she's asking your advice on what to name her new poodle." He paused and laughed aloud—a hollow laugh that held no humor, only sarcasm. "No, I know. Maybe it's your agent asking you how many millions you want for your next picture. That's why you left, isn't it? For fame and fortune."

Amy stopped and whirled around to face her accuser, ready to give him an answer he'd never believe—the truth. Wouldn't he be surprised to know that the real reason she'd taken the midnight bus to Denver then hitched her way to Los Angeles wasn't because of anything he'd suspected all these years?

Yes, she'd give him just enough of the ugly details to let him know why she hadn't been able to stay another night under the same roof as the drunken father who called her by her mother's name. Instead, she opened her mouth and the Lord rendered her mute. Not a word escaped her lips, though she fought to spit them out—to fling them at him then watch how terribly they would hurt.

No, Adam Chambers was a rescuer. Had he known why she left, he would have rescued her for sure. Instead, she'd banked on him following her to California back then because he loved her—not because she needed saving.

She'd been wrong.

Amy laughed when she realized she'd just wished for a rescuer. Hadn't she gotten what she deserved by calling up that plea without qualification? She wanted someone to get her out of her current fix, to somehow make everything right in California so she could pay her housekeeper, make her movies, and continue to support the missions and causes as the Lord prompted.

Ignoring the multicolored junk mail filling the mailbox, Amy marched up the cracked front walk and stabbed her key into the lock. "Mama always said to be careful what you wish for."

"What does that mean?" Adam had caught up again, although this time he kept his distance on the sidewalk.

Amy managed to turn the key on the third try, pushing the door open on hinges that protested loudly. The house still smelled musty, like Great-granny Foreman's quilts, and she made a note to air things out as soon as she found the time.

She stepped inside and turned to close the door, only to see Adam still standing at the curb. Obviously she could no longer deny the inevitable. Leaning against the frame, she focused on the persistent veterinarian then closed her eyes. "If you're going to fire me, Adam, do it now."

"Fire you?" Adam shook his head, trying to follow the logic of his newest employee. "I'll admit the thought occurred to me more than once over the past two days, but that's not why I followed you here."

Amy continued to lean against the door frame, her expression and posture indicating her displeasure. "All right then," she said. "Why *did* you follow me here? And while you're answering that question, you can tell me why you were hiding out in the Dumpster behind the clinic."

"First off, I wasn't 'hiding out' in the Dumpster." He patted his shirt pocket with his palm. "I was looking for an invoice my mother decided we didn't need. And as to why I followed you, well. . ."

"Well?"

He turned to stare up the street toward his uncle Willard's Fix-It Shop. "Honestly. . ."

"Yes?"

"I'm worried about you, Amy, and I don't know what to do about it." Again he shook his head. "No, that's not right. I don't know what to do about *you*."

Chapter 4

I really need to go inside, Adam. Are you going to stand on the sidewalk or would you like to join me?"

"Sure," he said to her dismay.

He looked a bit perplexed but managed to slip past her into the house before she slammed the door shut. When he stopped in the hallway to stare, she felt the urge to explain the disarray, to tell him that she really couldn't afford to redecorate with her bills piling up more each day. Instead, she offered him a cup of coffee and gestured toward the ancient sofa. Adam had seen her through circumstances worse than this.

She watched him test Pop's old tan corduroy recliner before gradually sinking into its patched and mended depths. To his credit, he remained in place despite the bent spring she knew must be working its way into his backside about now.

Maybe he won't stay long.

"I'll just be a moment." She slipped into the kitchen and closed the door. As she made all the appropriate noises of coffee making at the highest volume possible, she also dialed her cellular phone. "Hello," she whispered, "I'm returning a call from the detective at this number."

While the on-hold music played a show tune, the old silver coffeepot began to perk, settling into a rhythmic bubbling. Soon the rich aroma of the dark roast coffee she'd found in the freezer chased away the musty smell in the tiny kitchen.

The music stopped abruptly in her ear. "The detective isn't answering, ma'am. Would you like to leave a message?"

She paused and opened the door a notch. Adam seemed absorbed in a copy of last week's *Daily Variety*. "No," she said, "no message."

Slipping the phone back into her pocket, Amy poured two cups of coffee, added the requisite three spoonfuls of sugar in Adam's, then carried the mismatched mugs into the living room. "I hope I made it strong enough."

He took a sip and smiled. "Just right." He seemed to contemplate the dark liquid for a moment before turning his attention to Amy. "I've been rude."

She said nothing, choosing to settle in silence on the end of the sofa farthest from him. He was right about having been rude, but in her estimation, he was also entitled.

Adam ran his hand along the rough fabric of the chair's arm then shook his head and looked away. "It's just that seeing you here, in Tierra Verde, and well. . ." He returned his attention to her. "I have a lot of questions, Amy, and I don't even know if I can ask them."

Amy took a delicate sip of the strong, black brew and winced. Her taste went more toward lattes with more froth than teeth. "You can ask me anything, Adam." She set the cup down. "Doesn't mean I'll answer, though."

"Fair enough." He shifted positions, and for a moment Amy felt bad about the uncomfortable chair.

"You're a big movie star, Amy. You can go anywhere. What *really* brought you back here?" He leaned forward and placed his coffee cup atop the newspaper on the floor. "And I'm not buying the line about needing to work for me, so just be warned."

It was her turn to shift positions. Her discomfort, however, did not come from a chair spring but rather from a jolt to her heart. What to say? She'd been offered so many opportunities to tell the truth. Was this the one she should take?

Her cellular phone rang, precluding any further conversation. The screen showed a Los Angeles area code and an unfamiliar number.

"Will you excuse me a moment?" When Adam nodded, Amy slipped down the hall to the bedroom and closed the door. "Hello?"

"I'll get right to the point."

She sucked in a deep breath and let it out along with a single word, "Ed?"

"Yeah, kid, it's me, now listen. Here's how it's all going to go down."

"Wait a minute. I—"

"No, *you* wait a minute. I don't have time to listen, just to talk."

He paused as if to dare her to speak. She didn't.

"I got two calls coming in this evening, kid. One's a contact of mine at the *Times*." He chuckled, a low, throaty laugh that made Amy's skin crawl. "Guy's looking for a big scoop, and he's paying real well."

Amy resisted a quip regarding business manager Ed Moore's lack of a need for payment after stealing her money. Instead, she settled for a bland, "Oh, really?" even though the bile had begun to rise in her throat.

"Yeah," he said with enthusiasm, "and the other call's gonna be from the cops."

Now we're talking.

"I figure either way I win." Another maddening pause. "Or I conveniently fail to answer both of them. Your decision."

Amy heard the ancient recliner's springs protest and peered out the door in time to see Adam rise. He turned his back to her, picking his way across a floor cluttered with newspapers, junk mail, and the ratty slippers she'd shucked off this morning before work. He seemed to be staring out at the backyard, deep in thought.

"Did you hear me, kid?"

"What?" She ducked back inside the bedroom and sank onto the pink ruffled spread. For good measure, she flipped the clock radio on in hopes the oldies tunes might prevent Adam from overhearing. "Yes, I heard you," she said as the Supremes belted out a three-part harmony in the background.

"You have a little problem, see? I'm the guy whose been keeping that problem out of the press. That costs money."

Amy sniffed and tried to focus. The room smelled inexplicably of old roses and baby powder. "Ed, I have no idea what you're talking about."

The music turned abruptly from Diana Ross to Aretha Franklin, and the tempo picked up. So did the volume on the ancient appliance. Amy reached over to turn the music down a notch.

"Pills, baby. See, you got a little problem with pills. Bought 'em in Mexico and had that sweet little maid of yours bring 'em back after her weekends off. You spent half the money on buying the stuff, and I had to spend the other half on getting you off of it. Hence, the bank account's empty."

"Pills? What—"

"Don't overthink this, Amy. You know that woman who works for you could be doing anything on those visits back to Mexico. How you gonna prove I'm wrong?"

Maria Elena. It was bad enough he'd chosen to go after her, but to involve an innocent, young Christian woman who'd gone without full pay to remain at Amy's side was just too much to take. Amy already felt bad enough that she'd only been able to give Maria Elena enough money to go home to her family along with a small stipend and a promise to send for her when the dust settled on her current troubles.

She could go down in flames with Hollywood and the whole world watching, but Maria Elena Santos would never be touched by scandal. Amy would see to it.

"Ed, that is the most despicable, disgusting lie I've ever—"

"Listen. You or your maid disputes this, and I take it to the cops and you both go down—her for buying and you for using." He gave her a second, most likely to let his threat sink in. "A guy in Tijuana'll be happy to testify she spends her weekends getting wild at his cantina then sleeping it off in his bunk behind the bar. So will a couple of border guards and a well-placed fellow in the Tijuana police force. On the other hand, you got no one who'll say it ain't true. You lose, kid. *Comprende?*"

Amy fisted the spread then let it go. Understanding rose, and with it, anger. Staying apart from the Hollywood social scene had kept her walk with the Lord intact. Unfortunately it had also left her with no close friends, except Maria Elena. If only Amy had taken the time to strengthen ties with the few Christians she'd met on sets or the acquaintances she'd made at church.

No time for regrets now.

"That's a lie and no one will believe you," she said without enthusiasm and at a volume she instantly regretted.

She leaned over and turned the radio back up to prevent Adam from hearing any further loss of control. Blaring horns vied with a guitar and piano to fill the room with up-tempo music.

"No one will believe you," she repeated.

"Won't they?" He paused. "This is Holly-weird. Nothing's too far-fetched."

He was right. The story of yet another pill-popping actress and her aiding-and-abetting maid would barely make a blip on the show business radar screen. Only the casting directors would take heed, and with their attention came unemployment, for no one wanted to risk running up the costs while an actor went for yet another unsuccessful stint in rehab.

She'd be done for—a Hollywood has-been who'd let everyone down, especially those who depended on her.

The room began to spin, and Amy fell backward onto the lumpy mattress. Aretha serenaded her with a song about fools.

Amy's breath shortened into gasps, and her eyes closed of their own accord.

Gradually, a realization dawned on her. "If I keep quiet about the money, this nightmare will end, right?"

Silence on the other end of the line.

Amy opened her eyes and rolled over on her stomach then held the phone back up to her ear. "Ed? Did you hear what I said?"

"Yeah, and I'm thinking about it." Another pause. "After all, you're the next Audrey Hepburn, right?"

Tired. So very tired. She closed her eyes again. "Actually, it's Grace Kelly."

"Whoever. There could be a lot more cash where this came from, right?"

Panic gnawed at the corners of her mind, begging entrance to her thoughts, her words. *Please, Lord, guide me gently, safely.* "What do you want me to do?"

Had she spoken the words to her business manager or, rather, had the plea flown above the patched roof of the little house on Third Street to reach the very ears of the Father? She certainly hoped it was the latter.

"Amy?" Adam called from the living room. "Are you all right?"

"Who was that?" Ed asked.

Amy rolled over and jumped to her feet, nearly dropping the phone. "I asked you a question, Ed. What do you want me to do?"

"No, kid, I asked *you* a question. I heard a man. Who is he?"

A soft knock and Adam opened the door a crack. When he

saw she held the cell phone in her hand, he stepped back.

"I'm sorry. I didn't realize you were still talking."

Amy offered a quick smile as the door closed. His retreating footsteps thudded above the pounding of her heart and the musical stylings of Aretha and her backup singers.

Chapter 5

Adam heard a desperation in Amy's voice that made him want to break down the door and whisk her away from whatever troubled her—to play knight in shining armor, rescuing her from the villain on the other end of the line.

How to go about this was another question entirely, one for which he had no answer. God would know, but so far He wasn't saying a word.

Walking back into the living room, he scooped up his empty coffee cup then went to the kitchen to rinse it out. A thought struck him hard, and he had to lean against the cabinet to absorb it.

She remembered how he liked his coffee.

What did that mean? What else did she remember about him? About them?

"Nothing, idiot," he grumbled as he headed back to the living room to retrieve her almost-full mug. "And it's just coffee."

He poured out the black liquid then debated a moment about pouring a fresh cup. No, he'd do that when she came out of her exile in the back of the house.

Restless, he grabbed the threadbare kitchen towel and spread it on the cabinet then reached below the sink for the unopened container of detergent. Without a sponge, he made do washing out his mug with a handful of paper towels and a spot of soap. Setting the mug upside down on the towel to dry, he wandered back into the living room to wait for Amy.

Waiting for Amy.

The story of his life.

I want to know who's there with you, and I want to know right now," Ed said. "Is he anybody?"

Only the kindest man she'd ever known. And the most honest.

"No," she said, although she hated saying so. "He's nobody."

To Ed's way of thinking, Adam *was* a nobody. After all, he had absolutely no connection to anyone in the film industry— except her, of course, and that relationship was tenuous at best.

"So let's cut to the chase," she said with an authority she did not feel. "You want something from me. What is it—other than what you've already taken, that is?"

"Taken is such a harsh word, Amy."

Amy ignored the statement. The word was mild in comparison to a few others she'd thought. She and the Lord would be discussing the issues of forgiveness and pure thinking tonight for sure.

"From now on, all monies go straight to me, kid, and you give up all rights to sign on your accounts. I get total control, and if you're a good girl, you get an allowance. Got it?"

Aretha finished singing and a used-car commercial followed. Amy walked over to shut off the radio. Suddenly she felt tired, weak, like all her bones had turned to rubber or, worse, to dust.

"I'm listening," she said.

"Anyone asks questions about our financial arrangement, I tell them it's a precautionary measure. So you don't go shopping on the all-you-can-eat-pill buffet." Another creepy chuckle. "Course, I don't mention the pills as long as you behave."

"Of course." Amy let the proposition—and the warning—sink in.

Softly, tenderly, Jesus is calling. Strange how the words her mother used to whisper in her ear as a baby in this very room came rolling back on a wave of nostalgia just when she should be thinking of how to save herself, or rather of how to save Maria Elena. She walked over to the ancient black wooden rocker with the missing arm and set it into motion.

Softly.

Tenderly.

Jesus.

The room's walls softened and her vision clouded. "Ed?" she asked softly and without emotion. "Why pick me to rob blind when there are so many others to choose from?"

"Why *not* you? Besides, who better to fall than the goody-goody, outspoken Christian? Do you know how many people have been waiting to find out that Miss Perfect has flaws?"

If only he knew how many flaws she really had.

Click. Thankfully the line went dead before she had to admit to any of them.

Amy dropped the phone then pasted on a smile and went

in search of Adam, praying she could fake an air of casual calm. It almost worked—until she saw Adam standing in the kitchen and fell apart.

His arms enveloped her as the tears began to fall. Amy sank into his embrace and cried until both of his shoulders were soaked.

"I'm sorry," she managed when she could find the words.

"Don't be." Adam held her at arm's length and shook his head. "Are you ready to tell me what's wrong?"

No lay just on the tip of her tongue, but somehow she nodded a weak yes instead. She allowed him to lead her back to the sofa then smiled when he rushed back into the kitchen and returned with a fresh cup of coffee and a slightly damp dish towel.

"Sorry." He shrugged. "It was this or the roll of paper towels." He settled on the opposite end of the sofa and waited for her to begin.

Waving away the coffee, she curled her feet beneath her and stared out the window into the lush, green backyard. Finally she swung her gaze to meet his. He now sipped gingerly at the coffee he'd brought for her.

"I don't know why I'm telling you this."

His features softened, and a slight smile tilted one corner of his mouth. "Does it matter why?"

"No, I suppose it doesn't." Amy thought a moment then shook her head. "That's not right. I'm telling you because I trust you." She let out a long breath and punctuated it with a brittle laugh. "Do you know how long it's been since I've trusted anyone?"

She started slowly, telling him about last fall's unexpected blockbuster movie and the corresponding monies that should have flowed into her bank account but somehow did not. Contacting her business manager became harder and harder until he'd begun to ignore her completely.

"Checks started bouncing, and I began to receive threatening calls from the mortgage company. Three weeks ago I finally managed to get into my online accounts." She held the dish towel to her chest and refused to cry. "I discovered I'm broke."

"Broke?" Adam asked. "How can that be?"

She sniffed and wiped her nose with the towel. "I wondered the same thing so I showed up at Ed Moore's office—he's my business manager—and told his receptionist that I'd take my problem to the police if Ed wouldn't see me."

"And?"

"And he admitted everything."

Adam set the coffee cup on the floor and scooted a hair closer. "That's great. What did the police say?"

"I didn't go to the police." She let the towel fall into her lap then stared at it rather than brave a glance at Adam. "I couldn't."

"But you said a Detective Miller left you a message."

"I know," she said, "and that's what scares me."

"Why didn't you go to the police, Amy? One call and that business manager of yours is out of a job and behind bars. Let the police do their job. I know this might come off as cliché, but God really is in control. With Him on your side, what are you afraid of?"

Amy pondered the question a moment. Of course Adam was right, and this *was* a matter for the police to handle.

"When the detective calls back, I promise I'll tell him everything, all right?"

And if he doesn't call back, even better.

Chapter 6

He said he'd tell everyone I was. . ." Her voice failed.

Adam leaned toward her to offer comfort then froze when she shifted away from him to continue her story. He sank back against the stiff cushions and closed his eyes as Amy spoke. Never for a moment did he doubt the creep's claims were lies. Amy Foreman might not have been dependable enough to stick around Tierra Verde and marry him, but she was certainly no pill popper.

When she finished, he opened his eyes and caught her wiping her nose. "This guy obviously doesn't know you."

She looked perplexed—and a little relieved. Had she expected he might not believe her?

"Because if he knew you, he would know that your absolute last drug of choice would be pills. Just ask anyone in Mrs. Landon's fifth-grade class." Her sideways glance and look of slight amusement spurred him on. "Remember how your mom used to send those chewable vitamins in your lunch because you couldn't swallow the other kind?"

Her grin turned up only one corner of her mouth, but it was glorious all the same. "I used to trade them for cookies."

"Until you got caught and Mrs. Landon made you take your vitamin right there in the lunchroom."

"And I got sick." She leaned forward and chuckled. "Oh, Adam, I'd forgotten all about that. How do you remember these things?"

How indeed? It was a curse he'd asked God to remove, this ability to recall the slightest details about Amy Foreman while regularly forgetting important things like his lunch or where he put his truck keys. So far, however, the Lord just seemed to keep putting more memories into his mind rather than taking them away.

Rather than answer directly, he merely shrugged. "So how are we going to fix this, Amy?"

Amy lifted a brow and frowned. "We?"

Just let her try to argue. "That's what I said."

"All right." She looked away. "Even though my agent and my attorneys are hopeful, I don't see a fix. An actress in rehab isn't exactly an unusual event. It's Ed's word against mine, and I have no proof while he's got all sorts of supposed witnesses against me." She paused. "And it's not just about me. There's an innocent person involved."

White-hot jealousy slammed him. "A man?" he asked before he could stop himself.

She didn't seem to notice his discomfort. "Her name is Maria Elena and she works for me. Ed says he's going to implicate her in this, too."

"So there's not a man involved?" *Idiot!*

If she thought his question strange, Amy didn't let it show. "No," she said softly.

He let the situation sink in for a moment. "So when you

came to me, did you want a job or someone to take care of the problem?"

Amy's face registered surprise then contemplation. "Honestly, I thought I just came for the job. I didn't think you would turn me away, and I needed an income while I laid low and tried to decide what to do next."

"And now?"

"And now I guess it's a little of both. I need the job, and I—I can't believe I'm saying this." She paused to fiddle with the dish towel in her lap. "I know I don't deserve it, but I'd be grateful for your help."

"Of course I'll help." Adam stood and reached to grasp Amy's hand and pull her to her feet. After seeing her on the big screen the past few years, he'd almost forgotten how tiny she was in person. A lone tear traced a path across her cheek. Adam captured it with the back of his hand. She leaned into his arms and he caught her.

"I'm sorry. . . ."

Adam let her cry herself out then fetched a clean dish towel. He sent her off to wash her face while he rummaged in the kitchen for something to feed her. By the time Amy emerged from the bathroom, eyes dry but rimmed in red, Adam had retrieved a can of vegetable soup and a box of saltines.

Amy dropped the dish towel in the sink and watched him light the fire on the front burner of the ancient gas stove. "What are you doing?"

He pressed past her to find a saucepan then dumped the contents of the soup can inside. Adjusting the flame, he turned to offer her a smile. "I'd like you to eat, okay? If you're going to fight this, you have to take care of yourself."

She returned his smile then unceremoniously blew her nose into the washcloth she held. "Would you like to join me?" she said when she finished.

"Thanks, but I've made other plans." Was it his imagination, or did she look the slightest bit disappointed?

What other plans?

Amy frowned as she watched Adam's retreating form. She'd only been in Tierra Verde for a short while, but the thought of Adam having other plans seemed a bit far-fetched. From what she'd gathered at the clinic, the town vet was practically a hermit. You could set your clock by his comings and goings, and his mother insisted he'd been born with a watch on his wrist.

A quick check of the clock above the refrigerator revealed she still had time to phone her attorneys in Los Angeles. Afterward, she would call her agent and check in. Good news on both fronts would make her night, she decided as she turned off the heat under the soup and retrieved her cell phone.

Unfortunately, Joyce, her agent, had no news at all until she finally called her nearly a week later. She offered an apology for the lack of communication then claimed she had an incoming call. They would finish their conversation very soon, she promised.

"Very soon" turned out to be a full week later when, on a Tuesday afternoon, Joyce caught her at work. With Mrs. C. manning the receptionist desk, Amy knew she'd best slip outside to find some privacy.

"The director's still interested so I'm overnighting the script." Her spirits soared. "That's great."

"Maybe." Her agent's reticent tone sent Amy's hopes into a nosedive. "I have to tell you that it's not looking so good for you out here, Amy," the plainspoken transplanted Midwesterner said.

"Oh?" Amy shifted positions. "Why?"

"Word on the street is that the Christian actress has a pill problem. Most of us don't pay any attention to this sort of thing, but with a high-dollar movie shoot coming up and a director who's still under fire from his last budget fiasco, I'd say right now your chances are fifty-fifty that you'll land the part."

"It's a lie, you know, what they're saying."

"Yes," Joyce said. "I know."

Relieved, Amy sank to the curb beside Adam's truck and leaned against the cold metal of the front bumper. At least someone in Hollywood believed her besides her lawyers. "But how did the rumor get out?" she asked, although she guessed the answer.

"Who knows? Someone took a call on set, maybe, or forgot to close the office door then someone overhears. Maybe a grip talks to a gaffer. The next thing you know, the studio head's got the scoop, and he's selling the story to the highest bidder."

"Ed?"

"Or maybe someone else. He might not be in this alone."

As she hung up, her heart sunk even deeper. A chill October wind blew across her face and turned her thoughts to winter. It would be November in less than a week, with Thanksgiving and Christmas not far behind. Had she really been in Tierra Verde for three whole weeks?

If she didn't get the part, what would she do? Maria Elena had offered to take her in, but that would be a temporary fix at best. And in light of Ed's threats, probably the worst thing she could do to the kind woman. Could she imagine staying here in Tierra Verde indefinitely? Closing her eyes, she breathed in a frosty breath and held it until she felt her lungs would burst.

"Maybe I could."

"Maybe you could what?"

Amy's eyes flew open. Adam held her jacket in his outstretched hands.

"Here," he said. "Put this on. It's cold."

She rose and shrugged into the warm coat. "Thanks. I'll just be going back inside now. The Parkers' Jack Russell terrier needs a shampoo, and I still have to brush that sheepdog's teeth before he can go home."

Adam touched her arm. "Wait."

"Yes?"

"I was wondering—that is, I've been thinking. . . ." He looked away, his face pained. Finally he swung his attention back to her. "How long are you going to stay here in Tierra Verde, Amy?"

Amy snuggled into the warmth of her jacket and tried to put thoughts of sticking around this town indefinitely out of her mind. "Just until I get the part I'm up for."

His shoulders seemed to relax, but the lines on his face deepened. "I see."

She began to scramble to fill the silence. "Yes, it's a good part. A plum role."

Adam lowered his gaze and frowned. "So," he said slowly, "you're going to leave a perfectly good life washing dogs and sweeping my office to play a *fruit*?"

It took a moment for Adam's attempt at a joke to sink in. She feigned concentration then gave him a sideways look. "When you put it that way, it doesn't sound like such a great career move, does it?"

Rather than laugh, Adam pressed his palm to her back and led her toward the back door of the clinic. Inches from the door, he stopped abruptly.

"Then stay, Amy." He peered down at her with an expression that told nothing of his thoughts. "There'll never be a script that's worth it."

Was he serious or just playing along with her joke? Amy cleared her throat and contemplated a snazzy comeback. Before she could come up with something, he pressed past her and disappeared into the building.

A moment later, the door opened again and there stood Adam. "I was wrong," he said, his face unreadable. "There is another script that would be perfect for you. If you're interested in a rewarding career move, that is."

Was he making another silly joke? If so, Amy failed to get it.

"I see I've left you speechless." He chuckled. "Are you interested or not?"

She nodded.

"Then don't make any plans for Tuesday night. We'll catch a bite to eat after work, and I'll fill you in on the details."

Chapter 7

"Catch a bite to eat after work," Amy muttered as she closed the script she'd been trying to read while she ate. "What is he up to?"

She jabbed a fork into her chef salad and tried to concentrate on anything but Adam Chambers. Fortunately, the sparsely populated Tierra Verde Diner—the renovation a vast improvement of the old Quick Cluck—offered plenty in the way of diversion. But then, Monday night *was* "Free Dessert with Entrée" night.

In one corner a pair of ladies from the church choir finished their salad suppers with a shared piece of Double Trouble Brownie Delight and coffees with whipped cream and chocolate sprinkles. A slice of pie sat in a take-out box on the corner of the table. Two tables over, the mayor and the city manager pored over a set of blueprints while carrying on a heated debate concerning whether the meat loaf or the stew was the best item on the menu. In the booth behind her, a teenage foursome giggled as they recounted a recent weekend adventure over banana splits.

The rest of the booths sat empty. Amy had waited three

weeks for the "I can't wait to return to California" homesickness to arrive. As yet, it remained back on the West Coast with most of her possessions and the brand-new car she'd probably lose to the bank.

Funny how she didn't miss that car, or the big house, or any of the perks money could buy. After spending five years making sure she was not just another ordinary face in the crowd, she rather liked being one again.

Returning to the script, Amy gave thanks that she'd managed to accomplish a measure of anonymity in Tierra Verde. Somehow, the locals had finally begun to treat her like the old Amy. Only the occasional autograph seeker approached, and rarely was she stopped on the street or required to converse with strangers.

She sighed and stabbed another lettuce leaf. The script was good, very good, and she knew she was born to play the part of Rebecca. Unless the director chose to listen to the rumors, the part was all but hers—she could feel it. With the advance from the film, she would be able to pay off her mortgage and hire Maria Elena back full time. Joyce's note said that shooting was scheduled to begin in late March, but preproduction could begin at any time.

"Is this seat taken?"

Amy lifted her gaze to meet the spry older man. He might have grown gray around the temples and acquired a few wrinkles, but she would recognize Adam's uncle Willard anywhere. She rose with a giggle and a greeting then let him wrap his strong workingman's arms around her in a bear hug. As she inhaled the spicy scent of his aftershave, she felt an unexpected pang of loss for her father.

Uncle Willard slid into the booth, gazed intently at Amy, and steepled his hands. "So I close up shop and take the first vacation of my life and what happens? My favorite girl returns and doesn't even let me know she's coming. Now I enjoy my fishing as much as the next man, but if I'd known, I'd have made other arrangements."

"I'm sorry." She busied herself with replacing the napkin in her lap.

"You're wasting away eating that rabbit food." Uncle Willard waved for the waitress and ordered a pair of cheeseburgers with the works and a basket of fries for two before Amy could protest. "And bring us a couple of chocolate shakes, too," he called after the retreating young woman.

Amy pushed away her salad and suppressed a groan. If she stayed in Tierra Verde much longer, she'd never be fit to take on another movie role.

Uncle Willard gave her *that* look, the one that said he planned to ask her something and he planned to hear a proper answer. "So, I understand you're working for my nephew." He paused and began to inspect his fork. "How'd that happen?"

She took a sip of water. "I asked him for a job and eventually he came around."

"Eventually, you say?" Her companion smiled. "I'd be willing to bet it wasn't as easy as all that."

"No," she said. "There was a little more to it."

"Just like I believe there's a lot more to the fact that you showed up on Adam's porch instead of mine or someone else's." He gave her a level stare. "You think I couldn't put you to work just as easy as that vet?"

"Well, I, um—I guess I just didn't think of it." She'd only thought of Adam when she thought of returning to Tierra Verde. With Daddy gone, Adam *was* Tierra Verde to her.

Interesting.

The waitress returned with their shakes and a pair of straws, providing a much-appreciated distraction. "You plan on spending much time here?" He rolled the white cylinder of paper into a tiny ball and let it drop next to his fork.

"I'm not sure," she said. "So tell me what's new around here. Have you been fishing much lately?"

The question provided Uncle Willard with enough material to hold a one-sided conversation until the food arrived. Amy lightly salted the fries at Uncle Willard's insistence then dug in, all the while listening to the dear man's stories of his month-long visit with an army buddy in Colorado. By the time he finished, so had she—the entire cheeseburger and a good share of the fries.

It was delicious.

Uncle Willard insisted on paying the check and then declared his intention to walk her home. All the while, they made small talk and danced around the subject she most dreaded. She made it all the way to her front door before Uncle Willard finally asked.

"Why are you here, Amy?"

She shoved the key into the lock and turned it then pushed the door open and flipped on the porch light. Adam's uncle stood at the edge of the porch, studying her every move. His characteristic smile had vanished, and in its place an unreadable expression greeted her.

His expression softened into concern. "Does it have anything to do with Adam?"

Amy shook her head. "I'm just hiding out for a while," she said as she began a careful dance on the edge of the truth. "I needed a place to go, and home seemed like the right place."

"So you're not out to take up with Adam again?"

"No," she said. "Adam's a friend. I don't think it would be good for either of us to think of being anything more than that to each other."

Uncle Willard looked as if he might speak but instead nodded then added a smile and a hug. He waited until he reached the sidewalk to turn and address her. "You going to be here for Christmas, Amy?"

What to say? "I don't know," she finally responded. "Why?"

"Just wondering." He chuckled. "I bet you thought it was an accident that I ran into you in the diner."

She leaned against the door frame and palmed the keys. "I guess I did."

"There are no accidents, Amy Sue Foreman. You should have learned that by now." He turned and walked away, leaving her to wonder about the older man's curious statement.

The next day was Adam's half day off, so the office buzzed with activity until lunchtime. Mrs. Chambers had taken the day off, as well, leaving the remaining staff in blissful silence. Amy used the time to complete the inventory of the storeroom then headed for the kennels to put them in order. Before she realized it, the clock read quarter to five. She slipped into the rest room to clean up and change into her street clothes, emerging to find Adam waiting for her.

He wore denim and a smile. Amy's heart did a strange *kerthump* then settled back into its natural rhythm. Sometimes when she looked at Adam, it felt like no time at all had passed since she'd actually contemplated becoming his wife. This was one of those moments. She said a quick prayer that it would pass and shrugged into her coat.

"Ready to go?" Without waiting for an answer, he linked arms with her and led her outside. "I understand you had dinner with Uncle Willard last night," he said as he led her to his truck and helped her inside.

She waited for him to join her, suppressing a chill. When had her tolerance for the cold left her? Adam cranked over the engine of the ancient but neat-as-a-pin vehicle then adjusted the heater. With a grin, he shifted into reverse and began to back out of the parking space.

"Your uncle is as charming as ever," she said. "And protective of his nephew."

Adam cast a glance at her before putting the transmission in drive. "Why do you say that?"

"Because he was either pumping me for information so he could be assured I wasn't trifling with your affections or he was trying to fatten me up so you would lose interest." She offered him a smile. "Either way, the cheeseburger and fries were delicious. So was the shake."

"Chocolate?"

Amy nodded.

"Figured as much. Mine was chocolate, too." Adam brought the truck to a halt at the red light on the corner. "The one he fed me for lunch after church on Sunday, that is. And in my case, he was more worried about whether *I* was trifling with *your* affections." He paused to drum his fingers on the steering wheel. "I think he was awfully disappointed when I told him I wasn't."

She smiled. "Good old Uncle Willard."

"Yep, good old Uncle Willard," he repeated as the light turned green and he accelerated. They rode a few minutes in silence until Adam pulled up in front of a dark green building with a tin roof and a massive sign advertising the best ribs and worst service in town.

"It's a joke." Adam ran around the front of the truck to open her door and help her out. He gestured toward the sign. "The service, I mean. It's really very good."

Amy smiled and nodded then allowed Adam to lead her inside. Once seated at a booth in the corner, Amy pretended to peruse the menu while surreptitiously studying Adam. Even in Hollywood he would turn heads. Funny how here in Tierra Verde no one seemed to notice.

"Hi, Adam." The sultry voice of the waitress cut through her thoughts. Amy's gaze landed on a woman barely out of her teens and barely in her top. "Ma'am."

The waitress, whose name tag read Buffi, reached across Adam to grab his glass and fill it with water then leaned forward to place it on the table slowly. No wonder he thought the service here was good. The one performing it seemed to think he'd hung the moon. Repeating the process with Amy's glass took much less time.

Adam ordered a pair of iced teas then opened his menu and began to study the entrées. Amy followed suit but, in light of last night's calorie fest, elected to head to the salad section of the rather extensive menu. A moment later the waitress returned with the iced teas.

"Will you be needing more time, Adam? Because I've got all the time in the world." She sighed. "Well, actually I *do* get off at seven."

When her dinner date failed to notice the obvious ploy for his attention, Amy's heart soared. "The ribs, Buffi." He slapped his menu shut. "What about you, Amy?"

"I'll have the grilled chicken salad." She watched Buffi stride away without taking their menus then turned her attention to Adam. "She a friend of yours?"

The poor man looked clueless. "Who?"

"Buffi." She paused. "The waitress." His look told her all she needed to know. "Forget it."

Adam nodded. "Yeah, well, as I was saying, I had lunch with Uncle Willard after church on Sunday. He has this crazy idea that. . ." He looked away and shook his head.

"What?"

Swinging his gaze to meet hers, Adam let out a long breath. "He loves us both."

"I know that."

"And he *is* my uncle."

"Yeah, and my dad's dear friend." She emptied a packet of sweetener into her tea. "What are you getting at?"

Chapter 8

What *was* he getting at?

Adam cleared his throat and tried not to look directly at the woman who'd nearly cost him his membership in the Bachelor Club. How to turn the conversation—and his thoughts—in a safer direction? *Ah, yes, the play.*

"Actually, Uncle Willard had a great idea." He managed a wavering stare. "I thought I would run it by you."

She swirled her water with the tip of her straw then took a sip. "Sure. What's up?"

"Well," he said, "I really hate to make any presumptions, but you *are* the most qualified person for the job, and you *do* attend the church, even if you hide in the back and slip out early."

Amy's cheeks colored slightly. "I didn't want to be a distraction."

Adam suppressed a smile. As if leaving five minutes early would prevent anyone from knowing Amy Foreman graced the church. "Why don't you take a chance and sit with Uncle Willard and me next Sunday? I think it's probably past the point where you're a curiosity."

Considering the idea took a moment, but eventually she nodded. "Maybe I will," she said. "So is that what you wanted to see me about?"

He shook his head. "Actually, I had something else in mind, although it *does* relate to church."

She broke the tip off a bread stick and popped it into her mouth. "Oh? What's that?"

"Nope," he said as he spied Buffi heading their way with a tray of food. "You'll just have to wait and see. It's a surprise."

A moment later, with the food set in front of them and Buffi hovering nearby, Adam blessed the meal then reached for his fork. As Amy followed suit, Adam carefully steered the topic away from the issue at hand and into safer waters by mentioning last year's class reunion.

Filling Amy in on what she'd missed was almost as fun as watching her face while he told the stories. Listening to her laugh put him in mind of a time when making her laugh came easy and thinking of her leaving was near to impossible.

In fact, all he could think of was that he had to find a way to make her stay.

"Something wrong, Adam?"

He looked up and realized she was staring, all traces of laughter gone. "What—uh, no, nothing's wrong." He swiped his chin to remove any possible traces of barbecue sauce.

But as he paid the check and led Amy back to the truck, he knew he hadn't been truthful with her. From the moment she plopped her posterior in his favorite chair, she'd wiggled her way back into his heart.

The truth be known, she'd never really left.

Sitting in the restaurant talking to Adam about old times made Amy feel like she'd never left Tierra Verde. Now that he'd slid into the driver's seat beside her, she felt almost compelled to remember the days when riding around town in this manner had been the norm.

"So are you ready for that surprise?"

She nodded, and off they went toward the church. They passed the main church building and circled the block to stop in the back, where a smattering of vehicles sat in the lot. Noting the vintage and the presence of multiple stickers and various ornaments hanging from the rearview mirrors, she turned to Adam. "Youth group?"

He wore a look of concern on his face. "I hope it's all right, but I told them you might be coming along with me. See. . ." He paused. "It's a special occasion."

"Oh?"

The door flew open, and the sound of guitars being tuned and teenagers chatting greeted them. "Hey, Adam!" a kid in a dark T-shirt and baggy shorts called. Amy followed the sound to the stage, where a band warmed up. The boy motioned for Adam to join them, but he declined, hanging back to introduce Amy to the kids.

"Hey, Adam," another band member called. "What are you, chicken?"

Several kids began to cluck. Adam turned to Amy. "Go

on," she said. "I'll be fine."

For the next half hour, Amy was entertained by a side of Adam she hadn't seen in too many years. With little coaxing, he climbed onstage with the youth band and took over the background vocals and finally the drums. Amy settled onto a stool in the back of the room and watched her former fiancé's crazy antics while bittersweet memories threatened once more.

Only the presence of the Lord in that room kept her from going there—from thinking about what might have been. Instead, she focused on the lyrics and on Adam's voice when he sang.

Too soon the music ended, and Adam stepped around the drum set to take the mic. "Who're we praising tonight?" he shouted.

"Jesus," the group responded in unison.

"Okay, before we get started, I want to introduce a friend of mine. Amy, come on up here."

Amy felt her face flush. "What? No, really," she said, but before she knew it, she'd been led to the stage by several members of the crowd. Adam helped her up and handed her a mic. Standing center stage with Adam brought back more memories—thoughts of leading worship at VBS, being counselors together at church camp, and finally, the last time they sang together in the youth group. What was the name of that song? A bit of melody teased her but proved elusive when she tried to remember the words.

All good memories; all bittersweet. She pushed them back into the far recesses of her mind and turned her attention to the man beside her.

"So, you all know Amy, right?" He waited for the crowd's cheering to die down. "Well, she doesn't know why I brought her here."

Strange how being on stage felt good, so natural. Nothing like the soundstages where she now made her living. Correction: where she used to make her living. It had been so long. "Adam, what are you up to?"

Several kids in the back began to make catcalls, and the ones down front clapped. "Hey, Adam," one of the band members shouted. "You're right. She's way out of your league."

Adam clutched his chest in mock pain. "Hey, I never said that." He turned to Amy. "These guys are harmless, I promise. How would you feel about singing just one song with me?"

"Sure," she said over the sound of the kids. She smiled at Adam, and he returned the gesture. "I hope it's one I know."

The band struck up a familiar chord, and their gazes locked. For just a moment, the whole world telescoped into a space no larger than the small stage. The music swelled and so did her heart. It was their song.

He sang the first chorus, and she joined in on the second. By the end, the crowd's cheering nearly drowned out the music. When the band had played the last note, Adam gathered Amy to his side and bowed his head.

As Amy listened to Adam pray for God's blessings on the meeting and its participants, she felt a pang of loss—for what she had missed and for what she would miss when she left Tierra Verde. She added a prayer in silence for the ability to do the right thing when the time came then added her amen to the host of others echoing in the room.

While the teens broke for refreshments, Adam thanked the band, shaking hands and making a point of offering specific compliments regarding each one's performance. As the last boy stepped off the stage, Adam turned to Amy. His face showed a bit of worry.

"Did I do the wrong thing putting you on the spot like that? You look a little, I don't know, far away, I guess."

She reached for his hand and held it. "I was far away. Back at camp. Remember when we played that song for the first time?"

Adam chuckled and drew her hand to his chest. "My voice kept cracking all through the second chorus."

"And I kept messing up the words because I was looking at you."

Once again their gazes locked. "I never noticed," he said softly as he leaned toward her.

"That I was looking?" She paused to take a breath. "Or that I messed up the words?"

"Hey, Adam. Can you come here a minute?"

The moment shattered as the reality of the commotion going on around them returned. Adam lifted her fingers to his lips and kissed them softly. "To old times," he said.

"Adam? Hey, dude."

He released his grasp. "Excuse me a sec."

She nodded and watched him walk over to the corner where a group of kids sat in a circle. The talk seemed animated, but with the noise level so high, she could hear none of what they said. One of the band members wandered up and offered her a cookie and some punch. She accepted the punch and drank half the glass while watching the exchange in the corner. A moment later, Adam returned.

"Can we talk?" He gestured toward the exit door. "Out there?"

"Sure."

She set her cup on the stool and followed him into the hallway. The familiar church smell assailed her senses. *Funny how some things from childhood follow you no matter how far you roam.*

Adam took her hand once more. "Amy, I don't want you to feel pressured by what I'm going to ask you. I realize you don't know when you'll be leaving Tierra Verde, so don't think you'd have to stay just for me." He shook his head. "No—um—I mean for us."

Us? "Okay," she said slowly.

"Okay." He took a deep breath and let it out. "I know you have a lot going on in your life, and I don't want to add to that but. . ." He looked away. "I guess I was wondering—I mean it's for the kids and all, but I don't want you to think we'd just be asking because of what you do. The acting thing, I mean. . ."

He looked positively adorable, and Amy was tempted to let him stutter on indefinitely. Unfortunately, the crowd back in the teen room had begun to get exceptionally loud. Staying away for any amount of time probably was not a good idea.

"Adam, it's okay. Just say it."

"All right." He met her gaze once more. "Would you direct the Christmas play?"

Chapter 9

There. He said it. Obviously she would turn him down. She always seemed to.

"Sure."

"What?"

"I'll do it." Amy paused. "Or rather I will do it along with someone else so that person can take my place when I leave."

When I leave. Why did that phrase threaten to steal the joy from her affirmative answer? He opened his mouth to say something, only to clamp it shut when a door closed and footsteps echoed in the hall.

"Now that sounds like a right good idea, Amy, and I think Adam is the man for the job."

Adam whirled around to see Uncle Willard standing a few feet away. "I thought you weren't coming." He cast a glance at Amy. "He said he couldn't help with the youth group tonight because he was *busy*." With that last word, Adam returned his attention to his wayward uncle.

Uncle Willard smiled and pressed past him to take Amy by the elbow. "Well I'm here now, and it sounds like we'd better get in there before the joyous noise those guys are making wakes the dead."

The rest of the evening passed in a blur. Before breaking the kids into groups for Bible study, Uncle Willard made the announcement that Amy would be directing the Christmas play with Adam as her assistant. When pressed as to what Willard would be doing, his answer was, "Supervising those two."

For the next hour, Amy held her own among the kids. She signed autographs, posed for pictures, and endured more hugs than she thought humanly possible. It didn't take long for the youth group members to realize that, while the world might paint Amy Foreman as a star, God had made her a humble and giving young woman.

He'd also granted her a measure of grace and beauty, which one particularly cheeky member of the group noted when she turned him down for a date the following evening. "I came here with Adam tonight," she told the poor fellow. "Surely you don't think I would make plans with someone else under the circumstances."

Under the circumstances.

Adam could still hear the hoots and hollers of the kids echoing in his ears as he drove Amy home. Too soon he found himself walking Amy to her door, a copy of the script tucked under his arm. A sliver of moonlight illuminated her face and cast her profile into shadow.

"Thank you for a lovely evening." She took the script then fumbled for her keys. "I can't wait to read the play."

"My pleasure." A thought occurred. "Hey, are you sure I didn't overstep my bounds? I probably should have warned you before just tossing you to the wolves in the youth group."

"They are great."

He leaned against the hood of the truck and grinned. "Yeah, they are."

She shook her head and continued to dig for her keys. "You shouldn't be such a worrier. I really did have a terrific—"

The keys tumbled forth and bounced around his feet. Adam leaned down to retrieve them and bumped heads with Amy. The script landed between them. "Oh, no, I'm so sorry." He reached to help her up.

Somehow in the process of helping, he ended up doing just the opposite. Both of them went sprawling onto the driveway. They looked like fools in the glow of the truck's headlights.

Amy scrambled into a sitting position and rubbed her forehead while Adam remained very still lest he show himself to be an idiot again. When he chanced a look up at Amy, he saw she was biting her lip, one hand over her eyes.

Well, he'd certainly done it this time. She looked like she was about to cry.

And then she began to giggle.

Slowly she lowered her hand to show eyes that sparkled, not with tears but with mirth. He leaned up on his elbows and tried to affect a terse look. "Do you find this funny?" he asked, but before he could get the question out, he'd begun to laugh.

Amy rose first and reached for his hand to try to pull him to his feet. Instead he patted the place beside him on the driveway. "There's quite a view from here," he said as he pointed to the stars. "Look over there."

He felt her move into place at his side and nearly stopped

breathing when she reached for his hand. They lay there in silence for a moment, then Adam leaned up on one elbow.

"Adam, you're blocking my view," Amy said with mock irritation.

"Sorry," he said. Without warning, he kissed her.

It was a light kiss, chaste and soft. When he lay back beside her and tightened his grip on Amy's hand, he heard her sigh.

"Adam?" she whispered.

"Yeah?"

"Do that again. Just once, no matter what I say, and then promise me you will never do it again."

So he did—although he made no promises.

Amy had no idea how long they lay in the driveway side by side staring up at the stars. The next morning she found out it was long enough to have been spotted and photographed. The picture arrived by fax along with a phone number and a caption stating ACTRESS SHUNS SQUEAKY CLEAN IMAGE FOR PILL-POPPING PARTY. The image, though grainy, was clear enough to show her and Adam sprawled in her driveway.

The shaking began before she could return the paper to its resting place on the desk. Instead she let the awful image fall to the floor and watched as it landed upside down on the cracked linoleum.

What to do? After several attempts, she managed to dial the clinic to say she'd be late, then she punched in the numbers on the fax. A strange voice answered first before Ed came on the line.

"You had enough, kid?"

She held tight to the phone as she sank onto the sofa. "What do you want?"

"Call off your lawyers, and your boyfriend doesn't see his face plastered all over the place."

Amy fought to catch her breath. "You leave him out of it."

"Sure, Amy." Ed laughed. "How about we talk about this movie you're up for?"

"There's nothing to talk about." She clutched her knees to her chest. "There is no movie."

"I hear different." He paused. "Soon as you get the word, you call me. In the meantime, I'll just hang on to the originals."

She hung up and phoned her attorney. It was barely seven o'clock in Los Angeles, but she knew she could leave a message if necessary. To her surprise, she got a live body—a paralegal. She gave the woman all the details then sent a copy of the fax and waited for a call from one of the team of lawyers working on her behalf. In the interim, the paralegal explained that she would be sending a report to the LAPD.

Sitting drove her crazy, so Amy stood and began to pace, willing the phone to ring. When she tired of that, she headed into the kitchen and began to clean. When the phone finally rang at quarter to eleven, Tierra Verde time, she dropped her cleaning rag and ran.

Fifteen minutes later, she hung up with a seed of hope in her heart. If Ed thought to threaten her with blackmail, he should have done his homework beforehand. By sending her the fax from his office so soon after the photos were taken, he'd all but proven he had an accomplice. It would be almost impossible for him to fly out to Tierra Verde, capture the pictures, return to Los Angeles, and then send the fax without help.

Oh, it could be done, but Ed was definitely not the type to skulk around in the shadows with a telephoto lens. Not when he could pay someone else to do it for him.

With the fax number in hand, Detective Miller had told her attorney that it was a matter of time before the other party was found out. If the detective was to be believed, playing one bad guy against another often yielded the desired result of catching them both.

She showered and dressed for work, heading toward the clinic a little before noon with a sack lunch and a smile. To her surprise and relief, Adam's mom was nowhere to be found. Explanations could wait—a blessing as she had no idea how to account for the hours she'd missed. Fortunately, this was Adam's day in surgery.

She greeted Judy, who sat in Mrs. Chambers's chair, then headed for grooming, where she would have to work twice as fast to make up for the lost morning. Thankfully, the dogs cooperated, and the morning's work was done in short order. As she placed a bright red bandanna on the malamute and led him to his cage, her stomach growled. Somehow, in the rush to complete her work, she'd forgotten all about lunch.

After washing her hands, she grabbed her lunch sack and pulled a bottle of water from the fridge then called to Judy that she'd return in half an hour. The cloudless day beckoned, so she headed outside and settled in a quiet spot to read the script Adam had given her last night.

Last night.

Amy grimaced. There could be no more nights like last night. She was nothing more than a short-timer in this town. The last thing she intended to do was break Adam's heart again.

But what about your heart?

Ignoring the still small voice, Amy plunged into reading the script, taking the occasional bite of sandwich between scenes until she'd read the whole thing. The afternoon sun slanted toward her, providing a welcome warmth from the chill wind that ruffled her hair and lifted the edge of the pages. Soon it would be winter, and with it, the holidays. Where would she be? With whom would she celebrate?

In the past she'd spent the months either on location at some remote film site or back in California, alone. Why did the fact she might spend them alone again bother her now?

Setting the papers and the thought aside, she leaned back and reached for her apple. The play, entitled "The Rescue," was good, well written, and entertaining. The premise that a girl who comes to town on Christmas Eve in need of help only to end up helping her rescuer instead made her giggle—and warmed her heart.

As she put away her lunch and walked back toward the clinic, she began to think of who she might cast in the leading roles. Slipping in the back door, Amy checked the clock. A quarter to four. Time to get back to work.

"Amy? Where have you been?" Mrs. Chambers called. "I've been looking for you all over."

Chapter 10

Amy shrugged out of her jacket and dropped her purse and the script into her desk drawer. She followed the voice to the front of the clinic, where Adam's mother stood on a chair, inflatable pumpkin in hand.

"There you are," she said as Amy rounded the corner.

"I had a late lunch. Oh, Mrs. Chambers, that doesn't look safe." She reached for the older woman in time to help her down just as the chair began to wobble. "Please come down from there."

"Can't, dear," she said.

Assessing the situation—copious amounts of orange-colored decorations with a suspiciously pumpkin-and-turkey theme and several containers of tape—Amy deduced a decorating session was in the offing. "Oh, please let me do that," she said.

Not that she would actually *want* to decorate the office area for Thanksgiving. Rather she looked at the offer as saving a dear lady's neck. Five minutes after Mrs. Chambers handed over the loot and started directing the operation, Amy began to wish she could retract her offer. Still, she kept her word and followed the older woman's instructions until the last of the decor was in place.

"Come and sit with me, dear," Mrs. Chambers called as she disappeared down the hall toward the kitchen. "I'm brewing tea."

Amy cast a glance at the clock over the reception desk. Almost four thirty. Within the hour Adam would finish the last surgery of the day and at least a half dozen pet owners would arrive for their animals. She still had three dentals and a nail trim to do.

"Just for a moment," Mrs. C. said. "I know you're busy, but I have something important to talk to you about." She patted the place beside her on the break room's white wicker sofa. "Sit. You young people move way too fast."

Way too fast. Yes, that's exactly the way her relationship with Adam felt—like it was moving way too fast. She touched her temple with her fingertip then smiled. "I suppose I can spare a moment for the boss's mom."

After enduring the formalities of pouring and sweetening the tea, Mrs. Chambers pursed her lips and shook her head. "I certainly hope you can help me, dear."

She'd never seem Adam's mother the least bit bothered, so the concern on her face now was worrisome. "What is it? Is there something wrong?"

Deep blue eyes lifted to meet her gaze, and the worried look deepened. "I've done something dreadful, Amy, and I need to ask your help in righting it."

"Of course." She reached for the older woman's hand. "I'll do whatever I can for you."

The worry line on her forehead seemed to disappear as Mrs. Chambers smiled. "You will? Oh, that is *such* good news." She shifted to face Amy. "You see, it all started when Mr. Chambers bought a travel trailer. Well, actually, it was more of a little house on wheels. Well, anyway. . ." She paused to take a sip of tea then continued. "He's a sly one, my husband, and he got me hooked by telling me I could decorate our new place any way I wanted. Well, how was I supposed to know our new place's decor would include a steering wheel?"

Amy sat back and listened to the older woman's description of the new home on wheels her husband surprised her with this morning. All the while Amy thought about the dozen other things to do. Still, her mama had raised her right, and she knew that to stop Mrs. Chambers in mid story would be the height of bad form.

Just about the time the story wound down, the door opened and in stepped Adam. He leaned against the door frame just out of his mother's line of sight and watched in amusement as Mrs. Chambers described her first experience with backing up her new home.

As their gazes met and Adam's smile deepened, Amy opened her mouth to speak. When he touched his fingers to his lips in a plea for silence, Amy's heart skidded to a stop.

"Are you listening, dear?"

"Hmm? What? I'm sorry." She tore her attention from Adam and focused on his mother. "I'm listening."

"So as I said, I'm a bit worried about Adam. His father plans to keep to a rigorous travel schedule." She heaved a dramatic sigh as Adam silently cheered behind her. "I don't know how he will manage. He needs someone who will see he's taken care of."

She couldn't look at him. If she did, she would laugh for sure. "I'm sure Judy will do a fine job."

Mrs. Chambers's painted-on brows rose while her gaze lowered. "Well, dear, I'm sure Judy is a fine woman, but she's married." She met Amy's questioning stare. "It's not his veterinarian practice that needs a woman's touch. It's him."

"Oh?" Realization dawned. "Oh!"

"Mr. Chambers and I have always adored you, Amy, and Adam, well, he hasn't had a single date since you—"

"Mother, am I too late to join this tea party?" Adam turned his gaze on her. "Mr. Hawkings will be by for Rex in a few minutes. Is he ready to go?"

Amy rose on shaky legs and set her teacup in the sink with a distinctive rattle. "Yes, well, the conversation was lovely, Mrs. Chambers." She brushed past Adam, making a concentrated effort not to touch him as she made her way through the door. Still, the spicy smell of his aftershave chased her down the hall to the grooming room.

You can't have him, she reminded herself. But was that true?

"Amy?" She froze at the sound of Mrs. Chambers's voice.

"Yes?" she called.

"Come to Thanksgiving?" floated down the hall toward her.

She retraced her steps and refused to make eye contact with Adam. "Thank you, Mrs. Chambers, but I have other plans."

Thankfully the cell phone in her pocket rang, providing an escape. Only after she checked the identity of the incoming caller did she wish she'd continued the conversation with Adam and Mrs. Chambers instead.

Amy had other plans for Thanksgiving?

Adam found it hard to concentrate on being upset with his mother. His mind reeled with the possibilities of what Amy Foreman might be doing for Thanksgiving. Dining with a host of Hollywood heavyweights, perhaps?

"I just know she's the one for you, and I think she knows it, too. Adam, dear, don't be angry."

He looked down into a face so like his own. "Mom, I'm not angry." Pausing, he searched for the kindest words he could use. "I would appreciate it if you'd let me do this my way."

"This?" She grinned and slapped her knees with her palms. "So you *are* considering a relationship with her. I *knew* it. Why, I just told your father this morning that I was certain you weren't going to let that girl get away this time. Of course, he. . ."

Mom talked until she ran out of words—temporarily. Adam used that opportunity to make his excuses and flee to the privacy of his office.

Threading his fingers together, Adam leaned back in his chair, rested his boots on the desk, and stared up at the ceiling. Allowing a long breath to escape, he closed his eyes. Memories of what happened the last time he allowed Amy to steal his heart taunted him. The minor—and more prideful—concern of giving up his stake in the Bachelor Club also begged for consideration.

Was loving Amy Foreman worth the risk—both to his heart and to his pride?

"Excuse me, Adam." Amy's voice cut into his thoughts, and he opened his eyes to see her standing in the doorway. "Emergency call for you on line three. It's Mr. Jarrell."

A moment later he bolted from his chair. The owner of a greyhound was racing to the clinic. His dog had taken a nasty spill after chasing a postal truck onto the freeway. Operating on the high-strung breed was dicey at best, and this dog had a history of seizures that made her an even more difficult case.

"Judy!" he called as he raced down the hall to the operating room. "Scrub up. The Jarrells' greyhound's coming in, and she's in bad shape."

When Judy failed to answer, he stuck his head out into the reception area and found it empty. "Judy?"

His mother emerged from the office and shook her head. "She's already gone for the day, dear. What's this I hear about Daisy?"

"Mr. Jarrell is on his way in with her." He dashed to the reception desk to retrieve the phone list. "Broken leg. Possible internal injuries." Thrusting this list toward Mom, he whirled around on his heels and headed back to the operating room. "Try to catch Judy on her cell. I can't operate without someone to assist."

Adam began his pre-op preparations, all the while praying the Lord would bring him the help he needed. An eternity later, Amy burst through the door with Lynn Jarrell trailing behind her. He'd managed to wrap Daisy in a sheet, but the telltale signs of blood soaking the fabric urged Adam into quick action.

"Where's Judy?" he snapped as he directed Lynn to lay Daisy on the table then watched as the man skittered from the room.

"Phone's turned off," Amy said. "Looks like I'm all you've got."

Their gazes locked over the table. She only looked moderately afraid—not terrified as he'd expected. Adam paused a second then turned to attend to the whimpering dog. "All right. But you're going to have to do everything I say exactly as I tell you."

A half hour later, Daisy rested comfortably in a monitored cage, her vitals strong and her leg bandaged. Adam spoke to the dog's owner then returned to the OR to find Amy standing beside the gurney, her eyes closed and face tilted down as if in prayer. When she opened her eyes, he noted a tear.

"It's all right," he said gently. "You did an incredible job assisting me. Thanks to your help, she's going to make a full recovery."

For a moment he thought she might say something. Instead, she just stood still and allowed the tears to flow. Gathering her into his arms, Adam tucked her head beneath his chin and let her cry.

When she finally quieted, Adam kissed the top of her head. "Are you all right?"

"Yes. No," she whispered. "Oh, Adam, I'm so confused."

"What is it, sweetheart? Is it the surgery? I know I didn't handle my first time in the OR very well, but you were a champ."

She shook her head. "That's not it."

"Did I do something wrong?"

"No, that's the problem. You did everything right." She paused to take a gulp of air. "The part I was up for. Well, I got it."

His heart sank. "Hey, that's great," he managed.

"Yeah." She sniffed and wiped at her eyes with her sleeve. "The cops arrested Ed and a guy from one of the tabloids this afternoon. Turns out I'm not the first one they've tried this on."

"So everything's back the way it should be?"

"Almost. Except that I love you. I always have." Her tears began again, only this time he gladly held her while she cried.

"Oh, Amy." He leaned his head against her silky hair. "I love you, too." He paused to find his voice. "I always have."

"But I have to leave," she said. "Didn't you hear me? I got the part."

"I heard." His heart refused to wrap around the fact she might not be here forever. "But getting the part doesn't necessarily mean you have to leave, does it?"

"You could go with me," she said in a tiny voice.

"To Hollywood? No way." He chuckled despite the gravity of the situation.

"I don't care where we are, Adam." She snuggled closer. "I only know I don't want to let you out of my sight. Ever."

An idea dawned and he smiled. "I think I can make that happen, but you'll have to marry me first."

Amy froze then tilted her chin to look up into his eyes. "Don't tease me, Adam."

When she pulled away to face him, her cheeks stained with tears and her nose red, he did the only thing he knew to do. He dropped to one knee. "Be my wife, Amy. I don't care if we live in Hollywood, Tierra Verde, or Timbuktu. I just know I can't live without you."

She swiped at her eyes and frowned. "But what about the Bachelor Club?"

"I don't care about that silly bargain. I'd marry you tomorrow if you'd have me."

"Oh, I'll have you," she said, "but we can wait until Valentine's Day, can't we? Then you'll be an old man of *thirty*." Her eyes twinkled with mirth.

Chapter 11

Will Lovelace's laughter crackled on the other end of the phone line. He'd called Will, knowing his friend would be the only one of the three other members of the club who would answer at this early hour.

"Getting married on Valentine's Day is a stroke of genius," Will said. "You get the woman of your dreams and still keep your share of the Bachelor Club loot."

"Yeah, I thought so, too. With Amy out in California until the end of the week, I'm working on getting things taken care of so I can get away for a decent honeymoon."

"You, get away? How'll you manage that?"

"Remember old Doc Brown, the guy I bought the practice from? He's more than ready to come out of retirement and take over for me for a while. And Amy's got her housekeeper coming to stay here and take care of my place and the dogs."

He paused to pour his coffee, only to narrowly miss dropping the phone into his cup as it filled. "Hang on a sec."

Three spoonfuls of sugar later, Adam picked up the phone

and padded toward the back door, coffee cup in hand. "Okay, where were we?"

"You were asking me to be your best man."

"Oh, yeah, that's right." Adam opened the door and pressed on the screen, inhaling a deep blast of cold, fresh air. "So, will you—along with the other two members of the Bachelor Club, of course?" The dogs raced past him out the door then froze and began to bark at something—or rather someone—on the deck. "Hey, I'm going to have to call you back." He clicked off the phone and went back to pour a second cup of coffee.

The last thing he expected to see was Amy sitting in his favorite chair. She was also the best thing he'd seen all week, and he told her so just after setting the mugs on the porch rail and lifting her out of his chair to kiss her soundly.

When he pulled away to push a strand of hair from her face, he noted a look of sadness. "What is it, Amy? What's wrong?"

Amy shook her head and refused to meet his gaze. "I'm sorry, Adam. I can't marry you on Valentine's Day."

His heart sunk. Amy Foreman was leaving him—again. Somehow, he managed a "Why?"

"Because the shooting schedule's moved up. I have to be on location in New Zealand two days after Christmas."

"But Christmas is in two weeks." He collected his racing thoughts. "How long's the shoot?"

"Five months in New Zealand and another six weeks of postproduction work in Sydney. I won't be back until June." She fell into his arms once more. When she calmed, she stepped back, leaned against the rail, and looked up into his eyes. "I can't ask you to move up the wedding date, and I'll understand if you want to call the whole thing off. I know the Bachelor Club has meant a lot to you. Maybe the Lord's trying to tell you I'm just not the one for you."

Adam looked past Amy to the purple mountains and the orange glow of a new day dawning atop their peaks. Tierra Verde was home, and his deal with the members of the Bachelor Club went way back, well before Amy Foreman disrupted his life—twice.

"Well," he said slowly, "this is a problem. I'm going to have to give it some thought."

She nodded and offered a shaky smile. "I understand."

"Good." He sank into his rocker before she could steal it again and reached for his coffee cup. "So, since you're back early, will you be at dress rehearsal tomorrow night at the church auditorium?"

Amy settled beside him and sipped gingerly at the strong brew and seemed to wince. "Oh, Adam, I forgot. What time?"

"Eight," he said, knowing full well it started at seven. Once again, Amy Foreman had thrown his entire life into complete chaos. He would need that extra hour—maybe more—before he could see her again.

Amy walked into the auditorium and stopped short. The house lights were down, throwing the room into darkness. At center stage, a single spotlight shone. The backdrop looked phenomenal, its artificial snow and shimmering white snowflakes providing a stark contrast to the shadows.

As her eyes adjusted to the light, Amy could see forms in the seats near the front. She began to make her way toward the front, touching the back of each aisle seat as she followed the path of tiny safety lights. When she reached the front row, a hand grasped her wrist and stopped her. A second later, she felt herself being led up the stairs onto the stage. As she stepped into the circle of light, she realized it was Adam who held her hand.

What?

The cast of "The Rescue" appeared from the wings and formed a semicircle behind them. From somewhere offstage, soft music began to play.

Adam clasped her hand and touched her fingers to his lips. "Ladies and gentlemen, the play these kids have been preparing is a story about a woman who comes to town in need of help, only to end up rescuing someone instead. When I wrote the play—"

"You wrote it?"

"Yes, last year, actually." Adam squeezed her hand. "As I said, when I wrote the play, I had no idea the plot would turn out to be taken directly from my life." He turned to look down at Amy. "Amy Foreman, you rescued me, and I didn't even know I needed rescuing. I know we had plans for a big wedding with all the fuss and frills, but it looks like that's not going to happen, at least not in time for you to make your flight on the twenty-sixth."

"I'm sorry," she whispered.

"Don't be." Adam motioned with his hand, and the house

lights went up. Seated in the auditorium were many familiar faces. One stood out among the rest as the biggest surprise of all.

"Maria Elena?" She nodded and waved as Amy turned to Adam. "What's going on here?"

"A wedding." He grinned. "That is, if you'll have me."

"But I don't understand, I—"

"I had already arranged for Maria Elena to surprise you with a visit for Christmas, so it was pretty simple to get her ticket changed to a noontime flight today. As for the other things, the food, the cake, and of course, your dress, well, that took a little more doing, but I managed that, too.

"We'll be here until the day after Christmas, then you and I head for New Zealand. I have this Easter play I've been thinking of writing, and I can't imagine a better place to get started on it. I'll fly back every once in a while and see how Maria Elena's treating my dogs and how Doc Brown's running the clinic, but you've pretty much got me to yourself for the next six months." He paused. "Do you think you'd mind living in Tierra Verde when you're not off making movies?"

"Of course I wouldn't mind, but. . ." Tears blurred the man she held tight. She tried to continue speaking but failed miserably.

"So is that a yes?"

"But the Bachelor Club. You'll lose your part in it."

Adam gathered her into his arms. "I might be resigning from the Bachelor Club, but I have another club I plan to join."

"What's that?"

"The Happily Ever After Club."

KATHLEEN Y'BARBO

Kathleen Y'Barbo is an award-winning novelist and sixth-generation Texan. After completing a degree in marketing at Texas A&M University, she focused on raising four children and turned to writing. She is a member of American Christian Romance Writers, Romance Writers of America, and Writers Information Network. She also lectures on the craft of writing at the elementary and secondary levels and conducts distance learning classes on the university level.

Stealing Home

by Rhonda Gibson

Dedication

I want to thank Colleen Coble, Jean Kincaid,
Kathy Velarde, and all of ACRW for their love and support.
Most importantly and above all,
I want to thank the Lord my God for all things.

Set your mind on things above, not on things on the earth.
COLOSSIANS 3:2 NKJV

Chapter 1

Will Lovelac e leaned against the fence. Boys of all ages gathered on the greening baseball field to practice. Warm spring air that held hints of summer in its feathery breeze cooled the perspiration beaded on his forehead.

He shut his eyes and relished memories of childhood. Spring and summer days filled with ball practice, games, and picnics. His parents supported him no matter what the sport of the season, but Will had to admit baseball was his favorite game of the year.

"I want to play, too."

Will opened his eyes and searched the area for the owner of the demanding voice.

"You're too little, Joey. Go home."

He spotted four boys coming through the side gate. Will's gaze found Joey immediately. If he was too little, he had to be the one with red hair and freckles who looked to be about seven or eight. And a scrawny seven or eight at that. They were less than five feet away, and their voices rang out loud and clear.

"I don't want to go home." Will watched as Joey stuck his lower lip out and crossed his skinny arms over his chest. "And you can't make me." The belligerent expression on Joey's face warned of his determination to stand his ground.

"You don't even have a glove," one of the boys taunted as he ran across the field to join more of his friends.

Joey ran after him. "I don't need no glove."

Will felt a smile tickling his lips. He enjoyed the spirit of the kid. Joey reminded Will of himself as a young boy.

The coach walked up to home plate. He held a ball and bat. "Okay, boys! Spread out! A couple of you get in center field."

The boys scampered into different directions, but Joey didn't move from the position he'd taken in right field. A loud crack echoed on the morning breeze, and the ball curved through the air in Joey's direction.

Will's heartbeat quickened with adrenaline. The game never ceased to excite him. He pushed off the fence and watched Joey position himself under the ball. Another boy ran toward Joey.

"It's mine," Joey yelled.

Will held his breath as the two boys ran, heads up and arms raised high. Both yelled repeatedly, "I got it! I got it!"

The bigger boy bumped into Joey, and Will watched him refuse to give ground. The ball came down on top of Joey. It slid through his hands and hit him in the chest.

Missed it!

The ball rolled down Joey's small stomach and landed at his feet. Joey grabbed his chest and looked at the ball.

Will was too far away to hear what the other boy said, but he saw Joey look up and scowl. The older kid scooped up the ball and threw it back toward home plate.

"Joey!" the coach yelled. "Don't try to catch the ball without a glove! You'll get hurt!"

Will's gaze followed Joey, who ran through another side gate exiting the field. His heart went out to the boy. He wondered why Joey didn't have a ball glove with him. Will felt sure that if Joey had used a glove, he would have caught the ball.

He exited the field by the gate closest to him. Will hurried to his truck and hopped inside. He drove around the block and found Joey walking down the sidewalk.

The last thing he wanted to do was scare the boy, so he pulled a few feet in front of him and parked the truck. Will got out and leaned against the front fender. When Joey came even with him, he spoke.

"You almost had that ball back there."

Joey continued to walk with his head down. "Yeah, but almost isn't good enough." His voice sounded choked and low.

Will fell into step beside him, close enough for conversation but far enough away to be nonthreatening. "True. But all you need is a good glove."

Joey stopped. He looked up at Will. Tears filled his emerald green eyes. "You think so?"

Will got down on one knee and looked the boy in the eyes. "I'm sure of it."

"My sister says it's not *necessary* and won't get me one." Joey started walking back down the sidewalk. His shoulders slumped.

Will stood up. "Joey?"

The little boy stopped and turned to face him. A tear

slipped down his cheek. "What?"

"Do you think your sister would object if I gave you my old glove?" Will wanted to go hug the boy but instinctively knew that was an inappropriate gesture from a stranger. His mind swirled with questions. Why would someone object to him having a ball glove? Was it a money issue?

His gaze moved over the little boy's clothes. They looked new. He wore a clean red shirt, blue jeans, and white tennis shoes. Not the attire of a poor kid.

A smile brightened Joey's face. "I'll go ask Charisma—that's my sister." He turned around and headed back the way they'd come.

Joey stopped. "Mister, what's your name? I'm not supposed to talk to strangers. And Charisma will ask me your name and then I'll have to say I don't know and then I'll get in trouble."

Will tucked his hands in his back pockets. "She's right, you shouldn't talk to strangers." He could kick himself. In his hurry to give the boy some comfort and reassurance, Will had forgotten to consider the risks strangers too often represented.

"If you tell me your name, we won't be strangers and then we won't get in trouble."

The big grin on Joey's face worried Will. "Listen, Joey." Will moved closer to the little boy. "My name is Will Lovelace, and if she asks where we met, you tell her the truth. It's wrong to lie."

"Okay, Will. I won't lie." Joey continued down the sidewalk.

Once more, Will fell into step beside him. "Great, is she home?"

"Naw, she's at work." Joey's footsteps increased in speed.

Will stopped. "And where does she work?"

"The Diner," Joey called over his shoulder.

"Joey, don't talk to any more strangers."

"Okay, Will." Joey started running.

"I'll go get the glove and meet you there," Will called after him. He walked back to his truck and climbed inside.

"Charisma, Jackie just threw her order pad down and walked out."

Charisma Diner looked up from the floral arrangement she was working on. Lynn Hartford, her teenage floral assistant, stood in front of the desk with her hands on her slender hips. "Why did she do that, Lynn?" Charisma added a few sprigs of baby's breath to the greenery.

"I'm not sure, but you should get out there. Old man Morgan isn't happy." Lynn moved to a vase of red roses and began pulling several out.

"Lynn, calling Mr. Morgan old isn't very nice." Charisma set the new arrangement on the counter.

"Well, he *is* old," the teenager shot back.

Charisma chose to ignore Lynn and headed to the front counter. She peeked through the door at Mr. Morgan. He paced the front entryway like a groom before his wedding. She pushed through the swinging doors and entered the room.

"Good morning, Mr. Morgan."

"That girl is impossible!" Mr. Morgan declared, spinning around on his heels to face her.

Charisma offered what she hoped was a warm smile. "I'm sorry Jackie upset you. Can I help you?" Without being told, she knew he was there to get his wife's morning carnation. Every day he chose a different color. It was really romantic. Charisma could just visualize the beautiful bouquet sitting in their home.

Her smile must have done the trick, or maybe it was the way she spoke, for Mr. Morgan's voice softened and he asked, "Do you have a blue one this morning?"

"Dark or light blue?" She made her way to the cooler that held vases of various colors of carnations.

He followed her. "Do you have one of those that have a mixture of lights and darks?"

Charisma felt him leaning over her shoulder as she bent into the case. The cool air felt good on her cheeks. "Sure do." She pulled out two so he could choose. One was dark blue with light blue streaks and the other was light with dark streaks.

"I think my Mazie would like the lighter. Don't you?" He took the light one from her hand and bent to inhale its sweet fragrance.

Charisma didn't answer his question; instead she asked one of her own. "How is she this morning, Mr. Morgan?"

He lifted his head. His gray eyes filled with moisture. "She's doing as good as can be expected. The doctor says she could go any day now."

"Don't you give up hope. He's been saying that for weeks now, and we haven't stopped praying for her at church. You and I both know God can still create a miracle." Charisma moved to the register. The tears in his eyes filled her with sorrow.

Lord, why do bad things happen to good people? That same prayer had been on her heart and lips for three years now. That was when her father and stepmother had died, leaving Charisma to care for her beloved half brother, Joey.

"Thanks, Charisma. You always know how to brighten my day. Sometimes I forget there is a whole church full of people praying for my Mazie. We might lick that cancer yet." He handed her the money and turned to leave.

When he opened the door, Joey dashed in.

"Whoa there, little fella." Mr. Morgan stepped back to avoid getting knocked down.

"Joey. What do you say to Mr. Morgan?" Charisma scolded, coming around the counter.

"Oops, sorry, Mr. Morgan."

"That's okay, Joey. You must be in a big hurry this morning." He ruffled Joey's hair.

Joey stepped away from the old man's hand. "I am. I got to ask Charisma if I can have a baseball glove."

"I see; then I'm going to get out of here so you can talk to her about that." Mr. Morgan winked at Joey and left the store.

Charisma knelt down in front of her little brother. "Joey, where is Marla?"

He studied the toe of his shoe. "She's putting a new diaper on Mary. I asked if I could go to the ballpark for a little while and she said I could."

She made a mental note to look for a new baby-sitter. "Joey, you know you aren't supposed to be running around without an adult." Charisma waited for his nod before continuing. "Also, we've already talked about getting you a mitt. A ball glove is not something we need. I'm sorry, sweetie, you know we don't have the money for that right now."

Tears filled his eyes. "I need it and it's free." He wrapped his thin arms around her neck. "Please let me have it, Charisma."

The bell over the door announced another customer. Charisma wanted to know more about the glove, but she knew the customer came first if she was to keep the business going. She hugged Joey to her and whispered in his ear, "We'll talk about it as soon as I finish with this customer. Okay?"

He nodded then released his hold around her neck.

She stood up, her heart clenching at the sad expression on her eight-year-old brother's face.

Charisma turned her attention to the customer standing in the doorway. The morning sunlight created a halo around his blond head. His sea blue eyes scanned the store. "Can I help you?" she asked as recognition filled her.

Joey turned around to see who had come in and shouted, "It's Will!"

Will laughed and came farther into the store. He held the mitt out to Joey and looked about the flower shop. "When you said she worked at the 'diner,' I thought you meant a restaurant. It took me a few minutes to find the place."

Charisma stared at the man who seemed to know her little brother. She watched in silence as Joey took the glove and tried it on.

"How does it fit?" Will asked Joey.

Joey looked up at him with big, shining eyes. "Great!"

How could she tell her little brother he couldn't have the glove? Especially since it came from Will Lovelace.

Chapter 2

Will patted Joey's shoulder. "Good, I'm glad. I used it when I was about your age." Will's gaze met the woman's standing behind Joey. Some emotion he couldn't identify shone in her eyes. Was she afraid he was a threat to Joey?

"I'm sorry, Mr. Lovelace. He can't keep it."

Before Will could utter a sound, Joey protested. "Why not? It's free!"

Will watched her expression change as she knelt in front of the boy. "Joey, that mitt belonged to Mr. Lovelace when he was a little boy. It means a lot to him. I don't want you to lose it or ruin it."

Joey pulled away from her and held the mitt tight against his chest. "I won't."

Will cleared his throat. Her brown gaze flashed up at him from where she knelt. Taken aback by the warning in her look, Will tried another approach. "I'm sorry. I should have asked before I gave him the glove."

She rose to her feet. "Yes, you should have." She bit each

word out between clenched teeth.

Joey eased up beside his sister. He put his small hand on her waist. "Please, Charisma. He said I can have it, and I'll take good care of it. *Please.*"

Will wanted to turn from the scene in front of him but couldn't pull his gaze away. Charisma's face softened. She reached out and lifted her brother's chin then bent down and kissed his cheek.

"Tell Mr. Lovelace thank you for the glove."

Joey jerked his face from her hand and approached Will. He stopped a few feet away from him and craned his neck back. "Thank you, Mr. Lovelace. I'll take good care of it, I promise."

Will watched Charisma Diner over Joey's head. She walked to the checkout counter and started arranging the small gift cards by the register. "You're welcome, Joey."

"I'm going over to the ballpark and see if I can play now." Joey ran out the door.

Charisma called after him. "Joey, be careful!"

Then she turned her brown eyes toward Will. "Is there anything else I can do for you, Mr. Lovelace?" He watched her cheeks turn into twin peaks of red.

"I really am sorry, Miss Diner. When I saw Joey out on the field with no glove and wanting to play so badly, I just didn't really think it through. I should have consulted you before offering him the mitt." He leaned his hip against the counter.

She wasn't thinking clearly. Charisma couldn't believe Will

Lovelace still had that effect on her.

She really needed to get him out of her flower shop. "Joey's been wanting a softball mitt all spring. I should have just gotten him a new one. What you did was nice; thank you." Charisma prayed Will didn't ask her how she knew his last name. She'd been so eager to say no, she'd blurted it out before he could introduce himself. Since he obviously didn't recognize her, she was sure he would find it amusing that she knew who he was.

She was one of the few girls he hadn't flirted with or dated in college. But all the same, she'd lost her young heart to him. It really wasn't his fault that he'd dated all her friends and never gave her a second look. Back then, she'd had crooked teeth and braces, owlish glasses, auburn hair so long she'd worn it in a bun fashion on top of her head, and was so shy and in love with him it hurt.

"It's Will. Please don't call me, Mr. Lovelace. That's my dad's name."

His smile could melt icicles, she thought as she nodded her acceptance.

The bell over the door chimed another customer's arrival. Charisma welcomed the distraction. Her pulse rate was entirely too rapid. She was sure Will was aware of her shaking hands.

Thankfully, he turned to see who had entered, too.

Joey stood in front of the door with a sad expression.

Will was the first to react. "What happened, sport? I thought you'd be out on the field catching some balls."

"They all went home. Coach said it was getting too hot to practice and to come back tomorrow morning." He walked over to the counter and crawled up on a bar stool by the window.

"It's not that hot, is it, Will?"

Charisma was amazed at how quickly her little brother had taken to Will. Come to think of it, he'd been full of surprises today. Joey never threw fits or argued with her, but today he had. She frowned. There was no way she was going to let Will Lovelace into their lives. He'd broken her heart once—whether he knew it or not—and once in a lifetime was more than enough for her.

"It is pretty warm out there. But I'm surprised the coach didn't call practice for later this evening. Did he mention that?" Will joined Joey by the window.

Joey turned to face the window, too. "No, he just said he had something he had to do tonight but tomorrow we would play. I wonder what he had to do. . . ." Joey's small voice trailed off in thought.

Will turned his head and met Charisma's gaze. His eyes twinkled, and she sensed he was up to something. Something she probably wasn't going to like. When the rest of his body turned and he started making his way back to her end of the counter, Charisma was sure of it.

"Can I talk to you a moment? Privately?" Will inclined his head toward the carnation cooler.

Charisma's gaze went back to Joey. He sat with his head and shoulders slumped in dejection, looking out the window. "Sure." The word was out of her mouth. The thought of investing in some duct tape for her lips was taking shape.

She joined him by the cooler.

He moved in.

Charisma felt the cool glass against her back.

He continued to move forward.

His lips were inches from hers.

Frantically her mind searched for something, anything but the thought that he was going to kiss her. Right here in her store. What would Joey think if he saw the kiss? Will's gaze met hers, and then he did it.

He leaned close to her ear and whispered, "Would it be okay with you if I practice with Joey this evening?"

His warm breath tickled her ear. Her mind still reeled from the thought of being kissed by Will Lovelace. Her tongue was too thick to speak. Panic choked her.

"We can play at your house if you are more comfortable with that." Will stepped away from her.

All Charisma could do was nod. So much for her duct tape theory.

He spun on his heels and walked toward Joey. "Hey, sport. Your sister says we can practice at your house for a little while this evening."

Joey jumped off the bar stool. "Really? You said that?" He ran and hugged her about the waist.

Charisma's cheeks felt on fire. She couldn't believe she'd thought Will was going to kiss her. Was she insane? Did he think she'd thrown herself at him? Her gaze moved to the small window that looked into her office.

Had the curtain just fluttered? The thought of Lynn watching that embarrassing display brought fresh heat to Charisma's cheeks. Out of the corner of her eyes, she saw Will make his way back toward her and the cooler.

"Sure did." Charisma needed to distance herself from Will's

approach so she moved behind the counter.

"Thanks, Charisma! Come on, Will." Joey was already headed for the door.

Will pulled his head out of the cooler. He held a pink carnation in his large hand. "Hang on, sport. Let me pay for this."

"Joey, you go straight home. I don't want you running around town any more today." Charisma rang up Will's purchase. Her hands were shaking so badly, she prayed he'd just lay the money on the counter.

"I'll drop him off if you'd like." He laid the money down.

She scooped it up and deposited it into the register while he took a pen and wrote on one of the small complimentary cards.

"You don't have to do that," she answered. Her gaze moved to his blond hair. It curled over his collar and looked soft enough to touch. She barely managed to keep from reaching out to run her fingers through it.

Will extended the flower to her. "This is for you."

Charisma took the flower and read the message on the card. "Thanks for letting me stay on first base."

Anger, hot and wild, flashed through her veins. How dare he! Charisma tossed the carnation down on the counter and spat out the words she would later regret: "You will never steal home with me, Will Lovelace."

Not giving him time to answer, Charisma hurried to the back room. Before entering, she turned and looked at her little brother. His mouth hung open as he stared back at her.

She slammed the door.

Chapter 3

Charisma leaned against the office door and took several deep breaths. *What is wrong with me?* She still held the card in her hand.

"Wow, I just knew he was going to kiss you." The overly dramatic, breathless voice came from Lynn.

The sound of the bell jingling over the door announced Will and Joey's departure. Lynn turned from the window. "Didn't you?" she asked with a sigh.

Charisma pushed away from the door. "Lynn, haven't I asked you not to spy out that window?" She walked to her desk and dropped the card onto its smooth surface.

"I wasn't spying." A silly grin touched Lynn's lips. "I was making sure you and Joey were safe."

"Uh-huh." Charisma slipped into a chair and rested her head against the soft, cushiony back. She closed her eyes and pretended the teenager wasn't there.

"He sure was nice-looking. What did he say to make you so angry?"

The sound of wire being clipped told her Lynn had returned

to the table where she worked at making her beautiful floral arrangements. She opened her eyes and offered what she hoped didn't look like a stressed smile. "Lynn, isn't it time for your morning break?"

Lynn stared at her for several moments. Charisma saw the confusion in the young girl's eyes before she answered in a soft tone. "Okay. I guess I can take my break now."

Charisma watched her scoop up her purse and leave by the back door. Her conscience bothered her. First she'd lost her temper with Will, and now she'd probably hurt Lynn's feelings.

Her gaze moved to the card.

She picked it up and went back into the store. The pink carnation lay where she'd tossed it earlier. Charisma touched the soft petals then held it to her nose. The light fragrance enveloped her raw senses. What a fool she'd been to react so badly.

There was no way Will would have known that carnations were her favorite flower or that pink was her favorite color. Why was she acting this way? After five years she should be over her crush. But just spending a few minutes with Will Lovelace proved she wasn't.

Will enjoyed driving Joey home. The little boy talked nonstop. During their short time together, Will learned Marla was a young mother who took care of Joey while Charisma worked at the Diner Floral Shop; Charisma was his guardian as well as his half sister.

He dropped Joey off at home with the promise of returning around six to practice again. As he drove past the flower shop, he wondered about Charisma's reaction to him.

She'd been angry, edgy, and angry again. Why had she been so offended by the card? It was just a thank-you for allowing him into Joey's life. He'd thought since they were talking about baseball that she would have thought his pun funny.

His thoughts turned to Joey. It seemed to him that Joey needed a male influence. After spending time with the little boy, he was sure of it.

Will parked his pickup in front of the hardware store and made his way inside. He'd started a miniature garden behind his house and needed a rake. The building was small, like most of the stores in Sweetwater, New Mexico.

The rakes hung on the back wall, so he made his way down the aisle. A small hallway led to what looked like a couple of small offices and a public rest room. He could see an older gentleman sitting behind a cluttered desk and a young woman standing beside him.

He pulled one of the heavier-looking rakes down and studied the prongs.

"Honestly, Daddy. I wasn't trying to be rude. I was just teasing her." The young voice carried to where Will stood.

"Honey, Charisma is your boss. You shouldn't be asking her personal questions."

Will hung the rake back up and reached for another one. The mention of Charisma's name caught his attention and held it. They had to be talking about Charisma Diner. Surely there wasn't more than one Charisma living in Sweetwater. The name was unusual.

"I hope she doesn't fire me." The sound of papers ruffling around couldn't cover the worried plea in the girl's voice for reassurance.

"Lynn, you're overreacting. Charisma is a good Christian girl who isn't going to fire you for being nosy. But it won't hurt if when you get back you apologize." A chair scraped against the hardwood floor.

Will took the rake and moved back to the front of the store. It wouldn't do to get caught eavesdropping. He shouldn't have listened in the first place. But he had learned Charisma was apparently having a bad morning—which might explain her odd behavior—that she was a Christian, and that people in Sweetwater thought highly of her. For the most part, very good traits.

"Can I help you?"

He turned to see the store owner come from the back office. Will held up the rake. "Got what I need right here."

Will followed him to an old-fashioned register that clanked and clattered as the man punched its buttons.

He tucked Will's money into the metal drawer and asked, "Is there anything else I can do for you?"

"As a matter of fact, I'm looking for a church and wondered if you could recommend one. It doesn't matter what the name is over the door as long as the people who attend love God and want to live for Him." Will had seen a couple of churches on his way into town, but knowing Joey and Charisma attended the same one as this man made it the most appealing.

A smile brightened his face, and it was like a dam of words burst from the store owner. He extended his hand. "I'd be happy if you'd consider attending my church. Name's Bob Hurt."

Will shook his hand. "Will Lovelace."

"Well, Will, my family attends the First Community Church of Sweetwater. It's kind of a big name for such a small congregation, but we are a caring bunch and we'd love to have you visit."

Will left the store with a warm feeling in his heart. Bob Hurt had given him directions to the church. He climbed into his truck and drove the short distance home.

It was an old house that needed lots of repair. Will was glad he'd decided to use his full month off to settle into his new surroundings before starting his new job.

The house needed to be painted and the shutters repaired. Even the interior could use a few good coats of paint. He shook his head. It was times like these that he wished his dad lived closer. Willard Lovelace could fix anything and in less time than the average Joe. A smile touched his lips. Maybe it was time to call Dad.

Chapter 4

The rest of the day proved uneventful. Charisma and Lynn apologized to each other when the teenager returned from her break. No more was mentioned of Will. Charisma had called home and made sure Joey had arrived.

"Marla! Joey! I'm home," she called as she entered the house.

"Shh, the baby is asleep." Marla, a young woman in her early twenties, hurried into the entryway. "Joey isn't here. He went off with Will. They said you told them he could."

Charisma tried to hold her temper. "Marla, you just let them go? It never occurred to you to call me?"

A soft cry came from the living room.

"Now look what you've done. The baby is awake again," Marla accused as she practically ran to the infant.

Charisma went to the kitchen. Joey had been neglected. Since the birth of Marla's child, Joey's importance in Marla's life had diminished. Charisma had to admit she was guilty, too. Her business had taken over, and she really hadn't noticed the changes in Joey's world—until today.

She pulled hamburger meat from the refrigerator. Charisma opened the package and dropped it into a skillet. She poured hot water into a pot, set it on the stove, and turned the burner switch to HIGH. "Things are going to change," Charisma muttered as she reached into the cabinet, her fingers closing around a package of spaghetti.

"I hope so." Marla stood in the kitchen doorway. Her hands were on her wide hips. "Do you have any idea how long it took me to get her to sleep?" Her voice held a demanding tone.

Charisma opened the pasta and took a deep breath. "Marla, you and I need to talk." She measured out the spaghetti and laid it to the side.

Marla slipped into a chair. "I'll say. I need a raise. Baby formula, diapers, and doctor appointments aren't cheap. What do you say to a dollar more an hour?"

"I'm sorry, but no." Charisma took a deep breath. Firing people was not something she enjoyed.

Marla stood back up. "I'd hate for you to lose me over a dollar an hour, Charisma. After all, who would you find to replace me?" The smirk on her face said she thought she had Charisma over a barrel.

Charisma dropped the pasta into the boiling water and turned her attention back to Marla. "You're right, it would be a shame to lose you over a dollar an hour, but that isn't why I'm letting you go. I'm letting you go because you no longer give Joey the kind of supervision he needs." She hated to admit it, but a small twinge of satisfaction rippled through her at Marla's shocked expression.

"You're letting me go?"

Charisma walked to the chair where she'd placed her purse when coming into the kitchen. "You said yourself you need more money, and I need someone who will give Joey her full attention."

She pulled out her checkbook and wrote out a check. Charisma handed it to the stunned girl. "So yes, I'm letting you go. That should be enough to cover this week."

Marla snatched the check out of Charisma's hand. "Don't call me when you can't find someone else to watch him." She pointed at Joey, who was standing in the doorway.

Will stood with his hands on the boy's shoulders. Marla pushed past them.

"Charisma?" There was anxiety in Joey's voice.

She smiled at her little brother. He was covered in dirt and grass stains. Charisma really hadn't wanted him to witness the distasteful scene between herself and Marla, but nothing could be done about it now. She held her arms out to him.

Joey stepped into her embrace. She gently rubbed his back. Charisma pulled him back a little and smiled. "It's okay, Joey. Go upstairs and wash for dinner."

Will stepped away from the wall. "I'll go with you, sport. I could afford to wash off some of this dirt, too."

"Okay." Joey's smile returned. He hurried back to Will.

Will placed his hand on Joey's shoulder.

Charisma mouthed, "Thanks."

He nodded in her direction and then allowed Joey to lead him away. Charisma stared after them for several moments. Will Lovelace hadn't changed much in the last five years.

She turned the heat down on the boiling water and went in search of Marla. The young woman met her in the hallway. Marla carried her small daughter and a diaper bag. "I only took what was mine," she muttered.

"I know." Charisma opened the door for her. She touched the baby's blanket. "Take care, Marla. God bless you both."

Marla looked at her for several moments. "Thank you. I will. I'm going home. Daddy will take us in. He won't be happy that I'm coming with a child and no husband, but he loves me, and he'll take us in." She continued out the door.

Charisma watched as Marla put the baby into her car seat and then got in herself. Marla waved good-bye and smiled. A genuine smile, as if a heavy load had been lifted from her shoulders. When Marla pulled out of the drive, Charisma whispered a prayer. "Lord, please be with them and let Marla discover Your love is even stronger than that of her earthly father."

She returned to the kitchen to find Will standing at the stove, frying ground beef and onions in the skillet she'd set out earlier. Joey stood on a stool by the counter. He was buttering bread and talking to Will.

"Do you think they'll really let me play tomorrow?"

Will stirred the meat. "I think they will let you try out. But if you don't make the team, what should you do?"

Joey tapped the butter knife against his chin and screwed up his freckled face. "Be a good sport no matter what."

"Right. Now, where does Charisma keep the sauce?"

Charisma answered, "It's in the pantry. I'll get it." She moved to the small closet. What was she going to do? There was no sitter for Joey, and Will seemed to have made himself at home.

As if he could read her mind, Will announced, "I'll be on my way. I was just keeping Joey company until you returned." He started to walk out of the kitchen.

"Charisma, can Will have dinner with us?" Joey asked as she came out of the pantry with a large jar of spaghetti sauce. "I made lots of bread. See?"

How could she refuse? He'd helped her with Joey when she'd needed him to. The least she could do now was to invite him to dinner. "Why don't you stay, Will?"

Joey jumped down from his stool. He led Will to the small table that sat in the breakfast nook. "Yeah, stay, Will."

Will laughed. "How can I refuse such a nice offer?" he teased Joey. "But if I'm staying, I'm going to help out. Deal?"

"Deal," Joey answered for the both of them.

After his meeting with Charisma that morning, Will expected dinner to be awkward, to say the least. He was pleasantly surprised as the three of them prepared the meal. Charisma returned the job of mixing the sauce with the meat to him while she tossed a salad. She'd given Joey the task of setting the table.

The little boy chattered nonstop about his new glove and the game of baseball. "Will said I might be able to play on the team. Huh, Will?"

"You sure might. But if you don't make the team this year, you're going to be a good sport about it. Right?" Will placed the pot of spaghetti on the trivet Charisma had provided.

Joey put the last plate on the table. "Uh-huh."

"Did you thank Will for practicing with you today?" Charisma placed three glasses of iced tea on the table and sat down.

"Oh, thanks, Will." Joey pulled his chair out and sat down, too.

Will was the last to take his seat. "Anytime, Joey."

He watched Charisma place a paper towel on her lap.

His gaze met hers.

"Would you offer the blessing, Will?" She ducked her head and closed her eyes.

Will said a simple prayer of thankfulness. When he finished, all three echoed, "Amen."

Joey was the first to speak. "Will you go to practice with me in the morning?"

Charisma served the boy's food. "What time do you need to be there?"

He crinkled his nose when she added a big helping of salad to his plate. "I was asking Will, Charisma."

Will watched the wounded expression cross her face. His heart went out to her. "Joey, I think you may have hurt your sister's feelings. There has to be a nicer way to say that," he corrected.

Joey frowned around a mouthful of spaghetti. "But she has to work tomorrow."

"That is no reason to be rude to your sister." Will pointed his fork at the boy and gave him what he hoped was a stern look.

He swallowed hard. "I'm sorry, Charisma. I didn't mean to be rude."

Charisma took a sip of tea. "It's okay, Joey. You're right. I do need to work, but since I fired Marla, I'm going to ask Lynn to work in the morning so I can go watch you practice."

Her smile brightened the room but not Joey's face.

"I really want Will to go with me," he mumbled around a leaf of lettuce.

Will watched the smile vanish from her face.

"Oh, I see." Charisma tried to bring the smile back into place. "Will probably has to work tomorrow."

Joey turned toward Will. "Do you?"

"Actually, I don't but—"

"See, Charisma, he can go. So you don't have to."

Will held up his hand. "Slow down, sport." He waited until he had Joey's full attention before continuing. "If Charisma wants to watch you practice, maybe we can both be there."

Chapter 5

The next morning, Charisma dressed in a pair of jeans and a blue T-shirt. She pulled her hair into a ponytail and applied light makeup. As she pulled on her tennis shoes, Charisma prayed she would be able to find a sitter for Joey soon.

Joey stood by the front door waiting for her. He scuffed his shoe on the rug. "You don't have to go if you don't want to."

Charisma ruffled his red hair. "I'm going, Joey. Besides, you can't go to the park alone; you shouldn't have gone alone yesterday."

"I don't need a baby-sitter, Charisma. I'm eight years old. I'm not a baby, ya know." Joey opened the door for her.

Charisma picked up her cell phone and clipped it to the backpack she carried. "Yes, but you do need someone to supervise you until you're older." She dug inside the bag to make sure she had a water bottle and sunscreen.

"I hate having a sitter." Joey followed her out the door.

"Well, I feel better knowing you aren't alone during the day. So that settles it. You, young man, are getting a new sitter." She walked beside him on the sidewalk.

Joey walked with his head down and his shoulders slumped. He kicked tiny rocks and pebbles as they made their way to the baseball field.

Charisma hated seeing him sad. Yesterday, for the first time since his parents' death, Joey had expressed genuine confidence. She hadn't realized how important baseball was to him. Or had it been Will and the attention he'd given the boy that had made Joey so happy?

"I'm sorry, Joey. Just think of the sitter as a new friend. Not as a baby-sitter." Charisma put her hand on her brother's shoulder. "I'll try to find a dependable teenager, not an older person with a baby or someone too old to do fun things with. Okay?"

Joey looked up at her and grinned. "Someone like Will?"

"Someone like Will? Honey, Will isn't a teenager. He's the same age as I am." Charisma thought about her twenty-eight years. She wasn't that old. Why couldn't she be fun like Will?

"I have fun when I'm with Will."

Charisma dropped her hand from his shoulder. "I know."

Joey stopped walking. "I have fun with you, too, but it's different with Will." He tucked his toe into a crack in the sidewalk.

Charisma wasn't thrilled that her brother found Will more fun to be around. She knew what he meant, though. In college, Will had been the highlight of every party. Everyone enjoyed being around him, including her.

"How is it different?"

He started walking again. "I can talk to him and tell him stuff. Guy stuff." Joey's freckles paled under his pink cheeks.

"Guy stuff, huh?"

"Yeah."

They arrived at the field. Charisma followed Joey through a side gate and looked about. Bleachers stood off to one side, so she made her way to them. What kind of guy stuff did Joey need to talk to Will about? The question swirled in her mind as she sat down on one of the wooden seats at the bottom of the stands.

Her gaze moved about the field in search of Will. He'd promised Joey he'd be there. Charisma wasn't sure if she was more disappointed for herself or Joey when she didn't see him.

Joey stood off to the right side of the field talking to several boys that looked to be his age. She turned her attention to the job of finding a new baby-sitter. Charisma pulled her backpack off and dug inside for her address book.

She flipped through the pages and sighed. Where would she find a new baby-sitter? Everyone in her book was either family or older people. There were old friends in it, but they didn't live in Sweetwater, so that did her no good. And there were—

"Any luck?"

Will's voice shocked her from her worry. She looked up and found him scanning the baseball field. Charisma took advantage of his distraction and really looked at him. He wore a red baseball cap, white T-shirt, and blue jeans. Like Joey's, his feet sported tennis shoes.

"I'm not sure. I don't think they've started playing yet." Charisma's gaze moved to Joey. He still stood with his friends, but now they were throwing a ball back and forth between them.

Joey noticed Will and came running over. "Hi, Will. We're just practicing while we wait for the coach." He pushed his ball cap back and smiled up at them.

Another little boy ran up and smiled.

"This is my new friend, Austin." Joey introduced them. "This is Will. I told you about him."

Charisma felt like a fifth wheel as she listened to Will's warm voice. "It's nice to meet you, Austin." She watched as he shook the boy's hand.

"Can I practice with you and Joey?" Austin pushed his chest out. "I'm pretty good. I want to play catcher."

Two other boys ran up. The newcomers pushed Joey and Austin in the back. Soon all four of the boys were wrestling around on the ground.

Guy stuff, Charisma thought.

Will watched the boys. They reminded him of days gone by. Summer days of fun with Joseph, Isaac, and Adam. His thoughts turned to the Bachelor Club. They were about these boys' ages when Joseph had come up with the idea.

Adam was the first to cave. He and Amy were now married and living happily. After the razzing Joseph and Isaac had given Adam, Will was even more determined to stay single. It wasn't the money. It was the principle of the thing. As a boy he hadn't wanted to be in a club without girls, but now that he was, he'd vowed to stay single until he was thirty and the winner.

Charisma called to the boys. "Hey, fellas, is that your coach over there calling you?"

The boys jumped up and scampered off to join the rest of the kids and the coach. Joey turned around and waved in their direction.

Will heard Charisma's deep sigh. "Something wrong?" he asked, giving her his full attention.

"I can't think of anyone to baby-sit Joey. Most of the high school kids that haven't left for the summer already have jobs, and everyone else is too old or working the same hours I do." She frowned down at her cell phone.

A light breeze tugged several strands of dark red hair from her ponytail. The sweet smell of fresh peaches teased his senses. Will realized the fragrance came from Charisma. He sat down beside her and watched the boys.

His mind went back to the Bachelor Club. For years he'd believed he could date and have fun with the girls. Then when they'd start to get too serious, he'd simply step away. In his young mind, he'd never realized the harm he was doing, until the day he'd gotten saved, and the Lord had convicted him for his behavior toward women. At that point he'd promised himself and God he wouldn't date until after he was thirty and the game completed.

Now, sitting beside Charisma, he reminded himself of that promise. He glanced in her direction. She stared out at the field. Worry lined her smooth brow.

Will couldn't quite put his finger on why, but he felt the Lord urging him to help her out. The wind shifted once more, giving him an even stronger sense of her scent. Could he do it?

Could he spend the next month around Charisma and not get her heart broken or his own?

He ignored the questions and stated, "I could help you out."

Her brown gaze turned toward him. He could see the distrust in her eyes and wondered why it was there. What had he done to cause her to feel that way?

She tilted her head to the side and blocked the sun from her face. "Don't you have a job to go to?"

Will relaxed. Of course she would be leery of him. She didn't know him from the man on the moon. "I took a month of vacation time to get settled here. I'm a park ranger for the San Juan National Forest."

She continued to eye him with caution. "I don't know."

Will wished he could read her mind. Her brown eyes were like pools of chocolate as she studied his face. He wondered what she found in his features. "I will be happy to supply you with references." He offered what he hoped was a reassuring smile.

Charisma pulled her gaze from his smiling face. "Will, the money isn't anything close to what a park ranger makes."

"I don't want your money. I'd be doing what I feel the Lord wants me to do and that is to help you and Joey." Will's gaze moved out to the field, where the coach divided the kids into teams.

He felt Charisma's gaze upon him again. Her voice held a hint of unbelief as she whispered, "You're a Christian?"

Will gave her his brightest smile. "Yes, I am. I received the Lord about three years ago."

She searched his eyes. "I'm glad."

They stared at each other for several long moments. Will

felt drawn to her in a way he'd never felt before. He pulled his gaze away first.

"Are you sure you don't mind watching Joey for a few days? I'll keep looking for another sitter. I might even ask at church Sunday morning."

Will found Joey on the field. He stood with his hands on his knees in center field. His gaze focused on the pitcher and the batter. "I enjoy spending time with him. But don't tell him I'm his baby-sitter. He hates that. How about I just tutor him in baseball? We'll spend all day together, and after you close the shop, I'll bring him home."

Charisma chewed the nail of her index finger. "That sounds good. I can't let you watch him for nothing. At least let me pay for whatever food you supply."

Relief washed over Will. She'd agreed. He didn't want or need payment for watching Joey. Will was sure the Lord sought him to spend time with the boy, and he couldn't put a price on the Lord's will. "Whatever you decide will be more than enough." He would have taken fifty cents but didn't say so.

"Thank you, Will."

He simply smiled and said, "You're welcome."

Chapter 6

She stepped onto the stool to screw in the bolt that would hold up the new porch swing. It was a frivolous buy, but she'd wanted one for a long time. And since Will wouldn't accept payment for taking care of Joey, she'd decided now was the time to buy it.

If Charisma had known a week ago that Will Lovelace would be at her house so much, she felt sure she wouldn't have asked him to take care of Joey. As she worked, she reflected on Joey. Her brother was happier than he'd ever been. He walked around with confidence, especially since he'd made the Little League team.

The stool tipped to the side. Charisma gave a little squeak. Wood scraped against wood as the step stool slipped on the wood floor and flew out from under her. Her squeak turned to a blood-curdling scream. She closed her eyes and her arms flung out.

She felt strong, warm hands wrap around her waist just as the stool clattered to the floorboards. "Easy does it," Will's comforting voice breathed across her ear.

Charisma buried her face in his chest and allowed him to hold her for several long moments.

"Are you okay, Charisma?" Joey asked.

She pulled her cheek from the sound of Will's pounding heart. Her own was galloping from her near fall as well as the warmth of Will's touch. Charisma nodded. Her gaze locked with Will's. She was aware of his hands leaving her waist. Charisma missed the warmth of being near him.

Charisma felt Joey's gaze upon her. Heat filled her cheeks. "I'm fine, Joey. I don't know what happened."

Will picked up the stool and examined its legs. One support had apparently rotted and splintered, causing it to break off to one side under her weight. "Looks like you need a new step stool." He handed it to her.

Charisma took the broken furniture. "Thanks for catching me." She felt the heat leave her face and travel down her neck.

"Anytime."

He gave her a warm smile, his blue eyes twinkling. Charisma's pulse picked up the beat. She inhaled deeply and then released it slowly as his gaze moved to the four-foot swing, the large chains that held it up, and the ceiling. "Looks like you could use a hand with this."

"Can I help, too?" Joey joined Will and imitated his stance.

"Sure you can. Grab those instructions and we'll get started." Will turned to Charisma. "That is okay, isn't it?"

What could she say? It was obvious she couldn't do it by herself. Well, she could, but Charisma had to ask herself why she would want to. Besides, Will would think it odd if she refused his help. "I'd love the help; thank you."

Two hours later, Will and Joey sat on the porch swing, testing it. "Seems to work pretty good, don't it, Will?" Joey swung his legs back and forth.

Charisma handed Will a glass of raspberry tea.

He took a sip before answering. "It sure does. Come sit down, Charisma, and try it out." He scooted closer to the arm of the bench.

Charisma watched Joey do the same. She sat down between them. Her feet barely touched the floor. The soft scent of honeysuckle filled the night air.

Joey chuckled. "Your feet don't touch the floor, either." He jumped off the swing.

The action caused the bench to jerk, and Charisma landed against Will's side. She quickly righted herself.

"I'm sorry about that, Charisma. I can lower it," Will offered.

She felt a new flush fill her face. "Thanks." Charisma smiled and scooted a little farther away from his warmth.

"Charisma, I'm hungry!" Joey called from the doorway.

"I bet you are." She stood up and smiled. "Will, would you like to have a sandwich with us? It's getting pretty late, and I'd hate to send you home on an empty stomach." She held the screen door open.

Will whistled as he stepped out of the shower that evening. Dinner with Charisma and Joey had been short and sweet. She'd set out lunch meat, cheese, and all the fixings for a delicious sandwich.

Joey entertained Charisma with stories of his and Will's day. Will enjoyed watching her smile and laugh at the boy's silliness. She didn't disguise her love for her little brother. Charisma touched and hugged Joey often.

He knew they were only half brother and sister, thanks to Joey's constant chatter. Will smiled to himself. He doubted there was much about the Diners that he didn't know. Joey talked from the time Will picked him up in the morning until they said good-bye later in the day.

As he readied for bed, his thoughts turned to Charisma. His heart had nearly jumped from his chest when he'd seen her falling this afternoon. Thankfully, he'd been there to catch her. He could still smell the sweet, peachy fragrance of her light perfume.

Will wondered if she was getting ready for bed now, too, or if she was still trying to get Joey to sleep. He shook his head. What was wrong with him? It seemed that every day he thought more and more about Charisma and what she was doing.

He reached for the alarm clock and set it for eight. Since the next day would be Sunday, Will looked forward to the extra hour of sleep. He also enjoyed the thought of seeing Charisma and Joey at church in the morning.

He told himself to stop thinking about her then turned off the lights and slipped in between clean sheets. He tried to force himself to think about something else, anything besides her warm brown eyes and soft, teasing lips.

He spoke aloud. "Focus on the Bachelor Club. If you're going to win the challenge, you have to stop thinking about

Charisma." Will closed his eyes tightly. A vision of her silky hair and the sweet scent of peaches continued to flood his thoughts.

He loved the way her eyes sparkled. The way the light reflected off her glossy auburn locks. The way she smiled at Joey with true love and happiness lighting up her face.

Will sat up. He shoved the covers back and knelt beside his bed. "Lord, this woman won't leave my thoughts. She is everything I've always wanted in a wife. She's smart, kind, and very loving. But best of all she's a Christian. Father, give me the strength to resist this temptation. I promised You I wouldn't date until after I'm thirty, and I haven't broken that promise, but Lord, I can't get Charisma out of my mind." He stayed beside his bed for a long time. Much later, Will fell asleep as soon as his head hit the pillow.

Chapter 7

"Hurry, Joey!" Charisma quickly slid into a light blue strapless dress. She pulled the matching jacket on.

"How come we're late?" Joey ran into the room. "Did ya forget to set the alarm?" his young voice accused.

"Yes." She could have added she'd gotten very little sleep the night before but instead held that tidbit of information.

Joey sat still while she combed his hair down. "I hate when we miss Sunday school. That's the best part of going to church."

She smiled. "The best part should be hearing the message from the pastor." Charisma's gaze met his in the mirror.

"Your hair's sticking out all over." Joey snickered behind his hand.

Charisma jerked the brush through her curling hair. This was Will's fault, too. If she'd been able to sleep last night, she wouldn't have thought a warm shower would help her rest, and she wouldn't have fallen asleep with wet hair.

It was mainly the top of her head where the hair was the most unruly. Charisma grabbed a long barrette and pulled that part of her hair up and clamped it down. Wavy locks fell about her shoulders. She quickly brushed them and pulled her bangs down. With the hot curling iron, she straightened them, but they insisted on curling slightly on the ends. "How does that look?" she asked Joey.

Joey smiled. "It looks good."

They arrived at the church just as Sunday school dismissed. Charisma led Joey to a pew and sat down. She hated being late for Sunday services and blamed it all on Will Lovelace.

It was his fault that all she could think about was how he'd changed and the fact that he hadn't asked her out on a date. In his college days, Will Lovelace asked every breathing girl out for a date. Well, all of them except her. Maybe she just wasn't his type.

Joey fidgeted in his seat. "I wish I hadn't missed Sunday school," he muttered.

"I was beginning to think you two weren't going to make it this morning."

Joey's head jerked upright, and he smiled at Will. "Charisma didn't set the alarm, and she went to bed with her hair wet. This morning it was sticking up all over the place."

Joey! Mortified by her brother's candor, Charisma pasted on a smile and looked up at Will.

Will smiled at a red-faced Charisma. "Well, her hair looks very pretty to me," he said, and it did. He loved the way the reddish brown locks curled around her shoulders.

"Are you gonna sit with us?" Joey scooted over. He nudged Charisma until she moved down, too.

Still smiling at Charisma, Will asked her, "Do you mind?"

She fussed with the skirt of her dress. "Not at all."

"Thanks." Will sat down just as the preacher stepped behind the pulpit. He kept his focus trained on the pastor during the whole service. Will felt Joey's gaze upon him and knew he was setting a behavior for the young boy to follow.

When the last amen was spoken, Will turned his attention back to Charisma. She smiled sweetly at him as she gathered up her purse and Bible.

"Want to go with us to Frosted Freeze? Charisma said we could go if I behaved in church." Joey stepped in front of Will.

Will searched Charisma's face. A slight frown marred her face as she focused on her Bible. *Lord, if it's not meant for me to go with them, let Charisma come up with an excuse not to go.* He shifted his focus to Joey's expectant face. *I don't have the heart to turn him down.*

"Sure. Why don't you join us, Will?" Charisma's gaze was on the little boy, too. They made their way through the crowded aisle.

The Frosted Freeze was packed with people. Joey pushed his way through the crowd. Will stood quietly in line with Charisma. The scent of fresh peaches teased his nose. A few minutes later, Joey made his way back to them.

"Guess what?" He didn't give them time to answer. "Austin is here, and his mom and dad said we can sit with them. Is that okay?"

"I don't—"

Will laughed. "Too late, Charisma. He's gone."

She frowned. "I'm not sure we should impose on Austin's family." Charisma's gaze followed Joey.

Will placed his hand on her shoulder. "Don't worry about

it. It's going to take a few minutes to get our order." He smiled as she caught on to his way of thinking.

Her soft brown eyes twinkled up at him. "They might even be done eating by the time we get through the line." A grin touched her lips, too.

"Maybe." He couldn't keep his smile from spreading over his face. Her soft curls tickled the back of his hand, and her shoulder warmed his palm.

He left his hand in place as they moved forward. Will enjoyed the sensation of feeling like they were a couple. His gaze moved about the Frosted Freeze.

It was a small establishment with old-fashioned round tables and metal chairs with red cushions. Pictures of ice cream and malts lined the walls. Several booths rested against the far wall.

The menu consisted of sandwiches, burgers, hot dogs of every kind, and lots of choices in ice cream. The smell of french fries caused his stomach to rumble. He heard a soft chuckle come from Charisma. He leaned down and whispered in her ear. "Woman, are you laughing at a starving man?"

"Nope, I'm laughing at you and your loud stomach."

Will enjoyed the way Charisma teased back and forth with him. She seemed more relaxed now that they were in a crowded restaurant. He didn't have time to dwell on the thought as they stepped up to the counter and placed their orders.

Charisma ordered Joey a corn dog and fries. For herself, a ham sandwich with a small bag of chips. Will stepped up and ordered a cheeseburger with fries.

"Where is Joey?" Will grinned as she turned to look for her brother and he paid for the food.

"He's still at Austin's table." She turned back to Will, and seeing that he'd taken care of the bill, frowned.

Will picked up the tray full of food. "Do you see an empty table?"

Charisma sighed. "Yep, there's one right beside Austin and his parents." She led the way to Joey and his friend.

"Well, if it isn't Will Lovelace." Austin's father stood up and extended his hand.

Will set the tray down and clasped the other man's hand. "Mark Zummer, I didn't realize you'd moved here. It's good to see you." Will automatically pulled a chair out for Charisma.

"Will, I'd like you to meet my wife, Lisa. Lisa, this is an old buddy of mine." He clapped Will on the back.

Lisa shook hands with Will and smiled at Charisma. "How are you doing, Charisma?"

Charisma set the food out on their table. "I'm good, Lisa. How about yourself?"

Lisa patted her swollen abdomen. "I'm ready for this little gal to greet the world."

Will continued his conversation with Mark and listened to Charisma and Lisa at the same time. His gaze moved to Charisma. A dreamy look entered her eyes.

"When are you due?" Charisma asked. "Joey, sit down and eat." She placed his corn dog and half her chips on a paper napkin.

Lisa sighed. "Last week. This little one is in no hurry to face the world."

Mark caught his attention again. "So what have you been doing with yourself and what are you doing in my neck of the woods?" He sat back down and draped his arm over the back of Lisa's chair.

Will took a seat beside Charisma. "Well, I just took a job with the San Juan National Forest. I'm a park ranger now. I decided I was tired of the commute and decided to move closer to my work. What about yourself?"

Mark patted the camera on the edge of the table. "I work for *National Wildlife* magazine. Maybe I can go to work with you and get a few pictures."

"Sure, why not?" Will took a bite of his burger. He'd noticed Charisma had gone very quiet and seemed nervous again.

"I'm sorry, Charisma. How are you doing?" Mark asked.

Once more she answered, "I'm good." Charisma handed Joey a napkin. The boy ignored her, preferring to visit with Austin.

Lisa smiled at Will. "So how do you know this clown?" She thumbed her finger at Mark.

"We went to Tierra Verde Community College together." Will laughed at the way Mark tickled his pregnant wife.

"Hey! That's where Charisma went to school. Huh, Charisma?" Joey's young voice stopped all activity.

Will turned to stare at Charisma. Her cheeks flamed, and she wouldn't look at him. Had she known him in college? Why hadn't she mentioned it if she had? Surely he would have remembered a beauty like her.

If only the ground would open up and swallow me, Charisma

thought. Why hadn't she told Will she knew they'd gone to the same school? That she knew who he was? She chanced a glance at him from the corner of her eye. His face was turned toward her, and one light eyebrow lifted.

She pulled her gaze from Will and decided it would be better to focus on Joey. "Yes."

"That's right. You were there at the same time Will and I were. I'd almost forgotten that." Mark began helping Lisa clean up.

"Funny. I don't remember you." Will's voice was close to her ear. He picked up the ketchup he'd been reaching for and poured a generous amount over his fries.

Charisma took a large bite of her sandwich. With her mouth full, she couldn't answer him.

Austin tugged on her arm. "Can Joey come over to play?"

She swallowed her food. "I don't know—"

Lisa interrupted her. "I don't mind if he comes over. It will give him something to do while I take a nap."

Charisma looked from Joey to Lisa.

"Please, Charisma. I'll be good," Joey promised.

She felt like they were all ganging up on her. The last thing Charisma wanted was to be left alone with Will.

Mark helped his wife stand. "I'll keep an eye on the boys," he reassured her.

She looked from one expectant face to the other. "Well, if you're sure."

"Yea! Thanks, Charisma."

"Come on, boys." Mark led his small family and Joey out of the café.

"You be good," Charisma called after Joey.

"I will." He ran out the door with Austin.

She focused on the rest of her meal. The sandwich felt dry in her throat. Charisma grabbed her diet soda and washed the bread down.

Will's steady gaze on her face unsettled her. "I really can't place you." His voice sounded puzzled.

Charisma felt a moment of anger. She wanted to yell at him. *How hard could it be to remember the one girl you didn't treat like a queen?*

Instead she offered, "It was a long time ago, Will. I've changed."

"But you remember me—don't you," he stated bluntly.

Was that accusation in his voice? Or was she just being extra sensitive to her own guilt?

"Sure, I remember you. You haven't changed a bit." Charisma picked up Joey's wrappers and then her own.

Will seemed to study her while she worked. "Why can't I remember you? Tell me about yourself." He added his trash to the tray.

Charisma forced what she hoped was a light laugh. "Nope. I'm going to take Lisa's plan and put it into action." She deposited the tray's contents in the trash can then set it on top.

He followed her from the café. "What's that mean?"

She continued walking. "It means I'm going to walk home, and I'm taking a nap when I get there."

Will laughed. He caught up with her and fell into step. "Why don't you skip the nap and go with me to an afternoon movie?"

Charisma stopped. She turned to face him. Had he remembered who she was? Was he offering her a mercy date? His expression was one of innocence.

"No thanks. Maybe some other time." Why had she said that? She continued walking, now angry with herself for hoping that Will Lovelace really wanted to date her.

It was driving him crazy. Why couldn't he remember someone as lively and lovely as Charisma Diner? Working in the garden wasn't helping him remember her. Will tossed the small rake down and stood up. He dusted the dirt off his jeans and headed for the house.

He opened the fridge and grabbed the tea pitcher. His mind reviewed all the girls he'd dated in college, but Charisma's face wasn't among them. He poured the tea into a glass of ice and gulped it down. Frustrated, he made his way back to the bedroom.

From the top of the closet, he pulled down a box. Will carried it to his bed, where he opened it up. Inside were letters, pictures, and other things from his college days. After his mother's death, Will hadn't had the heart to get rid of the box she'd so carefully packed for him after college. Now he was thankful for her thoughtfulness.

For the rest of the afternoon, he dug through the box and memories. Will felt ashamed to see all the pictures of himself with a different girl on his arm in each one. Instead of confronting those feelings, he went to make a sandwich.

Later in the evening, it continued to nag at him like a scratch he couldn't reach. Will picked up the phone book. He flipped to the back. Zummer was the only Z listed.

Half an hour later, Will walked back to the box on his bed and searched until he found a picture that he'd seen earlier. Mark had described her as a quiet girl, with owlish glasses and braces.

He'd seen such a girl in one of the photos. Will hadn't paid any attention to her because she was standing in the background behind him and Sarah something. He felt immediate guilt. Sarah had a last name, but Will couldn't remember it.

Once more he regretted his past. He found the photo and studied Charisma. She stood in the background with her hands clasped in front of her. Will leaned closer to the snapshot. No wonder he hadn't recognized her.

Her hair was pulled taut in a bun at the back of her neck. She wore a shapeless dress, and large, plastic-framed glasses covered most of her face.

They also helped to magnify her large brown eyes—eyes that were focused on him. Why hadn't he ever noticed her before? Had he been so full of himself that he hadn't looked to see those around him?

Will decided then and there to make it up to her. He'd ignored her before but never again. As he stared at her image in the photo, his heart ached at the look in her eyes. She'd cared about him, and he hadn't known she existed.

He bowed his head. "Lord, thank You for delivering me from my selfish ways. I know I have a long way to go, but I thank You for the place I am today." Will remained with his head bowed. His thoughts turned to Charisma. What was he going to do about these feelings he had for her? He knew he'd cared about her long before he'd found out how she'd felt years ago. Did she still have the same feelings?

Deep down, Will knew that unless he was willing to give up his stake in the Bachelor Club, Charisma could have no real place in his life. At least not until he turned thirty. Less than two years to go. Could he keep her from stealing home in his heart for that long? Or had she already set up residency?

Chapter 8

J oey swung at the ball.

"Strike two!"

Charisma held her breath. She chewed her fingernails. "This is crazy. It's only a game." She exhaled into the palm of her hand.

Will laughed. "True, but I do love this game." He approached her with caution, not sure how to let her know he remembered her.

The bat made a cracking sound as Joey hit the third pitch. The crowd went wild. Will watched Charisma. Her face lit with excitement as she called encouragements to her brother.

"Run! Joey, run!" Charisma screamed as Joey ran around the bases. The other team fumbled the ball and dropped it. She watched as Joey slid into home plate.

Wrapped up in the game, Will cheered along with her. "Yes!" He punched the air above his head.

Charisma jumped up and down. "He made it home! We won! We won!" She hugged Will around the waist and continued jumping around. She released him and screamed down at the field. "Way to go, Joey!"

Will watched Joey turn and wave. His teammates pounded him on the back. Charisma sunk down onto the bleacher bench. "This game is exhausting," she declared.

"Don't tell me you've never played baseball or softball." Will sat down beside her.

She laughed at his shocked expression. "Nope, never. This may sound even crazier to you, but I've never even been to a game before today." Charisma moved her feet to the side so the other boys' parents and friends could pass by.

Will clutched his chest and pretended to be having a heart attack. "Tell me it isn't so," he declared with mock horror.

"Brace yourself. It's true."

Will wanted to keep that smile on her face forever. He watched Charisma turn her attention back to Joey. His favorite sport had turned into a nice icebreaker. *Thank You, Lord,* he silently prayed.

"We won!" Joey yelled.

Charisma moved down the wooden steps. "You sure did!" She grabbed Joey and hugged him.

Joey pulled away from her, looked around, and then squared his shoulders. He focused on Will. "You said we could get ice cream if we won."

Will clasped him on the shoulder. "Yes, I did. How about it, Charisma? Shall we go celebrate the first win of the season with ice cream?"

"I could go for something cold right now," she agreed. Charisma's eyes sparkled. "But you know what I really want?" She tapped the top of Joey's ball cap.

"What?" Joey pushed the hat back off his eyes.

"I want a hot dog."

"A hot dog?" both Will and Joey echoed.

Charisma started walking in the direction of the Frosted Freeze. "Yeah. Isn't that what you're supposed to eat after a ball game?"

Will laughed. He jogged to catch up with her. "Well, normally you'd eat a hot dog during the ball game."

"I know, but they don't sell them during the game. So I want one now."

Joey laughed. "Hey, can I have one, too, Charisma?" He pushed his way between the two adults.

"Sure. We'll have hot dogs for dinner and ice cream for dessert." She smiled at Will. "We can eat them after a game, can't we?"

"Well, you can, but they're not as good after the game as they are during." Will stopped beside his truck. "Hey, how about we take the pickup? I'll drive you home later."

Joey hurried to the passenger's side and got in. "Come on, Charisma."

Charisma made a mental note to have a talk with Joey. It was nice of Will to drive them to the café, but Joey should have made sure it was okay with her first. If given the chance to respond, Charisma felt sure she would have declined Will's offer of a ride.

She wiped a glob of mustard off Joey's cheek. "Joey, you're

going to have to get in the tub when we get home. You've got mustard and ketchup all over your face."

"I think I put too much mustard on it." He smiled, showing his yellow teeth.

Charisma laughed. "Maybe you did."

Will pulled the truck into their driveway. He groaned and patted his stomach. "I can't believe I ate three of those things. I haven't eaten that many since I was a kid."

She had to smile. Charisma couldn't believe she'd eaten two. "Thanks for the ride home, Will."

Joey hopped out of the truck behind Charisma. "Are you coming over tomorrow?"

Will laughed. "I'll be here. Hey, Charisma."

She stopped on the porch and turned toward him.

"I'd like to take Joey out to the ranger station, if that's okay with you." Will leaned out his truck window and waited for her answer.

"Can I go? I'll be good," Joey promised.

Charisma felt torn. She hated for Will to feel like he had to take Joey to the ranger station. "Do you have to go to work? I'd hate for Joey to be in the way, Will."

"No, I promised Mark I'd take him out there tomorrow. We're going to look for white-tailed deer. He needs a picture for his latest magazine article."

The mention of Mark reminded Charisma that she and Will hadn't talked about their college days since Sunday afternoon. Mark was as much a part of that past as they were. Would Mark refresh Will's memory of the quiet wallflower of years gone by?

She doubted it. Mark had been just as unaware of her as Will had been. Charisma realized both Joey and Will waited for her answer.

"If you're sure he won't be any trouble, Joey can go. What time will you be home?" Charisma realized she'd asked Will when *he'd* be home not when Joey would be home. She prayed he didn't read anything into it.

"Before dinnertime. Hey, Joey, you need to pack a lunch and maybe a snack for tomorrow." Will started the truck.

"Okay," Joey called. He waved at Will as he backed out of the driveway.

Joey ran past her and into the house, then he called over his shoulder, "Charisma, can I take my school bag with me?"

Chapter 9

Will watched Joey run ahead of them on the path. "I'm sorry, Mark. I hadn't thought about how an eight-year-old behaves in the woods."

"It's okay. I'm getting several pictures of the foliage. But just so you know, you owe me one. When Joey tells Austin he came with us, I'll be the evil stepdad." Mark took a picture of a pale ivory flower on a blooming yucca plant.

Will watched Mark move about the flower and snap several times. "I hadn't even thought of that." He scratched his chin. Joey chased a butterfly into a meadow.

"You like him a lot, don't you?" Mark stood at his elbow watching Joey, too.

"Yeah, I do."

"Be careful; that's how Lisa caught me. She had this cute little boy that I couldn't resist helping, and the next thing I know, I'm part of a family." Mark laid his hand on Will's shoulder, his expression one of fake sorrow.

Laughter bubbled up in Will's throat. "Yeah, and I see you suffering from the exposure, too."

Their laughter caught Joey's attention. He ran back to them. "Hey, Will. I'm getting hungry. Can I eat my sandwich now?" He dropped down on the ground at the men's feet.

"That's a good idea. Why don't you two have your sandwiches? I'll mosey off this way. Maybe I can get a shot of something besides flowers." Mark walked off toward the meadow.

Will dropped down beside Joey and pulled off his backpack. "I think I'm ready for lunch, too."

"What's he going to shot?" Joey asked around a mouthful of peanut butter and jelly.

"Shoot." At Joey's quizzical look, Will continued, "What is he going to *shoot*?" He peeled a banana.

Joey swallowed, a smirk curling up the corners of his mouth. "I don't know. I thought he was gonna take some pictures." He laughed and twisted the lid of his water bottle.

Will shook his head and laughed. "All right, you got me. Mark's going to see if he can find some deer, so we need to eat quietly."

"I want to see the deer." Joey started to rise.

"Wait a minute, Joey. Mark wants to take a picture of them, and if we go running into the woods, we'll scare them away." He watched the boy sink back to the ground.

"We'll look for the deer next time we come out. Okay?"

Joey pulled out a fruit snack. "I guess so."

Watching Joey reminded Will of experiences he'd almost forgotten. The boy ran through mud puddles and did battle amid imaginary dragons armed only with a stick. He played enthusiastically and enjoyed his day in the woods. His young mind absorbed much about the plants, insects, and other wildlife.

Will rested his head against a tree and watched Joey play in the meadow. His eyes drifted shut. The air was warm and smelled of pine. Sleep drew him in.

"Will? Will?" Joey shook his shoulder.

Will opened his eyes and yawned.

Joey leaned against Will's side. "I don't feel so good. Can we go home now?"

"Where's Mark?" He stifled another yawn and then glanced down at his watch. Shock brought Will into full alertness. Two hours had passed since he'd sat down.

"I think he's still looking for deer." Joey groaned. "Will, my stomach hurts. I want to go home." Joey clutched his stomach tighter.

Will pushed himself up off the ground and called, "Mark!"

Joey groaned again.

"Did you eat something besides what Charisma packed for you this morning?" He leaned down to be at eye level with Joey.

"Just some berries. They were good, but now my belly hurts." Joey groaned again and closed his eyes.

"What did the berries look like, Joey?" Fear and guilt caused his words to come out harsher than he intended.

"I brought you some." He dug in his pocket and pulled out a sandwich bag full of smashed berries.

Will took the bag.

"Did you yell?" Mark ran into the clearing where they stood.

Will tasted the purple and green mush Joey had given him. He released the breath he'd been holding and smiled. "They're blackberries."

Joey clutched his stomach and moaned again.

"What's going on here?" Mark knelt down beside Joey.

"My stomach hurts," Joey complained.

Will knelt beside him, too. "Our friend here ate too many blackberries."

He opened the pickup door and waited for Joey to scoot to the middle of the seat. "Buckle up, Joey," Mark ordered as he clicked his own seat belt into place.

Once they started down the road, Will asked, "Did you eat the green or red berries, too?"

"Yeah, I like the sour taste." Joey attempted a smile.

"Austin likes them, too, but he's learned that if you eat too many of them, they give you a stomachache. I'm afraid that's a lesson you're learning the hard way." Mark patted Joey on the leg.

Will winked at Joey. "We'll get you something for that and fix you right up."

Mark rolled his window down. "Maybe some fresh air will help." He ruffled Joey's red hair.

"I'm sorry you didn't get any pictures of the white-tailed deer." Will pulled out on the highway.

Joey groaned his discomfort.

"Now who said I didn't get my pictures? While you napped and Joey ate too many berries, I found a large herd of deer, and I have two rolls of film to prove it." Mark held up his camera with a wide grin.

Charisma sat on the front porch, gently rocking back and forth in her new swing. The scent of honeysuckle drifted in the warm afternoon air.

"Good afternoon, Charisma," Mr. Morgan called from the sidewalk. He held a red leash in his right hand. Coco, a small dachshund, sat at his feet.

She pushed herself upright and joined the elderly man by the fence. "Hi, Mr. Morgan. How is Mrs. Morgan today?"

"Can you believe that woman got up this morning and did the breakfast dishes? Charisma, God is healing Mazie right before these tired old eyes." Mr. Morgan leaned down and rubbed the little dog behind the ears.

"Oh, what wonderful news! I'm so happy for the both of you." Charisma plucked a honeysuckle blossom from the vine along the fence.

"Will you be at the shop in the morning, Charisma?" He stood up and focused on her.

She frowned, wondering where this was leading. "Yes, why?"

"Well, I need to come get two flowers in the morning, and I wanted to be sure you would be there. Jackie is disrespectful, and I'd rather work with you than her. I'm not telling you how to run your business, but you really need to find a better person for the front counter." He gathered the little dog's leash in his hands.

"I'm sorry, Mr. Morgan. Jackie said you'd come by this morning. I just assumed she'd waited on you."

He twisted the leash in his hand. "She did."

"But?" Charisma prompted.

"Well, the truth of the matter is, she doesn't listen. The flower she gave me wasn't good enough for my Mazie, and when I told her I wanted a different one, she acted like I was an old fool. So I took the flower, but I threw it in the trash." He raised sad eyes. "I won't give Mazie flowers I'm not happy with."

Charisma's blood boiled. Jackie would have to go. She wouldn't put up with employees hurting her customers' feelings. "So you didn't give her a flower today?"

He shook his head.

"Hold on a second, Mr. Morgan." Charisma hurried inside and called the florist shop. Lynn was working late on a bouquet. Charisma just hoped she'd answer the phone.

She sighed with relief when Lynn answered. A few moments later, Charisma hung up the phone. She hurried into the kitchen and made two glasses of tea.

"Mr. Morgan, would you join me for a glass of tea?"

The old man hesitated for a moment then agreed. He opened the gate and made his way to the porch. "Thanks, I could use a cool drink."

Charisma sat back down on the swing. She wondered where Will and Joey were. It wasn't like them to be this late.

"I'm really sorry about Jackie. I'll try to be the one to wait on you from now on, and I'll give her a good talking-to." She took a sip of tea.

Mr. Morgan took an ice cube from his drink and gave it to the dog. He stood up and took another gulp of tea. "I'd hate for that young woman to ruin your business, Charisma."

"Me, too." She saw Lynn drive up to the curb and get out of the car.

Lynn carried a large vase of carnations in various colors. She waved as she came up the walkway.

"I can't take back what Jackie did this morning, Mr. Morgan, but I'd like to make it up to you and Mrs. Morgan." Charisma took the vase from Lynn and handed it to the gentleman.

Mist filled his gray eyes and he swallowed hard. "Now, Charisma, I can't take this."

"Yes, you can. I'm sure your wife was disappointed this morning when she didn't get her flower. This way, you can give her a full bouquet of carnations in celebration of her healing." Charisma gave him a quick hug.

"Thank you. You are a sweet girl." Mr. Morgan took his leave.

Charisma and Lynn watched him amble down the street.

"Mrs. Morgan is a lucky woman." Lynn sat down on the porch swing.

"Yes, she is. He loves her so much." She joined Lynn on the seat. "I'm glad the Lord is healing her. I'd hate to see what her death would do to Mr. Morgan."

The thought of someone loving her that much brought Will and Joey to mind. Where were they? She checked her watch. It was a little after six.

Charisma wanted to be angry with Will, but his gaze was soft and full of sorrow. She hated to admit even to herself, but her worry hadn't just been for Joey. What if something had happened to Will? Her heart skipped at the thought of losing him.

She knelt down to Joey's level and hugged him to her. "Why didn't you call? I was getting worried."

Will cleared his throat. Both Joey and Charisma looked up at him. "I'm sorry; it was my fault. Mark and I got to playing ball with the boys after we stopped to drop him off, and we sort of lost track of time."

She stood. "It's okay, Will. Just please call next time."

He nodded.

"Have you two eaten yet?" Charisma hoped to stall Will's departure.

Will's face lit up, but Joey dashed the look with three simple words. "Yep, sure did."

She couldn't contain a smile of her own. "Good. Then how about some cake? I made a blueberry angel food cake about an hour ago."

"All right!" Joey rushed to the house. "Come on, Will. Charisma makes the best blueberry cake in the world."

Will's warm laughter washed over her like a summer rain. He looped his arm over her shoulder and gave her a slight tug. "We better hurry or he'll eat the whole thing. Trust me on that."

Charisma wasn't sure what to do with his arm around her. Her experience with men was limited, to say the least. Thankfully, when they got to the steps, he released her.

A few minutes later, they were inside, savoring the cake. Charisma enjoyed the look of pleasure on Will's face. The gentle smile he offered melted whatever ice was left in her heart.

"Joey, don't eat too much of that. I'd hate for your belly to start hurting again," Will warned.

A frown touched Joey's features. "Yeah, I didn't like that much."

"What are you talking about?" Charisma set her fork down and looked from one male face to the other.

"I had a stomachache today," Joey offered around a mouthful of blueberries and cream.

Charisma watched her brother shovel in another scoop. "What caused it?" She turned her attention to Will.

"He had a few too many green and red blackberries this afternoon, but Lisa fixed him right up. Didn't she, sport?" Will winked at Joey.

"Yep." Joey grabbed his milk and gulped it down. "Charisma, can I go watch TV?" He scooted down off his chair.

"May I," she corrected.

Joey looked at her, puzzled for a moment. "Yeah, may I?"

"Yes." Charisma picked up his plate and empty glass.

She watched Joey dash out of the kitchen and called after him, "Put one of your tapes in. I'm not sure what is on TV tonight."

"Okay."

Will gathered his own plate and glass. "Here, let me help you with those." He followed her.

She ran hot water into the sink and added soap. "You don't have to do that. I'll have them done in a snap."

He reached around her and slipped his dishes into the sudsy water. Her pulse pounded in her ears at his nearness. "I'm good at drying."

Charisma released a shaky laugh. "Thanks, but that is one of Joey's chores."

"Well, then I guess I'll be on my way."

Charisma walked him to the door. "Thanks for taking care of Joey today. I'm sorry he was so much trouble."

"Joey is never a problem." Will opened the screen and stepped out onto the porch.

She followed him. "Will, I've been thinking." Charisma paused. What was he going to think of her next statement? She sat down on the porch swing and kicked off gently. "I'm going to ask Jackie from the store to take over watching Joey during the day."

He leaned against the post in front of the swing. "I see. Won't that make you shorthanded at the shop?"

Charisma decided to be truthful with him. "I have to do it. Jackie is great with Joey, but with customers, let's just say she leaves a lot to be desired."

Will tilted his head to the side and searched her face. "So this has nothing to do with us being late today?"

"Of course not. One of my best customers came by earlier and told me Jackie was rude to him this morning. I don't think she meant to be offensive, but he's not the first customer to complain." Charisma lifted her gaze to the stars behind Will's broad shoulders.

"I see. But that still doesn't answer my question. Will that make you shorthanded at the store?" He crossed his arms over his chest. Will's sea blue eyes were filled with concern as they searched her face.

Charisma thought for several long moments. How much should she tell him? Did she really trust him enough to tell him her personal business? A small voice reminded her that she'd trusted Will enough to allow him to watch her most prized possession, Joey.

He pulled himself up straight. "I'm sorry. I don't have any right to question your decision." He started to walk down the steps.

"No!"

Will turned at the sharpness in her voice.

Charisma felt heat surge into her face. "I'm sorry. I didn't mean to yell. I just didn't want you to leave thinking you were interfering."

Will's warm laughter touched her deeply. "I'm the one who's sorry, Charisma. It's just that I have spent so much time with you and Joey that I've become a little protective. I shouldn't have questioned your decision."

"It's okay. Honestly, I'm not sure how it will affect the business. For right now, I'm going to work the front and let Lynn do what she does best, and that's make the floral arrangements." She took a deep breath and exhaled. Having said the words out loud made her feel better about her decision.

Will sat down beside her on the swing. "What if Jackie doesn't want to watch Joey? Then what?"

Chapter 10

Charisma got up early the next morning. As she dressed for work, her thoughts turned to her evening with Will. He was good company, and she felt at ease talking with him about her personal problems.

Will had changed over the years. He'd gone from being a carefree bachelor to a warmhearted man who seemed interested in her problems and how to solve them.

Over the past three weeks, Will hadn't dated a single woman in the small town of Sweetwater. A smile tugged at Charisma's lips. The only woman he'd spent any time with had been her.

Just as quickly the grin slid from her face. He'd also been with Joey. Charisma couldn't think of a time that Joey hadn't been with them, except last night—and when they were in the bleachers while he played ball.

Charisma brushed her hair. What would it be like to be totally alone with Will on a date? She was sure he'd be charming and a true gentleman. Hadn't her friends told her so years ago?

Her thoughts turned to their college days. Most of her

friends had dated Will Lovelace, and they'd all felt special, as if he only had eyes for them.

Until he dumped them.

She sighed and laid the brush aside. Did she really want to date Will?

Charisma stared into the mirror. She looked herself in the eyes. *Time to be honest,* she thought, and then she forced the words past her tight throat. "He's changed. I've changed. I want to get to know Will Lovelace better. If he ever asks me for a date, I'm going." That said, Charisma headed out the door.

How come I have to go with you?" Joey demanded as he climbed into the car with Charisma.

She made sure he was buckled in before answering. "Because Will has something he has to do today, and I told him you could spend some time with me at the flower shop."

Joey squirmed around in his seat until he was facing her. "Will Jackie be there?"

Charisma pulled up to the back of the store and shut off the motor. She spotted Jackie's bicycle leaning against the wall by the door. "She's here."

"Good. I wonder if she'll play catch with me." Joey grabbed the ball glove and pulled on the door handle to get out.

Charisma laughed. "Wait, you have to unbuckle your seat belt first."

Within moments Joey had run ahead of her and gone into the store.

Charisma took her time leaving the car. She silently prayed as she made her way into the building. *Lord, please let Jackie agree to watch Joey for the rest of the summer. You know how I hate conflict. Amen.*

What was wrong with him? Will glanced at the clock. He hadn't fallen asleep the night before. His eyes felt scratchy, and his brain just would not shut down.

Will pushed the covers back and sat up on the side of the bed. He rubbed his hands over his face. His thoughts turned to Charisma and Joey.

Last night, sitting on her front porch, he'd realized that he was in love with Charisma. Will had to admit he'd already been aware of the feelings but had tried to ignore them. But when she'd opened up, told him her problems, and then trusted him to help her solve them—Will knew without a shadow of a doubt he loved her.

He'd tossed and turned all night. What was he going to do? He wouldn't be thirty for another eighteen months. According to the Bachelor Club rules, he couldn't get married until he was thirty, and right now Will wanted to get married. He wanted to spend the rest of his life with Charisma Diner.

But Will also wanted to win the competition. The other boys had insisted on starting the club, and he hadn't really wanted to play the game. They had insisted, and being the youngest, Will hadn't put up too much of a fight. But he'd vowed when he was eight that he'd win.

Will groaned as he stood up. His back popped as he stretched. His thoughts returned to the game. He'd already beaten Adam, only two more to go. Will stepped into the shower. Warm water washed over him. Adam, Isaac, and Joseph were his best friends. He loved them all as brothers.

His cousin Adam was the first to get married. They'd really given him a hard time about it, but secretly Will was glad. Adam was happier than he'd ever been.

What if he gave up the game and married Charisma? Would he be that happy? Would the game really matter? What would his dad think of him? Willard Lovelace had always supported Will in everything he did, but would he support a decision to quit the club? Could he really do it? Give up his dream of winning?

The questions swirled through his mind as he stepped out of the shower and dried off. Why couldn't he answer the questions? They were the same ones that had plagued him all night.

Will slipped into a comfortable pair of lounge pants. Since Charisma didn't need him to watch Joey today, he decided to spend a quiet day at home. He pulled a tan T-shirt over his head. It matched the Mr. Potato Head pants he wore.

He went into the kitchen and stuffed two pieces of bread into the toaster. While he waited for it to toast, he started a pot of coffee. Would Charisma consider going out on a real date with him?

The toast popped. Will jumped. The phone rang.

"Hello," Will growled into the phone.

Willard's voice answered, "Well, hello, son. How are you?"

Will sunk into a chair. *Thank You, Lord. My dad is just the person I need to talk to.* "Not so good, Dad. I have a little problem."

An hour later, Will hung up the phone. As always, his dad had the answers. Willard had suggested Will follow his heart.

It wasn't quite the answer Will had been looking for, so he decided to take the last week of his vacation and go spend it in the cabins at San Juan Forest. It would give him time to think and put some space between himself and the Diners.

Will picked up the phone and called the flower shop. Jackie answered the phone. "Jackie, this is Will Lovelace. May I speak to Charisma, please?"

"I'm sorry, Mr. Lovelace. You just missed her, she and Joey went out to lunch," the teenager answered.

He paused. Should he leave a message? Will knew he couldn't leave Charisma without a baby-sitter. "Jackie, did Charisma talk to you about watching Joey for her?"

"Yeah, I think I'm going to like that better than working here." A loud pop filled the phone line. Will could picture the teenager chewing gum and blowing bubbles.

"So you're going to do it then?" he asked just to make sure.

"Yep." Another pop filled the line. "Want me to tell Charisma you called?"

With her problem solved, Will didn't see any reason to leave a message. At this point they weren't really dating. "No, I'll talk to her later. Thanks, Jackie."

He hung up the phone and prepared to leave.

Chapter 11

Charisma slumped into her chair. Her gaze moved to the clock on the wall. It felt strange not to have seen Will all day. Why hadn't they heard from him in the last three days? Had he gone back to work early?

"I locked the door and turned the sign over. Is there anything else I can do before I leave?" Lynn rested a hip against Charisma's desk.

"No, I think we're done for the day. I'm heading home myself." She pulled her purse from the bottom drawer of her desk.

"Got a date tonight?" Lynn teased.

Charisma knew Lynn was wondering where Will had been the last few days. It wasn't like him not to call or stop by the flower shop. They'd all gotten used to him being around. "Yep, with Joey. He has a ball game tonight."

"Hey, maybe I'll stop by the field and watch." Lynn waved as she left.

After a quick peanut butter and jelly sandwich with milk, Charisma and Joey headed for the game. They arrived at the park a few minutes early. Joey ran off to meet his friend while

Charisma moved to the stands to watch the game.

Her gaze moved about the field. At any moment she expected to see Will's lean body lumber across the field in her direction. He hadn't missed a game yet. A smile touched her lips. She'd missed him over the last few days and looked forward to seeing him again.

The game started.

Lynn showed up during the third inning and waved. She stood in front of the bleachers and yelled up to Charisma. "Hey, how's it going?"

Charisma smiled and shouted back, "They're winning."

"That's great. Where's Will?" Lynn frowned up at her.

Heat filled Charisma's face. "Not here yet," she called back, aware of the other people in the stands watching her.

"Oh, okay. See you later." Lynn waved good-bye.

Mark stepped down from the top bleachers and sat down by Charisma. He waited a few moments until the rest of the crowd was focused on the game again and then offered, "Charisma, Will isn't coming today. Didn't he tell you?"

All she could do was shake her head.

Mark's jaw worked for several long moments. "I'm sorry, I thought you were different and he really cared about you and Joey."

"I don't understand."

Mark turned and looked up into the stands. "Lisa, I'll be right back," he called.

Charisma heard Lisa answer and then felt Mark tugging her up. She followed him down the bleachers and out to the parking lot. What was going on? Where was Will?

He lowered the tailgate on his pickup and told Charisma to sit down for a moment. When she was seated, he paced in front of her.

"I'm sorry, Charisma. I thought Will had changed since college. But I guess not." He was agitated. Mark pulled his baseball cap off his head and ran a hand through his hair.

He slapped the hat back on his head and asked, "Did Will ever mention the Bachelor Club?"

Again she shook her head.

He sighed and sat down by her. "Well, then maybe he's given up the game."

"Mark, you aren't making any sense." Charisma turned to face him.

"I know. I'm sorry." He took her hands in his. Mark took a deep breath and then began. "Do you remember in college that Will dated a lot of girls?" At her nod he continued. "Well, the reason he did that was because Will was part of a small club called the Bachelor Club. He didn't keep a girl long because she would start to get serious, and he couldn't let them get that close."

Charisma's head was spinning. It almost sounded like the Bachelor Club was part of the mafia. He couldn't get close to a girl because he was in the club. She mulled the information around. It explained his behavior in school, but what did that have to do with her now?

"He once told me as long as he was a part of that club, he couldn't get serious about a girl. When I saw him with you, I assumed he was done with the Bachelor Club." Mark released her hands. "Did Will tell you he was leaving?"

"No." Her heart felt as if someone had reached inside her

chest and squeezed. She tried to put on a brave smile. "But Will and I aren't a couple. We've never dated, so he probably didn't think he had to tell me he was leaving."

Mark jumped off the tailgate. "Charisma, we aren't in college anymore, and people don't date like they used to, especially when children are involved. I know Will cares about you and Joey. When he stopped by the house the other day, he asked me to keep an eye on you."

She watched him pace in front of her. Did Will really care about her? If so, why hadn't he told her he was leaving? Did it have to do with this Bachelor Club Mark was talking about? "How long did Will say he would be gone?"

"He didn't." Mark stopped pacing and turned to face her. "All I know for sure is he won't get married until he's thirty years old."

The crowd in the stands went wild. "We better get back to the boys' game." Charisma slid from the tailgate. "Thank you, Mark, for telling me about this." She led the way back to the stands. The thought of never seeing Will again ate at her soul. She silently cried out to God as she climbed onto the bleachers.

Lord, why do You let bad things happen to good people? Haven't I been through enough? Why did You allow me to fall in love with a man who can't commit to me and prefers to run away than face me with the truth? Father, if this love I feel for him is real, please send Will back to me soon.

Will looked down at the cell phone. Dead battery. His gaze

moved to the clock on the wall. Joey's game was well under way.

He wanted to be there watching Joey hit the ball, seeing Charisma jump up and down with excitement. During the last few days, his thoughts hadn't been far from Charisma. Will knew deep down that he loved her.

"Lord, I really need Your help. I can't do this alone." Will felt the need to open his Bible. As he read, he realized that the Lord had placed Charisma and Joey into his life to love.

The Bachelor Club no longer held importance for him. Will realized that it hadn't for a long time. If it had, he would never have allowed Charisma to steal a home in his heart.

"Thank You, Lord, for showing me what is important."

The next morning, Will packed the truck and headed home. He drove straight to Charisma Diner's flower shop. "Lord, please let her feel the same way I do."

She held her breath. Was it really Will pulling up in front of the shop? Charisma watched him slam the door to his truck and hurry inside.

What would she say to him when he came in? She didn't know.

Will pushed the door open and came inside. He didn't say a word as he made his way to the cooler that held the carnations. Charisma couldn't take her gaze off of him as he pulled out a huge bouquet of her favorite flowers.

He walked back to the counter and placed the money on the counter to pay for the flowers. She wondered why he didn't say anything. Charisma's heart sank. Will wasn't even looking at her.

Will pulled a card from his pocket and attached it to the ribbon on the flowers. Then his sea blue eyes met hers. He held the carnations out to her. "Mark told me you were pretty upset that I left without saying good-bye. I'm sorry."

Charisma took the flowers. "Will, you didn't have to give me flowers. I—"

A soft smile touched his eyes and lips. "Please read the card."

She couldn't stop the smile that spread across her face. "Okay."

Charisma's fingers shook as she opened the card and read the words. *Thank you for letting me stay on first base. Will you marry me?* She walked around the counter, remembering the first time he'd thanked her for allowing him on first base. Charisma stopped in front of him.

"Well? Will you marry me?" His loving gaze searched hers.

"What about the Bachelor Club?" She held her breath and waited for his reply.

He took a step toward her. "The Bachelor Club was a silly game. My love for you is real."

In that moment, Charisma realized why God allows bad things to happen to good people. In her case, if she hadn't been Joey's guardian, Will may never have come into her life a second time. She silently thanked the Lord, then closed the gap between them and whispered, "Yes, I'll marry you."

RHONDA GIBSON

Rhonda resides in New Mexico with her husband. She writes inspirational romance because she is eager to share her love of the Lord. Besides writing, her interests are reading and scrapbooking. Rhonda loves hearing from her readers. Feel free to write her at P.O. Box 835, Kirtland, NM, or e-mail her at rgib2001@yahoo.com. Visit Rhonda's Web site at www.RhondaGibson.com.

Right for Each Other

by Bev Huston

Dedication

To my earthly shepherd, Dr. Barry Buzza,
who encouraged me when I grew discouraged.
I think Hebrews 6:10 (NIV) sums it up perfectly: "God. . .will
not forget your work and the love you have shown him as
you have helped his people and continue to help them."
Thank you, Barry, for helping this needy author with
research and encouragement and for never growing weary.

Acknowledgments

My heartfelt appreciation and thanks to Laura-Lynn Tyler (*The Coffee Shop Girl*), who allowed me to tour NOW TV studios and who answered my 1001 questions with patience and humor. Thank you, Laura-Lynn, Craig McCulloch, and staff.

Special thanks to my critique partners Carolyn, Jan, Lisa, Cheryl, and Jill. I appreciate your diligence and feedback.

Words could never begin to express my thankfulness to the ladies of the CDA2003 Yahoo group who support me through all the vicissitudes of writing with their unconditional love, strong faith, and endless prayers.

Fear of man will prove to be a snare,
but whoever trusts in the LORD is kept safe.
PROVERBS 29:25 NIV

Chapter 1

I saac Brooks tapped his foot and tried to whistle, but only a weak *whoosh* came out. Hoping to busy himself, he picked up a nearby magazine. He flipped through a few pages then tossed the glossy publication back down on the cluttered table. He normally didn't have attention problems, but he was out of his comfort zone.

Though it seemed like he'd been waiting an hour, Isaac knew it had only been five minutes. In that short amount of time, an interesting phenomenon had taken place. His mouth had become bone-dry, and his palms now manufactured moisture at an alarming rate. Maybe he had time to find a drinking fountain then a rest room to wash his hands. Or slip out a back way and give up his dream.

He opened the door of the green room and took a hesitant step.

"There you are. We're waiting for you."

Isaac balked as a short, balding man grabbed his arm and ushered him along. "You are?" Had he misunderstood the receptionist? Hadn't his appointment been delayed?

Instead of identifying himself, his escort nodded and led him down a narrow hallway banked with shelves of file tapes on one side. Nearly everyone they passed greeted them.

"Wait here," he said and waved Isaac into what appeared to be a hair salon.

Before he could reply, the guy disappeared. Isaac hoped he'd have a moment to pull himself together. He wished he could hide and pray. Better yet, he wished he'd stayed where the receptionist had put him.

Outside the room, Isaac could hear a loud discussion.

"We don't have time for makeup. Get him on the set."

"He needs work." This sounded like the voice of the bald man.

"Gallagher, if you don't get him on the set, you'll have to answer to Reid."

Isaac tried not to listen to the conversation but couldn't help himself. This was a whole new world to him, and it would be a serious understatement if he said he felt uncomfortable.

He pulled a tissue from the coffee table and wiped his sweaty hands then balled it up and tossed it, like a featherweight basketball, into the nearby garbage can. "Two points." He pumped his arm like he'd made an awesome shot. At the sound of applause, he turned around.

Brooke Hart. British diva. Complete with a lovely accent and sultry smile. He'd watched her show every week and had dared to entertain romantic thoughts of quiet dinners and long walks with her. But hadn't every guy on the planet?

She was stunning, even without the lights and special filters he knew they used in television. His heart did a jump shot while his tongue disappeared. Every sensible thought vanished from his brain.

"Brooke," the balding man said as he reappeared, "they're ready for you on the set."

She smiled at Isaac and left.

I'm an idiot. Why didn't I say something? I stood there gawking. Like a starstruck fool.

"She's amazing."

Isaac blinked then turned his attention to the guy he assumed was Gallagher.

"We'd better hurry. You don't want the PA—that's the production assistant—barking at us."

"I had no idea things ran on such a tight schedule," Isaac said as he hurried to keep pace with the man.

"On schedule and under budget is our motto. Reid's a tightfisted, mean sort if you cost him money."

"Is he Mr. Montague's right-hand man?"

"You would think he *was* Mr. Montague, the way he worries and carries on." Gallagher pulled on a large door, and they entered a darkened area. Once again a cacophony of voices permeated the air.

"Reid. Here he is."

"Don't just stand there, Gallagher, get him on the set!"

Isaac froze. *The set? I thought I had an appointment, not a TV interview. Did I misunderstand?*

Gallagher led the way onto a brightly lit stage. At the center stood Brooke Hart. Seated nearby in a row were seven people. Each paired, except one.

"Take your seat by your fiancée over there," Gallagher said, pointing to the empty spot beside a nervous-looking female with too much makeup and a mass of curly red hair.

"Anthony, you're late." The woman jumped up and hastened to his side. Her bright rosy lips formed a pout as she began to drag him back to where she had been sitting.

"I'm afraid there's—"

"Anthony, we've got to win this!" She looked up at him, her eyes silently pleading. "Please, don't tell them," she whispered as she dropped into her place and pulled him down into the seat beside her.

She looked as if she were about to cry. How could he disappoint her? He was always a pushover when it came to a damsel in distress. Of course, the pain in his chest made it difficult to argue. His body stiffened like a two-by-four as he willed himself to take a deep breath.

Gallagher moved off the set while the man Isaac assumed was Reid shouted at everyone. As the contestants eyed the director, Isaac's partner leaned over. "I'm Debbie, by the way," she said in a hushed and rushed tone. "You're my fiancé. You're a car salesman, and we've been dating for eight years. I like violets, chocolate, and sappy movies. What about you?"

"I like the truth."

She chuckled. "We don't have time for jokes. Hurry, they're about to start."

"My name's Isaac; I'm a cartoonist." He didn't know what else to say. There had been a time when he loved to hike, play baseball, and spend time with his friends. Now everything had changed.

Isaac straightened as Reid explained how they would film

the show. "Once the ladies are secured in a soundproof room, you guys will have to answer questions about them. . . ."

Isaac's thoughts drifted as he wondered what would happen when the studio learned who he was. Would Mr. Montague forgo any further discussions about his work? It had taken every ounce of strength and faith he possessed to even agree to such a meeting in the first place.

After the women were removed from the set, Brooke began asking questions. The format reminded him of *The Newlywed Game*. Though this show—*Are You Right for Each Other?*—was for engaged couples.

"Anthony, what's Debbie's middle name?"

Isaac jumped at the forcefulness of Brooke's question. Not only had she caught him daydreaming, but he'd forgotten his new name. He looked down at his feet as he struggled to think of an answer. "I don't think she has one," he said with about as much confidence as a little kid standing up to a bully.

Brooke raised her eyebrows and pinned him with her gaze. "How long have you known her?"

"Obviously, not long enough," he replied, wishing the lights weren't so hot.

Brooke laughed. He watched her closely and admired her quick humor and easy rapport with each contestant. Though some of her comments were a little too harsh for his liking, they did seem to be in jest. All too soon, she was asking him another question.

"Anthony, if Debbie likened you to an animal in the wild kingdom, what would you be?"

"I'd have to say a chameleon."

"Are you saying she thinks you're a lizard? Or you're cold-blooded?"

"Neither. I just have this ability to blend in wherever I go."

A slight smile spread to the edges of Brooke's full lips, and Isaac couldn't resist grinning back at her.

"Anthony, you look ever so bored. Do you think you've won this round?" Brooke asked after she'd asked each of them another question.

"Not at all." He resisted the urge to squirm.

"Jolly good." She looked directly at him. "This is the final question and worth double points. What fictional movie couple would best describe you and Debbie?"

Well, so much for helping Debbie win—or impressing Brooke, for that matter. He hardly ever watched movies. When he did, they were certainly not romantic ones. Sweat beaded on his brow while he racked his brain for something. Next thing he knew, he opened his mouth and blurted out an answer.

His words seemed to take everyone by surprise, and laughter filled the set. Was it his fault that, as a child, his mother had loved Paul Newman movies and made him watch every one of them? Repeatedly? Isaac wanted to slink off and hide. He wouldn't be that lucky. Gallagher ushered the women out of the soundproof room and back to their men. Isaac hoped Debbie wouldn't be mad at him for his dumb answers.

"Actually," Debbie began in response to the first question, "I don't have a middle name. My first name is Debra-Jo."

Isaac hooted. His response surprised him. Brooke made a comment he didn't catch, and then she moved on.

The next couple got the answer wrong and started arguing.

"You can't win your dream wedding and honeymoon that way," Brooke reminded the contestants then chuckled.

By the time they were at the last question, Isaac could tell Debbie wasn't too happy with him. She'd gotten every question wrong and punched him in the shoulder after hearing each of his responses. For a petite woman, she yielded a painful right hook.

"Okay, Debbie. It doesn't look good for you and Anthony. But if you get this question right, you have a chance to move to second place at the end of this first round."

Debbie nodded, smiled for the camera, and began to bounce in her seat as Brooke asked for her answer. "That's easy! Jack and Rose from *Titanic*."

"Oh, sorry, Debbie. Anthony thought you two best resembled Sundance and Etta."

Isaac braced himself for another punch.

"Who?"

"If I'm not mistaken, Debbie, they're outlaws. Not to be confused with in-laws, which you may not have if you keep going this way."

A few minutes later, the filming stopped, and Brooke rushed off the set. Isaac turned to Debbie. "I'm sorry we didn't do too well."

"We can still catch up. Sometimes they ask the same questions. What's your middle name?"

"Don't you think you should be telling me that?"

"Oh, right." Debbie bit her fingernail as she thought. "I think it's Mark."

"You're not sure?"

"Just answer Mark and so will I."

Isaac laughed. "You know, if you happen to win, won't you end up forfeiting everything once they find out I'm not Anthony?"

"Shush, here she comes."

"How do you think you'll do in the next round?" Brooke spoke directly to Isaac as she neared them.

Could she see his guilt? Was it written all over his face? As a kid, Will always knew when Isaac had not told the truth. It wasn't until they had grown up that his friend finally told what gave him away. Isaac's ears wiggled when he lied. No doubt they were dancing a jig right before Brooke's eyes.

Debbie piped up and took the heat off him. She rambled on faster than his beating heart, and he let her have all the attention she wanted.

Chapter 2

"P laces, everyone," Gallagher shouted and clapped his hands. The teleprompter scrolled while the cameras zoomed. After a brief explanation, the men were ushered to the quiet room.

Isaac could hardly wait for this game to be over. His skin felt like it was too tight, and he found it difficult to sit still. The other guys stuffed their faces with the food on the tables, but he didn't dare eat. He looked at the clock again and again, but the hands never seemed to move.

Eventually, Gallagher brought them back to the set. It took a moment for Isaac's eyes to adjust to the dark walls and ceilings and the bright spotlight focused on the contestants.

"Brian," Brooke began, "what side of the bed does Judi prefer?"

"My side," Brian answered. Judi glared at him. "I mean the left side."

"That's right. You've earned ten more points."

When Brooke got to Isaac, his throat felt dry, and he worried nothing would come out. Worse, he didn't have a clue how he would answer.

"So, Anthony, what side of the bed does Debbie prefer?"

"The middle." What a dumb answer. Why did he say that?

"That doesn't surprise me," Brooke said. "And you're right. That puts you in third place. Good work."

Isaac flinched as Debbie socked him in the shoulder. She'd done that every time they'd gotten a question wrong. But this time he got it right. What'd she hit him for?

If he'd been embarrassed by the first question, the second one—in his opinion—was worse. Obviously, he'd never paid close attention to this show.

"Roger, where does Hazel buy her unmentionables?"

Isaac chuckled to himself as the guy squirmed.

I know exactly how you feel, pal.

"Big Red Sale Mart," Roger said with a wide grin.

Hazel put her hands on her hips. "Big Red has been out of business for ten years!"

"Exactly."

Everyone laughed.

"I'm not even going to ask what that's all about, Roger," Brooke said with a frown. "In case you're wondering, Hazel shops at La Senza."

Isaac had been so caught up in Roger's discomfort, he forgot about his own. When Brooke asked him to answer, he rubbed his hands and leaned away from Debbie's impending swing. "Wal-Mart."

Debbie squealed in his ear, grabbed him around the neck, and crushed the air out of his chest. Then she thumped him.

Right for Each Other

"That's another ten points. You've held your position."

Isaac rubbed his shoulder. Right or wrong, Debbie seemed to be turning him into mincemeat.

"Right, then. Larry and Heather, this is the final question in this round, and you're in last place. Which is only good when you're playing hide-and-seek."

The group laughed while Brooke continued.

By now, Isaac couldn't concentrate. His head pounded, and his lungs had constricted. Sweat formed on his brow, and his moist palms reminded him of a water fountain.

"Get this right, Anthony and Debbie, and you'll move to second place."

Debbie clapped with obvious excitement.

"What famous fictional character do you remind Debbie of, Anthony?"

How should he answer that? Superman? After all, he did rescue her from embarrassment. Esau? Didn't he give up his career for a pretty girl? He didn't have time to contemplate his response. Everyone was waiting.

"Jack from *Titanic*," he blurted in desperation.

Debbie flew out of her seat and shrieked.

Isaac couldn't miss the smile Brooke offered. "Well, you've saved your girl from losing, so far, so I'd say she's accurate. But will you end up drowning in the end?"

He didn't know about drowning, but he did know it would be days before he could use his arm again. Where did she learn to punch like a stevedore?

"We've reached the bonus round," Brooke announced. "Each of you must decide who will answer while the other is

191

in the soundproof room."

After a brief discussion, Isaac found himself walking off the set with Hazel, Judi, and Heather. He hoped he didn't look as chagrined as he felt. Debbie had insisted that they were unstoppable with her at the helm. He hoped she was right. Though a part of him worried that he could be in big trouble for pretending to be Anthony. Sure, many shows used actors and weren't always on the up-and-up, but as a Christian, he had a responsibility to be honest at all times. Was it okay to help someone this way, or was it still wrong?

After rehashing what he should do for the umpteenth time, they were called back to the set for the final question. Soon, but not soon enough, it would all be over, along with his chance of a career with Montague Studios.

"Well, Anthony and Debbie, get this question right and you will tie for first place with Brian and Judi. Get it wrong, and you'll be in last place."

Debbie began to jump up and down in her seat. Isaac had come to realize that the woman wanted to win—with or without Anthony. What good was a wedding and honeymoon without a groom? A sadness crept into Isaac's heart.

Tell me how to help her, Lord.

"Anthony, what is the number one reason you and Debbie know you're *right for each other*?"

In his head, Isaac could hear the *Jeopardy* theme. The pressure increased. What had she said? Anthony was a salesman? Nope, nothing he could use there.

Think, man!

"You'll have to answer, Anthony."

Isaac nodded. "I'm something right out of her imagination," he blurted.

Loser.

"Are you saying you're her dream guy or her worst nightmare?" Brooke asked.

"Probably the latter."

"I'm sorry, Anthony, but Debbie thought the one thing that confirmed you two were *right for each other* was your ability to understand her."

Isaac looked at Debbie, whose shoulders were now slumped. His heart ached for this stranger.

"Quite frankly, Anthony, if Debbie is right, you might want to share your secret with the rest of the men out there who are clueless."

Isaac couldn't laugh along with everyone else.

"So, congratulations, Brian and Judi. You're our winners and have proven that you're *right for each other!*" Brooke's voice rose in volume and excitement while the winning couple hugged and kissed. Balloons and streamers drifted down from overhead and music began to play.

Isaac looked at Debbie and reached for her hand. "Sorry."

Moments later the spotlight beamed back on Debbie and him. "Our last-place couple, Debbie and Anthony, win a consolation prize. I'd suggest, Debbie, if you want to keep that caring man of yours, you'll need to start paying attention to him."

Brooke's comment caused Debbie to cry. Isaac clasped her hands in his.

"It's just a show. Brooke's paid to make those kinds of remarks; they mean nothing."

She buried herself in his arms, causing Isaac to feel obligated to embrace her. "Why not tell them I'm not Anthony and see if they will do a retake or something?"

Debbie pulled back. "Are you crazy? I never would have won with Anthony, either. He doesn't even know what color my eyes are."

"I still think we should come clean."

"I never want to see you again," Debbie shouted as she stood up. She lifted her chin and strode across the set as if she owned it, disappearing into the blackness offstage.

Isaac stood watching, certain his jaw had dropped in surprise.

Brooke walked over and put her hand on his shoulder. "That was quite a row. She'll come round, though. You did read the release before you signed it, didn't you?"

He stared at her, surprised that she didn't have more compassion. He had been certain many of her remarks were all an act. Now he had some doubts. Of course, what did he care? It wasn't like he and Debbie had just broken up.

So why did it bother him that this beautiful, spirited woman had not been more understanding?

Chapter 3

"B rooke!" Gallagher hollered and motioned for her to join him and Reid.

She froze. She didn't like the look on the floor manager's face. Had something gone wrong? She plastered on a smile to hide her fear and walked to the control room. Both men stood beyond the sliding glass door, which was wide open now that filming had stopped.

"Good work today," the production assistant said.

"What? A compliment from the PA? Thanks, Reid." She leaned against the door frame in the hope that it made her look relaxed and casual. She suspected it didn't. The sharp metal edge of the casing dug into her shoulder, but she ignored her discomfort. "The first couple was rather funny. The audience will be glad they won, I would imagine."

"Gallagher thinks you were a little too nice."

"I didn't waffle on, did I? I do hate it when I'm a bore."

Gallagher and Reid looked at each other then at her. Reid motioned for Gallagher to speak.

"Waffle on? Is that another one of your weird expressions?

Like *loo*?" Both men chuckled.

"Now, gentlemen, I don't make fun of your expressions," she said as she crossed her arms. "Waffle means to blather."

"Okay, then," Reid said. "So. Was there a problem with the losers in the first show?"

She blinked. Had Reid seen the couple fighting? Had he heard her ridiculously stupid comment? Why couldn't she have been sympathetic? The way she truly felt. "I believe Debbie's parting words were she never wanted to see Anthony again."

"Good," Gallagher said as he took a seat.

Brooke's stomach tightened. There was nothing good about breaking up a relationship.

Reid laughed as he ran a hand through his thinning gray hair. "This could work in our favor."

The man was a numbers mercenary, and she struggled—more times than she'd like to count—with his heartlessness. "How?"

Gallagher cleared his throat. "Ratings are low. Controversy builds viewership, Brooke. You should know that. You've been in this business a long time."

Some days, too long.

"How can we use this to our advantage?" Reid stared out onto the set.

"Reid," Brooke started then paused. She took a deep breath. "I don't believe it's right to get involved in what happens after the show. While the release makes it clear we're not responsible if they break up, nothing is ironclad these days. I should think we would risk a great deal if we push this."

Gallagher frowned at Brooke. "Okay, Reid, what do you have in mind?" he asked.

"I'll let you know at the production meeting next week. In the meantime, I want you both to come up with some ideas to boost our ratings. Bring me the info on that couple, as well." Without waiting for a response, Reid exited the control room.

"That went well, don't you think?" Gallagher winked.

Brooke stared at the bank of monitors and sighed.

"Everything all right?"

"No. Yes."

The floor manager laughed. "Are you sure about that?"

"I'm terribly concerned, Gallagher. Reid's plans haven't always been the best."

"Don't worry your pretty little brunette head about it. Montague knows all."

"Right. But he usually *knows all* too late." Brooke shivered.

Isaac closed the door to his small apartment and leaned against it, breathing heavily as if he'd just escaped the jaws of a wild beast.

His hands trembled, and he willed them to stop. "That wasn't so bad," he said aloud to the empty foyer and walked into the kitchen.

He stopped in front of the fridge and read the verse he'd posted there six months ago when he first returned from California. It was Proverbs 29:25: "The fear of man brings a snare, but whoever trusts in the LORD shall be safe."

Lord, help me.

Pulling a tumbler from the white cupboard, Isaac turned on the cold water tap and waited to fill his glass. His thoughts wandered back to the day's events.

He'd left the studio with the receptionist calling after him. He couldn't have stopped even if he had wanted to. She must have thought he was some sort of lunatic. And wasn't he? Pretending to be someone's fiancé? What had come over him?

Isaac jumped when the phone began to ring. The incessant sound grated on his nerves. He rushed to the living room, checked the caller ID, and scooped up the receiver.

"I didn't think you'd answer," the male voice said.

"You know me too well, Willard." Isaac heard the elderly man chuckle.

"I see you survived, so it couldn't have been that bad."

Isaac carried the handset back to the kitchen so he could talk and forage for food at the same time. "You wouldn't believe me if I told you. Suffice it to say, the entire day was worse than anything we discussed."

"Are they not interested now?"

"I doubt it." He grabbed a stick of hot pepperoni and took a bite.

"They must have recognized the potential to make this a successful venture. What's next?"

Isaac sighed. "I'll probably be sued or arrested."

"You didn't pull one of your pranks, did you?" Willard's voice rose in pitch.

"Those days are long gone," Isaac said as he jerked a paper towel off the roll and wiped his hands.

Willard remained silent for a moment then spoke. "Sorry, son, I'm praying."

Though Isaac wasn't Willard's offspring, their relationship had always been like that of a father and son. No matter what Isaac shared, Willard still offered unconditional love, just like his heavenly Father.

"Start at the beginning, Isaac. I've got lots of time."

Apparently I will, too.

When he finished telling Willard about the delay in the interview, his new television persona, and never even meeting Mr. Montague, he let out a sigh. Complete silence was all he got from the other end of the phone. Good thing he hadn't even mentioned Brooke Hart.

"Willard?"

"I'm still here, Isaac."

"Should I leave town?"

Willard roared with laughter. "Not yet. But you might need some damage control. Here's what I think you should do. . . ."

Brooke stared absently at her computer monitor. Her mind had drifted a million miles away as she contemplated how poorly she had behaved on the set a few days ago with Anthony.

He'd caused such a stir within her that she'd barely been able to follow the teleprompter. She liked his answers, his kindness, and his dark, sympathetic eyes. Most of all, she liked how he genuinely cared for his fiancée and ensured he never said anything that would offend her.

Unfortunately, if there was one thing Brooke knew best, it was not to let her feelings get in the way of her job. Even when she was just an anonymous street reporter in London, she'd learned this lesson well. Anthony would be no different.

"He was kind of cute, don't you think?"

Brooke turned around and eyed her assistant, knowing Jolene had probably noticed her reaction to Anthony. "I'm not sure who you're talking about, but every guy is cute to you."

"Not quite. Gallagher and Reid aren't."

They giggled.

"Did you see your promo in the *Santa Fe Times*?"

Brooke moved to Jolene's desk. "I didn't know they were running it yet. How does it look?"

"Impressive. It's a good photo."

"If you like that sort of thing."

"You amaze me. You're in the spotlight all the time and hate it. Why did you take this job if you dislike fame so much?"

Brooke looked down and picked a piece of fluff from her trousers. Why, indeed? Financially, she knew why. Was that a valid reason? Sadie would think so. But then her sister didn't have the capacity to weigh the rights and wrongs. She shook her head. "It's not that simple."

"Yep, if you can complicate things, you will. I don't know how you live with yourself."

Brooke knew Jolene meant it in jest, but her comment stung.

"Oh, oh, look at this week's *Bachelor Club*."

She leaned over and read the comic strip her assistant pointed out.

"Isaac Brooks is the funniest guy on the planet."

"Isn't this the cartoonist Mr. Montague is always on about?" Brooke asked.

"Yeah. He calls him Dear Abby with a Y chromosome. Something males can relate to."

"Right. Since when do men want relationship counsel?"

Jolene chuckled. "There's talk Montague wants to create an animated series based on this."

"Is the studio that desperate?"

"I heard that," Reid said as he walked toward them.

Brooke felt the heat of embarrassment flush her neck and rise to her cheeks. She didn't mean her comment to sound like an insult. "Don't you think there are too many adult animated shows already?"

"This guy's popular." Reid leaned over and looked at the paper.

"I've heard the president doesn't start his day without reading the *Bachelor Club* first."

"You have to stop buying those tabloids, Jolene," Brooke said as she stared out the second-floor window. A long, white limo pulled up and stopped.

"Brooke?" Reid waved his hand in front of her face.

"What have you done?" Her heart beat thunderously in her chest.

"Nothing."

She pointed to the limo. "Isn't that the guy from the show a few days ago?"

Reid moved closer to the window and watched. "It looks like him. What's he doing here?"

"I asked you first."

Chapter 4

An hour had passed since the limo first appeared. Brooke had been unable to concentrate and had continued to watch for the vehicle's return. As soon as the luxury car eased toward the building like a slow-moving eel, she jumped up, grabbed the papers from her desk, and dashed down the stairwell like a little child rushing to meet the ice cream lorry.

Opening the main floor door, she slipped out into the hallway and attempted to walk calmly toward the receptionist's desk. Susie was a wealth of info and more than willing to share anything she knew. Sometimes even things she didn't know.

As Brooke neared, she spotted Anthony and stopped. Her feet refused to move forward. What if he were here to have her fired? After all, hadn't Reid said ratings were down? Hadn't she been horribly cruel to him after Debbie's comments? She wouldn't blame him if he were asking for her head on a silver platter.

She turned to leave.

"Miss Hart."

Oops. He must have seen her. Brooke spun around and waited for Anthony to approach. He seemed unsure of himself, almost nervous as he shifted his weight from one foot to the other. She seized on this opportunity. "Anthony, is it?" She started to continue but paused when she thought she saw his ears wiggle. She suppressed a smile and without waiting for his response said, "I'm so very sorry about the other day. I do hope you and Debbie have patched things up." His eyes clouded, and Brooke wondered if he would berate her with an angry outburst. She held her breath.

"Things aren't always as they seem," he said. He looked around. "Is there someplace we could talk?"

His voice was low yet determined. Brooke shuddered. Should she be afraid of this man?

"Brooke, Montague and Reid are looking for you," Gallagher interrupted.

She looked at Anthony then at the floor manager.

"Now!"

"I'm sorry," she said and left with Gallagher. It took every ounce of strength she possessed not to look back at Anthony. What caused her to feel such mixed emotions?

"Is that guy bothering you?"

Gallagher's words interrupted her thoughts. "I don't think so. Do you know why he's here?"

"I think he had a meeting with Montague."

Her heart sank. Anthony must be trying to have her fired. Her boss didn't see just anyone. He was a busy man with a huge empire to run, both here in America and in the U.K.

Even though she worked for him, she only saw him when there was trouble.

It had been such a surprise, years ago, when he'd said hello one morning and knew her name. An even bigger surprise when he offered her the job of hosting *Are You Right for Each Other?*

Her show had been a big hit back home, but it somehow lacked the same fun and energy here. Was it because she felt different living in New Mexico?

When she spoke, people stopped and stared. Some commented on her accent, while others said nothing. A part of her wanted to tell them they were the ones with the twang in their dialect, but she knew they would simply laugh. Still, she had embraced the uniqueness of the people, this town. Why couldn't they do the same for her?

"Go right in," Alice Wells, Mr. Montague's secretary, said.

Not a good sign. Brooke stepped behind Gallagher as he entered first. Her stomach tightened. She'd never been fired before.

"Have a seat."

Nothing had changed in the opulent office. Atworthy Montague sat behind a huge ebony desk, his burgundy executive chair tilted backward. The walls were covered with plaques and photographs. Brooke especially loved the one of Montague and Tom Selleck sailing off the coast.

"Brooke, how are things going?"

She struggled to answer. Was that a trick question? Hadn't Anthony already been in here? Didn't Montague know the truth? She swallowed and answered with the first thing that popped into her addled brain. "Hard to believe my year here in America is almost over."

"You don't sound disappointed." His thick lips tipped as a smile threatened to appear but never quite materialized.

"To be honest, sir, I'm a little homesick." She reached into her pocket and grasped the familiar coin she knew was there, holding on to it like a life preserver. "But I'm ever so thankful for this experience."

Montague laughed. "It's not over yet."

Brooke nodded, hoping she wouldn't cry. Wait. What did he say? She still had her job? Wasn't he upset?

"We've come up with a great idea. We're going to contact former contestants and see where they are now, a year after the show. Discover the fallout, that sort of thing."

Now she knew why Anthony had been here. He probably supported the idea. He would enjoy the opportunity to tell how poorly he had been treated. How the show cost him the only woman he ever loved. How thoughtless and uncaring she was. If only he knew the truth. With her hand still inside her pocket, she turned the silver coin over and over, thinking of the one who had given it to her.

"It will be live, and you'll moderate the show."

Montague's words caught her attention. "I'm not familiar or comfortable with a live feed. Plus we've all heard tales of disasters when the delay dropped or tensions erupted to an all-out brawl."

"Leave the logistics to us. I'm confident you can do it."

"What about my work visa? How will you get it extended?"

"We have three months to see about that," Montague said

as he waved them out of his office.

She and Gallagher were dismissed. Montague had said what he needed to say. He didn't care for idle chat. Brooke didn't mind. The sooner she escaped his fearsome presence, the better.

"I'm not sure Reid's idea is so hot," Gallagher whispered once out of earshot of the elderly Miss Wells.

"I don't have a good feeling, either. Do we want to exploit people's pain?"

"Let's hope most of the contestants went on to have a happy life together."

Yes. Especially one intriguing, recent contestant.

"I've had it."

Isaac's jaw went slack as his mind registered her comment. "What do you mean?"

"I mean, I'm tired of trying to make it here. I'm tired of the phoniness of it all."

"As soon as I finish my internship, we can leave."

"Isaac, I'm sorry. I'm tired of you, too." Melody said the words through quivering lips then began to cry. She turned and started to walk away.

Isaac raced to her side and reached for her arm. She wrenched free. "Wait. Can't we talk about this? I love you, Mel."

"Don't do this to me, Isaac." Melody turned and broke into a run.

He waited, not knowing whether to follow or give her time. A shriek pierced the air. Melody!

Isaac bolted upright in bed. The alarm sounded as he remained motionless. Every night he had the same dream. Every night Melody was taken from him.

He slammed the button on the clock, relieved at the silence that filled his room. His hair clung to his head, soaked with sweat, and he shivered.

Isaac threw back the covers and swung his feet over the edge of the thick mattress. He bent and lowered his head onto his palms, elbows supported by his thighs.

How long, Lord? How long will I feel this torture?

Could he take much more? Night after night, he lost Melody. Sometimes in a car accident; sometimes in a plane crash. Once, she'd even jumped from a bridge. No matter the scenario, the ending was always the same. She was gone. Forever. Nothing could bring her back. Not even in his dreams. And everything had been his fault.

He padded down the hall, his bare feet chilled by the hardwood floor. In the shower, Isaac considered Montague's idea. He'd presented Isaac with an opportunity of a lifetime, but could this new direction be something God wanted for him?

In time, his thoughts turned to Brooke. Had she seen him and turned to leave the other day when he had been at the studio? Did she dislike him so much she couldn't face him, or did she know the truth?

Even if he agreed to Montague's offer, he'd never see Brooke. Being a cartoonist meant he didn't have to leave his house for work. He e-mailed his comic strip to his publisher. They had the odd phone call, but personal contact was limited.

Sadly, that was the only way he could function these days.

Isaac spotted Brooke as the limo pulled up to the studio. He exited the vehicle and called after her.

She turned and started to wave then stopped.

"Hi," he said as he approached her.

"Anthony. I'm sorry. I'm late. I don't have time to chat." She whirled around, stiff as a drill sergeant, and left him alone.

Though her words were polite, he thought he'd detected a note of fear in her voice. Did she know about his past? He clenched his fists and wished he had Will's baseball glove to pound.

Isaac fought to ignore the familiar feelings that threatened to overwhelm him. His head pounded while his chest tightened and crushed his lungs. These and other debilitating symptoms had become his constant companions.

He needed to get this final meeting over with and, hopefully, never have to return here again. He should feel better, though. For someone who rarely left his home, Isaac had been at the studio almost as much as his apartment—and managed to survive each time.

Of all his visits to see Mr. Montague, this was the first time he wasn't put someplace to wait. The elderly secretary ushered him into the fascinating office in a timely manner.

"How much hands-on are you requiring?" Isaac asked after the salutation formalities.

"We were hoping for some script involvement. You'd be working with a team of writers so it wouldn't fall on your shoulders to come up with a whole episode."

Isaac nodded and took a deep breath. Not the anonymity he'd hoped for. Could he do this?

"I recognize you're not familiar with this type of thing. But I have no doubt you'll catch on quick."

"Thank you."

"You'll find—" He stopped as the heavy door to his office swung wide open and his secretary burst into the room.

"I'm sorry, Mr. Montague, but there's a problem that needs your attention."

"We're being sued," Brooke said as she entered, followed by the bald man who had dragged Isaac onto the set.

"The woman is a lunatic," Gallagher said then turned and stared at Isaac. "What are you doing here?" He didn't wait for a response. "You have to talk some sense into your fiancée. She's nuttier than a pecan praline out there screaming into the intercom."

Isaac looked to Brooke, whose eyes were wide and seemed to be sending him a message. Did she want his help?

"Has anyone called security?" Montague stood and opened a cabinet. Inside were six small black-and-white monitors. "Is that your fiancée, Isaac?"

"Isaac?" Brooke and Gallagher said together.

How he wished the floor would open up and swallow him. There was no way out of this mess. He had to confess. The opportunity before him would be lost, but he'd be relieved the truth was finally out. He shifted uncomfortably in his chair.

"Is this another of Reid's stunts?" Brooke stepped forward and planted her hands on her hips.

"Brooke, what are you talking about?" Montague barked.

"This man was on the show last week. His name is Anthony," she said as her head whipped back and forth like a tennis ball in a heated match. "That woman out there is Debbie, his former bride-to-be."

"They didn't win and had a fight," Gallagher added.

Isaac raised his hands in defense. "I can explain everything."

The scowl on Brooke's face subsided. "Reid put you up to it, didn't he?"

"Miss Wells," Montague shouted as he paced beside his desk. "Get Reid Jackson down here, now!"

Isaac shook his head. "That's not necessary, sir." He stared at his black leather shoes and prayed for strength. "You'd been delayed, and I was waiting for you. Gallagher found me and assumed I was this Anthony guy."

Brooke gasped while Montague sank into his chair.

"Why didn't you say something?" the floor manager asked.

"I tried, but I wasn't sure what was happening at first and then—"

"Don't blame Isaac for your troubles, Gallagher. You and Brooke are responsible for the final screening of the contestants. I'll deal with you two later. Bring that woman to me."

Guilt and remorse crept into his soul. "It's not their fault, sir. I didn't see any harm in going along with Debbie. She really wanted to win, and I must confess, I really wanted to play with Miss Hart." Isaac choked on his last words. "I didn't mean that the way it came out."

Montague smiled. "I understand. She's the reason we have so many male viewers."

Isaac's gaze met Brooke's, but her eyes were like stone.

Cold. He didn't have to be a genius to know that his actions may have ruined her career. Admitting his attraction only made matters worse.

What was it with him and women? Why did knowing him have to be so costly?

Chapter 5

Brooke threw a DVC tape onto the top of the box then dropped into her chair. She looked around. A part of her would miss this place. But secretly she was glad to be going home. Plus, Sadie would be delighted to have her big sister back. She slipped her hand into her pocket and touched the coin.

A sinking feeling overcame her. Without this job, what would happen to Sadie? Brooke couldn't go back to her old job as a retail clerk. Especially since she had become addicted to the chain's crisps. Every single one she ate had remained firmly deposited on her hips.

She looked down. It had taken a long time to lose those stones; she didn't want to gain the weight back. That was the good thing about being in America. Nothing tasted like home.

"Brooke, what are you doing?" her assistant asked as she approached.

"I'm being sacked."

"Fired? What for?"

"Montague's dealing with an issue, and when he's done, he'll be dealing with me."

Jolene seated herself on the edge of Brooke's bare desk. "Never. He's not that stupid."

Brooke envied her assistant's optimism. "He would be stupid to keep me after today."

"It's all over the studio that some guy wanted to be near you so he faked his way in here. Then he turns into a hero and defends your honor." Jolene sighed.

"Oh, this is terrible. What a bunch of rubbish."

"I hardly think so. Maybe he'll ask you out now that he's saved your job."

"Saved my job? He cost me my livelihood." Brooke clenched her jaw and tossed a notepad into the box. "He could have told us the truth. He lied. Now *I'll* have to pay the price." Why was she so angry? She was glad to be leaving.

"Well, you *are* a little overpowering, Brooke. Maybe you intimidated him."

"So why would I want to have dinner with a pansy?"

Jolene laughed and swung her legs. "Don't you think it takes a lot to stand up to menacing Montague? I'd say so. Besides, I saw him. Remember? I think he's dreamy with a great sense of humor. Number one feature in my book."

"He *was* rather funny on the show." Brooke shook her head. "But I should think it isn't worth what his actions have cost me."

"We'll see about that." Jolene winked and jumped down from Brooke's desk. "Here comes Mr. Menace, I mean Montague," she said under her breath.

"Isaac. You still work for this paper, don't you? Your messages are piling up; so is your fan mail. When are you going to drop by? For all we know, someone else could be writing your strip."

Isaac hit the SKIP button on the answering machine and moved to the next message. He could only take so much of Ernie.

"Wow. What sort of secret life are you living, pal? Brooke Hart has called twice for you. Va-voom! She's got a great—"

He skipped the rest of that message, too. As soon as he heard his editor's voice again, he stopped the machine. Why was Brooke calling him? Probably to scream at him. His mind wandered as he thought about the day she discovered his true identity in Mr. Montague's office.

There had been fire in her eyes when she looked back at him right before she left the room. Yet somehow that spark only made her more beautiful.

Isaac jumped at the double ring of his phone and without thinking reached to answer it. He hated unexpected noises.

"Hello." His voice sounded raspy.

"Mr. Brooks?"

He switched the handset to his other ear. "Yes."

"Mr. Montague would like to speak with you. Please hold."

Isaac could not stand still while he waited. He moved to his drafting table and began to doodle on the crisp white paper.

"Brooks?"

"Yes."

"I'd like to proceed with the series if you're agreeable."

Agreeable? He'd be a fool not to jump at this opportunity. So why the hesitation? Fear. Isaac gulped. "Yes, sir, I am," he said, hoping he wasn't making a huge mistake.

"We have a meeting here, tomorrow at ten o'clock, for you to meet the writers. I'll expect you."

"Yes, sir."

The line went dead.

In a daze, Isaac hung up the receiver.

Once the initial shock wore off, he realized this was good news. Good because it was the next natural step in his career? Or good because he might see Brooke?

If the latter, why didn't he return her calls?

"I have a secret," Jolene said as she strolled past Brooke's desk.

"It won't stay a secret if you keep that up."

"Maybe I *want* to tell someone."

Brooke laughed. "So why don't you just tell me?"

"A certain cartoonist will be here this morning."

"So?"

"Oh, c'mon, Brooke, I know you've left messages for him. Has he called you?"

Brooke's heart sank. Did everyone know? "I only wanted to thank him."

"Thank him? I thought you hated him." Jolene raised her eyebrows and seemed to be searching Brooke's face.

She looked away, uncomfortable with her assistant's scrutiny. "I do, but I'm not a boor."

Jolene stepped to the large window and glanced out. "Here comes the limo."

Brooke's heartbeat thundered in her ears. Though it had been a shock to learn Isaac was not Anthony and not engaged to Debbie, it had also been a relief. She'd fought her initial attraction to him—was still fighting it—but at least now it wasn't wrong.

She got up from her chair, sidestepped the boxes she hadn't unpacked from yesterday, and moved to Jolene's side.

Isaac exited the limo, straightened his tie, and raked a hand through his hair.

"Ooh, I can see why you like him. Look at that straight back. He looks like a football player with those shoulders. Nice. Very nice."

Brooke swatted Jolene. "Quit joshing. I don't fancy him any more than Gallagher."

"Did I hear my name?"

She blushed.

"Brooke's watching the *view*," Jolene replied.

Gallagher stepped between the two of them and glanced out the glass. "Not my kind of scenery," he said with a chuckle.

"I should think not." Brooke turned and headed back to her desk. "Did you want something?" she called over her shoulder.

"Yeah. Did you get that e-mail from Reid?"

"Haven't checked my mailbox this morning."

"She's been busy unpacking," Jolene said.

"What's all this about?" he asked as he motioned to the boxes beside her desk.

"She thought she was sacked."

Gallagher nodded. "I was sweating for a bit there, too."

"I can't believe he didn't eat you two alive and spit you out. Or at least dock your paychecks for having to redo that shoot."

"Don't give Montague any ideas, Jolene," Gallagher said as he started to leave. "Check your e-mail, Brooke."

She nodded.

"Guess I should get some work done, too," Jolene said then headed for the editing room.

"I do believe that's what you're paid for."

"If you didn't have me, who would make you look so good?"

"Right." She waved her assistant away and sat down at her desk. Her heart skipped a beat when she opened her e-mail program and saw a message. The subject line said *Forgive me?* and Isaac Brooks had sent it. She glanced around to make sure no one was nearby then clicked to open his letter.

Isaac logged off his computer and walked over to the leather sofa, dropping down heavily onto the cold cushion. The day had drained him completely. His head still spun from all the things he'd learned that morning: voice tracks, animatics, cels—something about transparent acetate and scenes, too. Everything blurred into one. Everything except the big shock: He was the director. He would be required to deal with staff writers and storyboard artists, as well. Isaac worried over this more than anything else.

He realized now that creating this series would be a big

production, and he knew better than to go into something so blindly, yet he had. He'd been distracted, obviously.

What troubled him right now, though, was that Brooke had not replied to his e-mail. Had she forgiven him?

He leaned back on the comfortable sofa and massaged his temples. There was so much to absorb, he didn't have time to think about Brooke. Yet that was all he wanted to do. Up close, she appeared very different than the acid-tongued hostess viewers saw each week.

He forced his thoughts back to the task at hand. It wasn't enough that he had a deadline for the paper, now he'd have to come up with ideas for the weekly series. There'd be no time for him to socialize. No time to think of Brooke.

His stomach rumbled, and he decided he needed to find food. After searching the cupboards and fridge, he remembered he hadn't bought groceries for several days. He glanced at his watch.

Should he slip out to the corner store or have a pizza delivered? The latter seemed the best option for him, and after calling in his order, he went back to the computer. He'd better visit his online grocer to have some food delivered tomorrow.

An airplane zoomed across the screen telling him he had mail and asking if he wanted to read it now. Isaac froze. Had Brooke responded? Probably not. More than likely the message was annoying spam.

He checked anyway.

Isaac's hands trembled as his clicked on a letter with the words *Forgive me?* in the subject line. Brooke had replied, and fear kept him from reading her response.

He jumped up and went back into the kitchen. He spotted the Bible verse on the fridge and read it. A few minutes later, he found himself back at his desk, staring at the screen.

Finally, he opened Brooke's e-mail.

Dear Isaac/Anthony,

Thank you for your e-mail. It was a pleasant surprise. I appreciated your apology, but it wasn't necessary. You'll probably laugh when I say this, but I was beginning to fear you were stalking me. What a relief to learn otherwise.

I've just heard the news about your new animated show. Congratulations. I should think you'll love working here at the studio. And don't worry, you won't be mistaken for someone else ever again. Though it's a shame we can't use the shoot. You did very well.

Fondest regards,
Brooke

Isaac read and reread Brooke's e-mail. Did *fondest regards* mean something more than *sincerely*? Or was that the way people from England signed their letters?

He sucked in his breath. Who was he trying to kid? He could never follow his heart. He couldn't even leave his home without some form of physical malady. How could he possibly start a relationship with someone?

Isaac clicked on a button and deleted Brooke's e-mail.

Chapter 6

Isaac entered the Red Rock Conservatory and glanced around. Thankfully, the place looked practically empty. He wandered along the cobblestone floor, always conscious of his surroundings and keeping a safe distance from people. He passed the gift shop then entered the café.

After carefully choosing a table, he sat with his back to the wall and a clear view of the entrance. His breathing sounded laborious to his ears as he fidgeted with a packet of sugar.

He glanced at his watch and wondered if she would come. It had been over two months since he'd returned Brooke's e-mail to his inbox and eventually responded. Since then, she'd written many warm and witty messages, which he'd saved and savored. Until she suggested they get together.

He didn't feel capable of handling her request, but his heart ached to spend time with her. His emotions battled back and forth, while his memories of Melody haunted him.

Lord, I feel like the wicked mentioned in Job. Terrors startle me on every side and dog my every step. . . . I know that is the place of someone who does not know God. But I know You.

"Been waiting long?" Brooke asked as she neared him.

He looked up and stared. The overhead spotlights caused her dark hair to glisten and her eyes to sparkle. Her complexion appeared soft, almost touchable. "Not at all." He stood and pulled out a chair for her.

Neither spoke for a few awkward moments.

"Would you like a coffee?"

"Actually, I'd love a cup of tea." She smiled. "Can you make sure the bag is in the pot first, please?"

Isaac looked around then cautiously walked to the service counter. He grabbed a clay-colored tray and slid it along, getting their drinks. The cashier handed him the change and a receipt, which he dumped on the tray then hurried back toward the table. Brooke was in the midst of a conversation with another patron when he seated himself.

"I'm glad you like the show." She autographed a napkin and handed it to the elderly man, who thanked her and left.

"I guess you get that all the time," Isaac said with a shiver. He placed an empty mug and a pot of hot water with the tea bag in front of Brooke.

"More so since we've started doing the live show." She picked up a little creamer, opened it, then poured the contents into her empty cup.

"Is that why I never see you at the studio?"

Brooke laughed. "You'll be seeing even less of me soon. Unless Mr. Montague can get my visa extended."

Isaac's heart seemed to seize up. She was leaving? He looked away.

"Isaac? Is everything okay?"

"I'm just surprised," he said. "When does it expire?"

"Next month."

Was it his imagination, or did she seem truly unhappy about leaving? "Is there a problem with keeping you here longer?"

"I haven't a clue. I've been so busy, and Mr. Montague is always out of the country." A soft, breathy laugh escaped her full, peach-colored lips.

Isaac watched Brooke dip the tea bag twice, close the lid on the pot, then pour the liquid into her cup. He smiled at the way she meticulously prepared her drink. "No doubt the entire studio would miss you."

"That's ever so sweet, Isaac."

He lowered his head. She had a nice way of saying things that made him feel self-conscious.

Brooke sipped her drink slowly and seemed to be watching him over the rim of her mug.

Isaac glanced behind him. When he looked back, she had picked up a quarter from the cafeteria tray.

"My father and I used to do this and then see if we could choreograph a coin ballet." She released the quarter, and it remained standing up on its side. Next, she picked up a nickel and made it stand, too.

Isaac watched in fascination then grabbed a dime and after a few attempts managed to have it upright beside the others. "Now what?"

"Now we make them dance," she said. Brooke grabbed a penny from the tray, placed it on the table, and with a flick of her index finger, sent it spinning. The copper piece connected with the dime, which spiraled into the nickel. Within a few seconds, all of the coins were dancing on the tabletop, then one by one they fell.

"That's impressive."

Brooke gathered up the money and handed it back to Isaac. "It's just a silly habit." She blushed a healthy pink.

"You should know that here in the U.S., coins are for table hockey or buying things. We don't consider them part of the arts."

Brooke's eyes shimmered with merriment, and Isaac liked what he saw.

"So shall we walk round the conservatory when we're finished?" she asked. "I'd love to see the desert pavilion."

Isaac's pulse increased. Couldn't they stay buried in this quiet corner? Did he have to expose himself to the unknown?

"You look very pale." Brooke's tone sounded solicitous as she reached out and touched the back of Isaac's hand.

He swallowed hard then laughed. "It's the lighting. It makes me look washed-out like on the set. Where's that makeup lady?" He pretended to be looking for her.

"I should think I must look poorly then, too."

"Far from it," Isaac said before he could stop himself.

"Thanks."

Isaac took a final sip of his coffee, put the cup down, and gazed up into her eyes. Something about her tugged at his heart, and he felt as if he'd known her forever. It was a nice feeling.

Their conversation flowed as they jumped from one subject to another. Isaac enjoyed her quick wit and gentleness—a very different persona than the one in the studio.

Brooke slipped her cup back onto the saucer then wiped

her lips with her napkin. "This was such a brilliant idea, Isaac." She started to stand, and he moved to assist her.

They returned to the entrance and purchased their tickets for the desert pavilion. Thankfully, only a few people milled about.

As they strolled slowly, they talked, but Isaac couldn't relax. His anxiety could not be ignored, no matter how inconspicuous his symptoms were.

Brooke ran her fingertips along the rough walls as if reading the pattern like it was Braille. "So how does one become a cartoonist?"

"Hmm, tough question." He turned his head and smiled at Brooke. "I was always a prankster, but I couldn't make a career out of it. For some reason, no one wanted to hire me to play tricks on their friends."

"Should I be worried, then? Or have you outgrown your penchant for practical jokes?"

"I still have a few things up my sleeve."

Brooke's laughter filled the air. "I've read some of your cartoons. They're funny. How did you come up with the idea?"

"The characters are loosely based on three of my childhood friends. When we were about eight, we formed the Bachelor Club since none of us was ever going to marry."

"And how do you feel about that now?"

"I'm still a card-carrying member," he said with a chuckle.

Brooke stopped to admire the bright blossom of a cactus. "And the others?" she asked as she turned and looked at him.

"Will and Adam are defectors."

They started to walk again.

"Who do you think will be the next turncoat?" she asked with a hint of amusement in her voice.

"Definitely Joseph. I'm holding out for the money."

"Money?" Brooke stared wide-eyed at him.

"It's not much. We started putting our allowance into the club. When we were old enough to get jobs, we still contributed for a little while. If we marry before we're thirty, we get nothing."

"Except a lifetime of love and happiness." She smiled as she said the words softly.

He stopped. She'd spoken in such a dreamy fashion, it made him want to reach for her, take her hand, and feel her lips against his. The desire was powerful. He trembled and took a step closer. She seemed to lean toward him.

His heart rate increased. As if in slow motion, Isaac moved to touch her cheek.

Brooke gazed into his compassionate eyes, the color of dark cocoa, and the world seemed to stop spinning. Her stomach was aflutter as Isaac inclined his face toward her.

Hang on. He's going to kiss me.

What should she do? Wasn't he rushing things? This wasn't even a date. She didn't even know Isaac. Maybe she should pull away or turn her head or start talking.

She did none of those things.

Everything seemed so perfect, so right to be with Isaac. His lengthy e-mails had been interesting, filled with tender thoughts and funny anecdotes. She knew more about him already than if they'd been dating for a year.

If she were honest with herself, it seemed perfectly appropriate to be awaiting Isaac's display of affection.

His nearness drowned out the world around her as she held her breath. He cupped her face in his hands and tilted her head upward. She closed her eyes.

I hope he can't hear how rapidly my heart is thudding in my chest.

His lips brushed her cheek with the gentleness of a feather.
Bang!

The loud noise startled Brooke. Her eyes flew open, and she caught a glimpse of Isaac's features. His eyes seemed wide with terror. Sweat beaded on his brow. His teeth were clenched. His face flushed.

Isaac's strong arms encircled her in a protective motion, shielding her from danger. His weight flung both of them to the floor. She cried out in pain as she landed on the soft dirt. The air in her lungs swooshed out.

Her throat tightened as fear gripped her. What was happening?

Isaac's breathing sounded as if he'd just run a marathon, and he said something she didn't understand. His stiff frame crushed her. She couldn't inhale the air she desperately needed.

He seemed to be trembling as she pushed up on his chest and tried to speak. "Isaac. It's okay."

He looked over his shoulder then down at her as if he were seeing everything for the first time. In an instant he stood then reached for her hand.

"Brooke, I'm so sorry." His voice cracked as he pulled her to her feet. "Are you all right?"

"I will be after a nice long soak in the tub." She rubbed the back of her head.

Isaac raked his hand through his hair as he looked around. "What a mess."

She reached for his hand. "Don't feel too bad. It's every girl's dream to get tackled by a cute guy."

He looked away.

"Did I say something wrong?"

"It's not you, Brooke. It's me."

A sudden disappointment rushed through her. She'd heard those words before and knew exactly what they meant.

Isaac cleared his throat. "There's something you need to know."

She shook her head and pulled at some of the debris entangled in her hair. This wasn't a brush-off, was it? "I think I already know. You're a secret agent, right?"

Isaac chuckled, causing his tense jaw to slacken. "I—I have this prob—"

"Excuse me, but what's going on here?" a woman in a red blazer asked as she approached them. "Look at this damage!" She whipped a walkie-talkie off her waistband like it was a weapon and called for assistance.

Brooke stepped in front of Isaac and hoped the woman would listen to her. "We're terribly sorry, but this gentleman just saved me from harm."

"I don't—"

Leaning forward, Brooke read the staff member's name

tag. "Candice, I should think I need to speak to the manager so I can complain. I could have been seriously injured."

Candice opened her mouth then closed it.

"It's my fault. I overreacted. I'll pay for the plants that were ruined."

"You'll do no such thing," Brooke said as she massaged her lower back and grimaced. "We'll sue. I'm sure I've been hurt." She took Isaac's hand and dragged him as she started to walk away. "My lawyer will be in touch."

Brooke glanced back as they made their escape. Candice remained rooted in place, her mouth still gaping.

Chapter 7

Before they left the conservatory, Isaac stopped at the cashier's window and explained what had happened in the desert pavilion. He gave the girl his business card and requested someone contact him so he could pay for the damage he'd inadvertently caused. He apologized then exited with Brooke.

"So what shall we do next?"

Isaac's throat constricted. He needed to explain all of the feelings and emotions he had just gone through, but she didn't seem interested. In fact, he was surprised that she seemed so apathetic about what had transpired. Had he overestimated Brooke's compassion? Had he read too much into her e-mails?

He was a fool. Why had he even agreed to meet her?

"Isaac." Brooke touched his wrist. "If I ever get set upon in a dangerous situation, you're the one I want with me."

Suddenly his annoyance faded. Was it the way she said things with her accent? Or was it the way she looked at him and smiled? Did it matter?

"Nothing you could say would make me think less of you

or feel differently," she added.

He felt as if she'd thumped him in the gut. In a good way, like he'd scored the winning goal and his buddies were walloping him on the back. "I suppose you're wondering what that scene back there was all about."

"Hang on. You have some rubbish on your trousers." Brooke reached out and brushed his pant leg then quickly withdrew her hand as if his clothing were on fire.

Isaac couldn't help laughing when he saw her face flush with embarrassment. "My car is over there. It's a nice night for a drive. I'll even put the top up if you're worried about your hair."

"That's your car?" She looked at the vehicle then turned to him, eyes wide with disbelief; she then stared back at the convertible.

Isaac disarmed the alarm as they neared his silver BMW Z4 roadster. He reached out and opened the passenger door for Brooke. She slid into her seat gracefully and looked around at the interior.

His smile mirrored hers. He closed the door and leaned on the fender. "With the moon as our guide, where would you like to go?"

"There," she said as she pointed a slender finger to a point high above them.

He laughed as he rounded the car and got in the driver's side. The engine roared to life with the turn of his key. Soft classical music emanated from the CD player, the sounds drifting through the quiet night air.

Within minutes they had left the conservatory and were

headed up into the mountains. The road had more curves than a row of hourglasses.

"Oh, Isaac, it's so beautiful." Brooke sighed and leaned back in her seat, watching the clear sky above her.

"Are you warm enough? I could turn the heater on." He glanced over at her and marveled at how natural it seemed to have her by his side.

She nodded then inhaled deeply. "What is that smell?"

"Aside from my inviting aftershave? That would be ponderosa pine."

"You've such a lovely country."

Isaac laughed. "Yes, well, it's not just mine. But I agree it's a nice place. I'll never understand why my parents moved to California."

"Can we stop there and get out?" Brooke asked.

She had pointed to a popular outlook, which, to Isaac's relief, seemed to be deserted. He pulled over and parked. Glancing at Brooke, he watched as she stared up at the clear, star-filled sky.

"Tell me about your mum and dad," she said.

"My mom is my number one fan. She laughs at all my jokes and pranks, even when she probably shouldn't, and loves every cartoon I sketch. Even the awful ones."

Brooke turned and gazed at him. "She sounds nice."

"She still has some of my stuff from my childhood."

"And your dad?"

"If I didn't know better, I'd think he was disappointed in me."

"I should think he's very proud of you, Isaac. Look at how well your series is coming together. Montague can't wait for it to air."

Isaac nodded, grateful that she recognized his hard work. "They've both been supportive and moved to be with me while I did my internship at W.D."

"W.D.?"

"Walt Disney." He turned in his seat and leaned his back against the door so he could see Brooke better. "They stayed, and I came home."

"That must have been difficult."

Isaac nodded while struggling with his thoughts. Should he tell her what really happened? Why spoil such a nice night? Though he already cared for her, it was too soon to dredge up his painful past.

"Isn't the moon absolutely stunning?" Brooke gazed up at the bright orb.

Isaac willed his arms to stay put, resisting the desire to reach for Brooke. He could easily imagine how comfortable he would feel with her tucked neatly beside him, his chin resting on her head and his hand gently caressing her hair. He needed a distraction. "What about your family? I know you grew up outside of London, but I don't know much about your parents."

"It's rather long and complicated. My younger sister, Sadie, started having problems—they diagnosed her with rapid-cycling bipolar disorder—which my mom couldn't handle. I think she felt responsible or guilty for Sadie's condition. She left a few months later."

Isaac rubbed the back of Brooke's hand. "I'm so sorry."

"My dad's worked hard to help her. I do what I can, as well. No one else in the family understands Sadie and her problems. They don't have much to do with us since they're afraid."

"I could see it being that way if we were still in the fifties, but these days we know so much more. People with mental health issues are not locked up anymore."

"Maybe not in a physical building," Brooke said, her voice quivering.

"Are you cold?" Isaac asked as he started the engine. "The seat has a heater, too. You'll be warm in a few minutes."

Brooke looked out over the valley while Isaac waited for her to continue. He sensed a struggle within her. Was there more to her family she wanted to share but fear kept her from opening up to him?

"We should head back, Isaac. I have an early morning taping."

He drove out and headed down the winding mountain-side. More than ever, he wanted to reach for Brooke's hand, but his own fears held him back. Where could their relationship possibly go? Not only would she be leaving the country soon, but he could barely leave his home. There were only so many places they could go that were quiet and out of the way. These days, it didn't matter where he went, people were there. Lots of people. And where there were people, there was anxiety. Lots of anxiety.

No, it would be best if he kept their relationship to one of friendship, thus ensuring neither of them would get hurt.

By the time they pulled into the parking lot at the conservatory, Isaac had cemented his resolve. He knew his course of action, and he would remain firm.

He walked Brooke to her car, and after she was seated, he leaned in through the open window to say good night. Instead, his lips found hers. The scary world around him vanished as he cradled her face in the palms of his hands. He searched her dark eyes while his heart swelled with feelings he hadn't experienced in a long time.

So much for my resolve.

He cared for Brooke more than he wanted to admit, but there were too many obstacles they would not be able to overcome. He wasn't being fair to her, and he needed to guard her heart as well as his own.

Isaac pulled away from her tender gaze, brushed his knuckles softly down her cheek, and whispered good night.

Once safely inside his apartment with the drapes drawn, Isaac tried to relax. He'd done well, being out with Brooke—until he'd stopped at the corner grocery store. Then anxiety hit him full force, and he couldn't leave fast enough. The store clerk probably thought he'd stolen something.

After sitting in the dark for close to half an hour reciting scripture to calm himself, Isaac decided to work at his computer. A few minutes later, while working on a drawing, an airplane icon zoomed across the screen announcing the arrival of e-mail.

He reread the beginning of the message several times.

Isaac,

I had such fun this evening, especially while we watched the city from the hill.

Until today, I thought you were a homebody—do you

use that word here in America? But tonight, after your overreaction in the conservatory, I began to wonder if it were something more. It felt rude not to ask what happened or if you were all right, but I didn't want to put you on the spot. I want to know all about you, your thoughts and feelings, but only when you're ready to share them. Not because you feel you have to explain something. Does that make sense?

A little pang of guilt hit him square in the chest. How could he have thought so poorly of Brooke when she had ignored the incident? The more he contemplated their evening, the more his lips turned upward into a silly grin.

Isaac leaned back in his chair and praised God for giving him the courage to meet Brooke in a public place. He prayed it would not be a one-time event.

"I can't believe you did this," Brooke said with a shake of her head.

Isaac liked the way her hair swished from side to side. "I don't like to be rushed."

"Look at all the little lights twinkling." She spun around and gazed into his eyes.

"You can go first," he said, ignoring the desire to kiss her. "It's a par three, but I'll bet you can do it in two putts."

Brooke giggled. "You'd be a poor man if you did."

He watched her place the bright orange ball on the tee and

position herself for the shot. Since it was midweek, it hadn't cost too much to rent the entire miniature golf course for two hours. Despite being sheltered, he could sense the anxiety threatening to rear its ugly head.

Silently, Isaac prayed Psalm 7:1. *"O LORD my God, I take refuge in you; save and deliver me from all who pursue me."*

"How many was that? About five?"

Isaac returned his attention to Brooke, who stood near her golf ball, far from the hole. She looked great in her black shorts and neon pink top with matching shoes. Her dark hair was pulled back with a similarly colored ribbon. "I lost count. Want to start again?"

She planted her hands on her hips. "Isaac, that would be cheating."

"Not really. We could say you were taking some practice shots."

"A lot of practice shots," she said with a little laugh in her voice.

"Besides, this place is paid for so we can make up our own rules if we want. Maybe the winner has to have the highest score."

Brooke hit her ball, and it rolled into the small hole with ease. She jumped up and down and screamed with delight. "Isaac, I sunk the silly thing. I'm brilliant!"

Isaac felt a matching silly grin spread across his face, certain he looked like a clown. He marked the scorecard then took his first shot. The blue golf ball zipped down the mini fairway, bounced off the middle obstacle, ricocheted off the edge, and zoomed over the hole.

"Oh, Isaac, that was so close."

He laughed. "I'd forgotten how badly I play this game."

"I hope you rented the place for several hours."

"I have more faith than that," Isaac said as his ball dropped into the hole.

Brooke leaned on her golf club. "Do you go to church?"

Her question caught him off guard. "Not too much these days."

She nodded.

"It's not because I don't want to or that I don't believe in God. Everything is kind of complicated."

"Back home, I went to Alpha a few times. Have you heard of it?"

"Yes, but I've never attended. Some friends did, but I think they went only because of the food."

"We had some lovely dinners, too." Brooke tapped the ball with her club and watched it slip down the green and drop with a *plunk* into the hole.

"Why, I don't believe it. You're a golf shark?"

"Excuse me?"

"I thought you couldn't play very well. Good thing I didn't bet any money." He chucked her chin as she stared at him.

"It was a pretty good shot, wasn't it? But I can assure you, I'm not a shark. Just wait."

He picked up the golf ball and tossed it into the air. Brooke snatched the orange sphere before it could land in Isaac's hand. "Guess it's true what they say," he said with a chuckle.

"Oh, and what would that be?"

"The hand is quicker than the eye."

"Especially when *the eye* isn't watching the ball at all," she said.

Isaac laughed. "Just because several thousand viewers watch you every week, doesn't mean I do, too."

"Oh, of course not," she conceded.

"I think it's my turn," he said, trying to change the subject. "So tell me more about Alpha."

"More about the food or the speaker?"

Isaac putted the ball onto the green. "Whichever you like."

"The preacher packed a lot of information into each night, and he had a great sense of humor. I quite liked him. Though I'm not sure I understood everything he talked about. I had hoped to take it again, but then I moved here."

"Perhaps we should go together."

Brooke stopped and stared at him. "To eat or to hear more about God?"

"Both." Isaac swallowed. How could he possibly go to such an event? What had he been thinking? Well, maybe she would turn him down.

"I'd love to."

Nope, that didn't sound like a no to him.

Chapter 8

And that's when I wake up." Isaac's voice cracked, and he could not continue. He rubbed his hands on his knees and waited.

"When are you going to stop blaming yourself?" Dr. Waters asked.

Willard had been asking him the same question and didn't charge an hourly fee to talk nor have an office that looked like it should be profiled in *Psychology Today*. Isaac stared at the silver-studded burgundy leather chair that seemed to enshroud the therapist.

"If Melody had not died," Dr. Waters said as he twisted the end of his gray mustache, "but lived with a permanent disability, do you think she would accuse you of causing her injury? Or be angry with you for her situation?"

"Of course not." The words escaped before Isaac thought about the doctor's question.

"Then why are you blaming yourself?"

"You don't understand. I should have reacted faster. I should have pushed her aside and taken the bullet. I should have kept her safe." He inhaled, forcing his lungs to expand, ignoring the sensation that the room was closing in on him. He could feel drops of perspiration dotting his brow while his heart rate increased.

This is not helping.

"Isaac, it was a drive-by shooting. No one knew what was happening, not even Melody. There is nothing you could have done. I think you know that."

Do I?

"You said Melody came from some small town in Oregon, right?"

Isaac nodded.

"What if she had gone home for a visit and been killed in a car accident, would you still feel like it was your fault?"

Ignoring the doctor, Isaac stood then walked to the large mahogany bookcase and stared at the leather spines. Was Dr. Waters right? He closed his eyes and willed his racing heart to slow. The room seemed to spin, but he kept his feet firmly planted.

A sharp pain suddenly pierced his temple, followed by a *thud* as something landed on the floor. His lungs refused to inflate. Like a caged, frightened animal, Isaac's muscles tensed as he hunched and looked around the room. He spotted a book on the floor nearby.

Dr. Waters seemed to be studying him. "So why didn't you stop me from throwing that book?"

"I didn't see you. I mean, I didn't know you were. . ." Isaac stopped.

"How could you have known I would do that, any more

than you could have known someone would shoot Melody?"

Isaac clenched his teeth and balled his hands.

"I suspect there is more going on here. How long have you suffered anxiety attacks?"

Moving closer to the corner, Isaac watched the doctor. Would he try something else to startle him? "Since it happened," his voice squeaked out, barely audible to his own ears.

"Never prior?"

Isaac shook his head. His mouth tasted like sawdust.

"Tell me what you were like ten years ago?"

"Someone else," Isaac said.

Dr. Waters raised his eyebrows but said nothing.

"What I mean is, I feel like everything happened to someone else. I used to love the outdoors. My friends and I hung out all the time doing crazy things, and everyone knew about my practical jokes." Isaac paced as he spoke. "I had a ton of ideas and was determined to be an animator for Disney."

"And now?"

"I think you can tell what I'm like now." He took two steps left, turned, and took two steps right.

"Which life would you prefer?" Dr. Waters asked as he scribbled on his pad.

"I know I should answer that I want my old life back, but. . ." Isaac stopped. *Brooke.* His old life would mean he never would have met Brooke. The one person—on earth, that is—who seemed to give him a purpose.

The doctor smiled. "Our time is up. I've written out the name of someone I think you should go see."

"I don't understand. Can't you help me?"

"You have two issues, Isaac. I'll continue to see you to help you through your grief. I think Matt will be able to help you with your posttraumatic stress."

"Posttraumatic stress? Isn't that for war veterans?" Isaac ran a trembling hand through his hair as he walked toward the doctor.

"Yes, but not limited to." Dr. Waters tore the sheet off of his pad.

"Is that why I overreact to noise and I'm afraid to leave my house?" There. He'd finally admitted it. That's what the chest pains and sweaty palms were all about. Twenty-eight years old and terrified of going outside. And if he did leave the safety of his home, he constantly watched his surroundings like some sort of criminal looking over his shoulder to make sure the police weren't descending on him.

Dr. Waters held out the paper. "And the reason you can't sleep and keep reliving the event."

Isaac took the offered sheet of information from the doctor. He glanced at the name and address then read the two words in bold print. "Exposure therapy? What's that?"

"I'll let Matt explain it to you."

"What's wrong with you?"

Brooke grabbed the coin balancing precariously on its rim atop her desk and slipped it into her pocket before Jolene would see it. "I'm tired, I guess." It wasn't a great excuse, but it would have to do. The lengthy evening phone conversations with Isaac were not conducive to early mornings.

"Too many late nights with Isaac?"

Brooke shook her head. "I haven't seen him all week." Which was the truth.

"I hope this isn't too serious. Have you given any thought to what your name would be? Brooke Brooks. That alone would stop me from seeing someone." Jolene laughed.

"Mmm," she muttered, not really paying attention since Brooke wasn't her real name.

"Do you know some people give their children weird names on purpose? I met a guy whose last name was Roberts. His parents named him Robert. Robert Roberts. Kind of dumb, if you ask me."

Brooke chuckled.

"I guess you wouldn't have to go by your married name. You could keep using Brooke Hart."

"I'm quite certain you're reading far too much into my relationship with Isaac. We're just friends."

"I've heard that before." Jolene smirked.

"Besides, I'm returning home soon." The thought of leaving caused an unwanted pang of regret to surge through her. Why now? Why after all this time? She'd been so lonely and homesick for so long. Then Isaac entered her drab life and made her smile again. Made her forget about the sacrifice she'd made for Sadie. She shook her head. Perhaps *sacrifice* was too dramatic a word. She'd do anything for her sister.

"Brooke, you're a million miles away," Jolene said.

"Hmm?"

"You know what? I think you're in love. You've lost weight,

you've lost your ability to concentrate, and you haven't lost your temper once this week. Even when you missed your cue and had to do a retake."

Brooke smiled. "Is that your professional opinion, Dr. Jolene?"

"Yes, I think it is."

"Shall I take two aspirin and call you in the morning?"

Jolene giggled. "No, I'm afraid not. There is no cure for what ails you."

"I hope you don't mind, but I'd like to get a second opinion."

"Be my guest. Shall I call Gallagher over?"

"Don't you dare!" Brooke jumped out of her seat and rushed to Jolene's side, her hand ready to cover her assistant's mouth.

Jolene flashed Brooke a knowing smile.

"You can't tell anyone about Isaac and me."

"I don't have to. Everyone knows he took you to Serenade Springs for a quiet picnic two weeks ago and a romantic dinner at the Hacienda on Friday."

Brooke could feel the heat rising to her cheeks. "What?"

"Shh." Jolene looked around. "I promised not to tell you."

Brooke staggered to a chair. Had the entire studio been chatting about her life, speculating or worse, as to what would happen between her and Isaac? Her stomach churned.

"They didn't mean any harm. They're happy for you."

Brooke nodded slightly.

"Are you okay?"

"No. Everything is so complicated."

Jolene got up, dragged Brooke into an editing room, and

pulled the sliding door closed. She leaned against the desk and pointed to the office chair for Brooke to have a seat.

"I really don't understand the way things are done in America."

"Like what?"

"You're right. I do fancy Isaac. He's funny and charming. But I'm worried there's a darker side to him."

"All artists are like that. It's what makes them so creative."

"I suspect this is something more."

Jolene's eyes opened wide. "Has he hurt you?"

"Never. I don't believe he would ever injure me." She paused. "On purpose, that is."

"But he's hurt you?"

Brooke took in a deep breath and explained to Jolene about the night at the conservatory. As if a dam had broken loose, she poured out her mixed feelings for Isaac. Her struggles because she would be leaving soon, her concerns because they always went to secluded places or alone—like at the miniature golf.

"You think he's leading some sort of double life, don't you?" Jolene asked, her eyes wide with disbelief.

"I have no idea."

"But it's too late. You're in love with him."

Brooke sighed. "I should think it's far too early for that sort of thing, but you may be right."

Jolene patted Brooke's shoulder.

"I'm so daft."

"Huh?" her assistant asked as she stared over Brooke's shoulder.

She turned and saw Isaac. He looked pale and uncomfortable. When he looked up, she waved him over.

"I'll leave you two alone." Jolene pulled open the sliding door.

"Thanks," Brooke whispered as she stood.

Jolene and Isaac exchanged greetings as they passed each other.

Alone in the room together, Isaac leaned down and brushed a little peck on her cheek. She looked past him to ensure no one was watching then slid the door closed.

"You look beautiful," Isaac said.

"I feel like rubbish," she blurted out as she dropped back into her chair. "Isaac, are you married?"

Isaac sucked in a breath. Brooke's question hit him harder than one of Adam's line drives. He searched her face for signs of humor, but her eyes were downcast and her luscious lips were drawn tight.

"Isaac?"

"I guess I owe you an explanation," he said with a heavy sigh.

Brooke stood and turned away from him. Was she crying?

"It's not what you think." He placed his hands on her shoulders.

She pulled away from his touch.

"Brooke, I tried to keep from caring for you, but I couldn't stop my heart." He swallowed hard. It was difficult to admit how he felt. "Who would have thought I'd let feelings outweigh logic?"

She didn't respond.

He rubbed his hand across his forehead. Did she really believe he would be so cruel?

A knock on the glass caught his attention.

Jolene slid the door open. "Brooke, we need you."

Without even looking at him, she said good-bye and left with Jolene.

Isaac's chest crushed his lungs and he struggled for air.

Not another anxiety attack. Please, God, no.

A sharp pain jabbed his neck then shot down his left arm. A throbbing at his temples sounded like drums on a warpath.

For the last two weeks, he'd seriously contemplated turning in his Bachelor Club membership card. How could he have been such an idiot?

Isaac gasped, loosened his tie, and dropped into a chair as the symptoms increased. Hunching over, he tried to calm himself. But the physical pain paled beside the emotional ache that cut so deep.

Would such a hurt ever go away?

Chapter 9

I don't understand. I've been working with Matt for a month now and things aren't any better." Isaac paced the kitchen as he spoke to his older friend, picturing Willard's easy smile and receding hairline.

"Give it time, son."

"I don't have time. Brooke has gone back to England." The urgency in his own voice shocked him. How had it happened that he'd fallen in love only to lose again?

"Have you spoken to her?"

"No one at the studio will give me her phone number or address or anything."

"You know how to use that fancy computer of yours. Can't you find her that way?"

"I tried. I found the studio address in London and sent a letter there explaining everything, but I don't think she got it. Apparently, Brooke Hart isn't her real name. I've left messages at Montague Studios here and in London." Isaac stopped. He wasn't ready to tell anyone about this. Even his friend.

"You've done all you can."

Isaac bowed his head and stared at the floor. "Willard, how can I have a mental illness? I'm a Christian."

"If you had leukemia, would you be asking this question? Or high blood pressure?" Willard paused. "You suffered a traumatic event. You lost someone you deeply cared for. If it had not affected you, I would have been concerned."

Isaac swallowed and clenched his jaw. He continued to pace and listen.

"As long as we are here on earth, we will suffer the things of this world. We will have sickness and death, but we also have a great big God who loves us. Who wants to heal us for His glory. Who wants us to walk by faith, not by our strength."

"When I am weak, He is strong," Isaac said.

"Exactly. Stop beating yourself up and start letting God help."

"How?"

"Let me tell you a story."

Isaac sat down on a kitchen stool and felt his mood lift a little. Willard had a parable for every situation, or at least it seemed that way.

"A few years ago, we had a nasty flood. My friend Barney had managed to scramble to his roof. Not knowing what else to do, he prayed that God would save him."

"A flood that high around here?"

"Don't interrupt, son."

Isaac nodded even though Willard couldn't see him.

"As the deluge continued, old Barney started to panic and begged God to rescue him. A motorboat drew up close, and the driver hollered at him to get in."

Isaac pulled a quarter from his pocket and stood it on end while he listened to his mentor.

"Barn waved the man on and continued praying for God to save him. A short time later, two men in a rowboat came by and suggested he go with them."

Isaac wanted to ask if the guy was insane, but given the current subject and Willard's admonition not to butt in, he remained silent.

"Barn let the guys leave, and he remained on his roof. When the water reached his toes, a small canoe with one passenger came near. 'You'd better get in,' the person called. Once again, he said no. The waters continued to rise and my good buddy drowned."

Isaac jumped off the stool, snatching up the coin from the counter. "I don't get it," he said.

"That's because I'm not done."

Willard's voice remained kind, but Isaac thought he'd detected a slight note of impatience.

"Now when Barney got to heaven, he asked God why He didn't save him. God said, 'I sent a motorboat, a rowboat, and a canoe. What more did you want?' "

"You had me until ole Barn got to heaven," Isaac teased.

"But it works well, doesn't it?"

"I'm not sure."

"The principle is simple. Barney was waiting for God to perform a miracle of supernatural proportion, which He could do, but God chose to use other people to rescue him."

"Oh."

"For now, you need to trust your doctor and this exposure

therapy guy. If God decides to heal you, you'll know it. If not, you'll work through this with God beside you. Either way, you'll get better."

"You think so?"

"You only need one more thing."

"Not another story," Isaac said, knowing Willard wouldn't be offended.

"No, I'm out of anecdotes right now."

Isaac heard the smile in Willard's voice.

"Just like with any other sickness, we need to pray."

He knew Willard had hit the mark. His words gave Isaac hope—hope he hadn't had in a long time. As soon as they finished talking and praying, Isaac was going to call Matt. He had grown tired of pretending his illness didn't exist—or shouldn't exist—and he was prepared to do whatever he could to get well.

Jolene, it's ever so nice to hear your voice!"

"Yours, too. When did you get that accent?"

Brooke giggled. It was the first time she'd laughed in the month since she'd returned to England. "I don't have to work to keep it hidden here at home. Nobody seems to notice it—fancy that." She flipped through some unopened mail from the studio as she chatted with her former assistant.

"That's good, I think."

"So what's new? Is Reid still acting like he owns the place?"

Brooke heard Jolene sigh. "Nothing ever changes around here. Oh, but have you heard the news about Isaac?"

She stiffened. Even the mention of his name caused a quickening in her stomach. How could she have fallen for a married man? How could she have been so daft?

"Brooke, did you hear me?"

"Must be a bad connection. Say again."

"No one knows for sure, but there's talk he's had some sort of mental breakdown. There's even rumors about shock therapy. Well, you know what they say about those creative types."

Brooke blinked back tears. Married and insane. Yet, it wouldn't change anything. Jolene could say Isaac had two heads and twelve toes on each foot, and she knew in her heart she'd still love him. She loved his wittiness, his tender touch. If she closed her eyes, she could see the pain etched on his face and loved how it made her want to comfort him. Forever.

But she couldn't. She could hardly handle Sadie. How could she care for two people with problems greater than she understood?

"For what it's worth, I don't believe any of that garbage."

Brooke sniffled and reached for a tissue. On her desk sat the silver pence she had carried with her in New Mexico. While there, it had been a reminder of Sadie. Now, as it stood upright here in England, it reminded her of Isaac. She could easily envision the gleam in his eyes when they'd made the coins spin at the conservatory. How it tugged at her heart.

"Look, I'd better go, Brooke. You know how Montague watches the budget. We miss you."

"I could hardly wait to return home, and now that I'm here, I'm wishing I was back with all of you."

"That's because you left your heart here," Jolene said softly.

"If it's still back in America, how come it hurts so much?"

"Have you called him?"

"I can't," Brooke whispered.

"He calls asking about you. One day, I'm going to break down and give him your number."

"Please don't." Brooke gritted her teeth. She'd have to tell Jolene the truth. No matter how much it hurt. "Isaac's married."

"What are you talking about?" Jolene sounded completely surprised. "He's not married."

Was Jolene right?

"Is that what this is all about? What's that word you use all the time? Rubbish. That's what it is. Rubbish." Jolene's voice blared from the receiver, causing Brooke to pull the phone away from her ear.

The constant ache she'd been feeling seemed to dissipate.

"So do I give him your number or e-mail address?"

Her heart screamed yes, but her brain wouldn't let her. "I'll let you know. Thanks, Jolene."

Brooke placed the handset into the old-fashioned cradle and dropped into a nearby chair.

Isaac isn't married.

She wanted to do cartwheels or twirl around the room. Instead she reached for a handful of potpourri and tossed it in the air.

"He isn't married!" Tiny acorns and small pieces of dried leaves, in various shades of purple, rained down around her like a shower of blessings.

Brooke leaned back in the chair. In her mind's eye, she could see Isaac's face. She wanted to reach out and run her fingertips along his strong jaw or brush a few strands of his dark hair back from his forehead.

She picked through the stack of mail and stopped when she saw an envelope from America. From Isaac. A longing to be with him filled her whole being. Somehow she had to return to New Mexico.

"You have to help me."

"I have to be honest, Isaac. I don't think you're ready for it." Matt put his coffee cup down then pointed outside. "See all those people out there?"

Isaac nodded.

"Right now you can escape them. On a plane for several hours, there is no place for you to go."

"Can't I take some drugs or something?" Isaac shifted in his seat, flexing his hands open and closed.

"You could, but your doctor would have to prescribe them. You'd need to take them for a week or so to ensure you don't have any adverse reactions."

"I haven't got a week."

Matt stared at him intently. "England will always be there."

"It's not the country I want to see."

"Aah," Matt said with a knowing nod. "What's her name?"

"Brooke Hart."

"The British diva?" His eyes opened wide and his brows arched in surprise.

Isaac laughed. "Be careful what you say from this moment onward."

Matt sat back and seemed to be lost in thought. After a brief pause, he said, "We'll start by going to the airport."

A rush of thunder resonated in Isaac's ears. How would he pull this off? What if he couldn't get to Brooke?

When I am weak, You are strong, Lord.

Chapter 10

I'm sorry, Miss Hart, but we've overbooked. You'll have to take a later flight or go on standby." The officious clerk stared down at her keyboard and never made eye contact.

"I can't take a later flight. I need to be on this one." Brooke fingered the small coin in her trouser pocket.

"We'll offer you a refund and discount your next flight, which would leave in about six hours."

Didn't this woman hear her? Everything had already been planned. If she didn't arrive on time, an unrecoverable disaster would occur. Well, maybe that was a little too dramatic. But still, the arrangements hinged on her arriving on time.

"Shall I rebook you on the next flight?"

Before Brooke could answer the woman, she remembered a phrase from the Alpha course she had been attending. *Pray without ceasing*. It was a strange feeling for her, as if someone had tapped her on the shoulder with a gentle reminder.

"You will need to decide," the clerk said then sighed impatiently.

"I need this flight. So if you don't mind, I'll go standby,"

Brooke said with a smile, knowing she would not stop praying until her feet were on the ground in New Mexico. Though such faith seemed foreign, a feeling of excitement stirred within her.

Maybe God was directing her path after all.

Isaac froze. His feet refused to move, and every sound sent adrenalin coursing through his veins. "It's no use, Matt. I can't do this."

"Take a deep breath and let it out slowly."

Isaac inhaled, waited, and then gradually released the air trapped in his tight lungs.

"I don't think you're ready, either." Matt led them to an empty seating area and motioned for Isaac to sit.

"But we've been here every day for two weeks." Isaac rubbed his moist hands on his jeans and glanced across the concourse toward his gate.

And every day I think I see Brooke disembarking from a plane.

"Like I said before, it takes time. You're pushing yourself too hard."

"Why didn't you tell me that before I bought my ticket?" Isaac jerked then rubbed his shoulder where Matt had smacked him.

"I did. Several times."

"Point taken."

Matt rested his elbows on his knees. "There's still time to back out. You haven't boarded yet."

"It's now or never."

"If you change your mind, it's not a crime." Matt smiled.

Isaac wanted to retreat, but when an earlier flight from Boston had landed, he was so certain Brooke had deplaned that he nearly ran to the woman. That's when he knew he couldn't wait any longer. He had to do this. "Will you stay with me until I board the plane?" Isaac couldn't miss the concern on his therapist's face. He hadn't needed to ask such a question.

Isaac tried to concentrate on his breathing. Over and over he told himself that he was safe. In fact, with all the security measures in place, it was probably safer here at the airport than in his apartment. Still, his mind refused to listen.

Would he have to admit defeat?

"You don't look too good." Matt took a sip of his bottled water.

"Thanks."

"Look. You've come a long way in a short time, but this is not something that will just go away. You can't make the problem disappear because you want it to be gone."

Isaac listened but said nothing.

"If she's as wonderful as you say she is, she'll understand."

Matt spoke the truth. Isaac knew from talking with Dr. Waters that he had a tough road ahead of him. Thankfully, Willard and the guys from the Bachelor Club were praying for him. As well as Amy and Charisma. Plus, he knew God would never leave him.

"Shall we call it a day? You can rebook your flight for another time," Matt said.

With a deep sigh, Isaac replied, "Sure." He stared out the

large glass windows, longing to board the plane. He needed to see Brooke. He needed to tell her everything. In truth, he simply needed her.

Isaac glanced down at his waist as his pager began to beep. Reading the display, he frowned.

"Something wrong?"

"An emergency at the studio." Isaac clenched the small device. "Though I can't understand what would be so important."

"Well, you know those cartoon characters. They're fairly picky about what you can and cannot put in their mouths."

Isaac groaned. "I'm the funny one, remember?"

"Want me to go with you, or will you be okay?"

"I should be fine. The studio is secured and safe."

Matt slapped Isaac on the back. "You did great, ya know? Why not give yourself another week before trying again?"

The two men parted, and Isaac headed for his car. Moments later, he pulled out onto the state highway in his BMW Z4 with the convertible top down. Music from a contemporary Christian artist's CD blared, and a sense of freedom surrounded him. A feeling he hadn't experienced in a long time.

God, I feel like You're giving me back my life. Thank You.

"Isaac!" Gallagher shouted to him as he entered the studio.

"Good to see you again." Isaac reached out and shook the man's tanned hand.

"What brings you here?"

"An urgent page from Montague."

Gallagher smiled. "Let me take you to him."

As they wandered the long hall to the animation studio, Isaac wondered if they had taken a wrong turn. Weren't they headed for the set of *Are You Right for Each Other?*

Isaac stopped. "Shouldn't we be going the other way?"

"Montague's in there," Gallagher said, pointing.

"Oh."

Gallagher stepped back. "You first."

Isaac walked ahead of him into the black room. Instantly lights clicked on, practically blinding him. Someone grabbed his arm and dragged him along. After a few moments, his eyes adjusted.

"Sit here," Jolene said.

Isaac noticed several other people seated on the stage. Everything looked like the first time he'd been mistakenly led to the set. Only this time, he didn't have a partner and neither did the other men. Had Debbie come back? He rubbed his arm in remembrance.

Reid stood in front of the camera. "Are we ready?"

Isaac looked around. His heart hammered in his chest. "Someone want to tell me what's going on?" he asked hesitantly.

"You know how it works," Jolene said as she stood behind the hostess podium.

"Did you take over for Brooke?" Isaac asked.

"Places, everyone. Rolling in ten, nine, eight. . ." Gallagher's voice trailed off as he continued to count down with his fingers.

"With the women secluded offstage, let's begin," Jolene said.

Isaac's anxiety caused him to tremble, and he let his mind wander, as Matt suggested, to a pleasant memory. He recalled the first time he'd met Brooke. He could see her, standing where Jolene now stood, with her dark hair glistening under the bright lights. He could even hear her voice. Her accent warmed his heart.

"Isaac, what habit do you have that your fiancée finds so annoying?" Jolene asked.

He stopped his daydreaming when he heard his name. "Could you repeat the question?"

Jolene did as he asked.

"I can't think of anything to say."

"You must have some fault."

Oh, he had many imperfections. Trouble is, he didn't have a fiancée that would know any of them. "I have no flaws whatsoever," he said. He hoped no one noticed his ears wiggling.

"Is that your final answer?"

"I think that's a different game show," Isaac teased. "Okay, I'd have to say my hermitlike nature is very exasperating."

Jolene flipped some papers then mumbled, "For a hermit, you clean up nice." Without waiting for a response, she moved along to the next question.

It seemed to take forever to get through the next round, and Isaac's anxiety increased. Something didn't seem right about this taping, yet he couldn't put his finger on anything out of the ordinary.

"Last question, gentlemen. If you could rewrite your personal history, who would you be married to?"

With a certain confidence, each of the men answered.

"Donna."

"Kathy."

"Lillian."

Then it was Isaac's turn. Couldn't at least one of the contestants need some time to think?

Jolene sighed. "We always seem to wait for you, Isaac. Are you the quiet, brooding type?"

"That's not what my yearbook said."

"So can we get a response?"

Isaac quietly replied then inconspicuously touched his ears. His answer was probably the most truthful thing he'd said all night. But it didn't hurt to check.

"Cut," Reid said. "Okay, everyone stay where you are. We're on a time crunch. Bring the ladies out, Gallagher."

Isaac watched each of them, waiting to see who would be his partner this time.

The last female in the line came into view. His muscles clenched when he spotted the bright red hair. Debbie? No, but she did seem familiar with her regal walk and gentle smile.

Get a grip, man. Every woman looks like Brooke to me these days, but she's in England. Where I should be.

She nodded when she sat down and Isaac caught a whiff of her perfume. She even smelled like Brooke.

"I'm Veronica," she whispered.

Isaac swung around to get a good look at his alleged fiancée. She smiled.

And he knew.

"In ten, nine, eight," Gallagher started.

Isaac couldn't show his feelings or do anything now that the cameras had begun to roll. His mind tried to assimilate a million questions.

"Veronica, what's Isaac's most annoying habit?"

"His shy, reserved nature."

"Would that include being hermitlike?" Jolene asked. Veronica nodded.

"Judges, will we give them that question?"

Isaac was confused. Jolene wasn't following the format.

Jolene nodded as she listened to the voice coming from her hidden earpiece. "Okay. They'll accept that answer. You earn five points."

Isaac tried numerous times to get a closer look at Veronica without seeming obvious, but all too soon Jolene had another question for them. What happened to the usual chatter that went on between the couples?

"Veronica, whom do you think Isaac reminds you of?"

"That's easy," she said. "Clark Kent."

Jolene laughed. "We'll have to get a ruling on this one, too. Isaac thought he reminded you of Superman."

When they didn't get the point, Isaac leaned away, out of arm's reach, assuming Veronica would slug him the way Debbie had the first time he played this game. Instead, she gave him a demure smile.

"We're down to the last question," Jolene stated. She quickly gave a recap of the scores and positions of each couple. Isaac and Veronica were in first place.

"Veronica, if Isaac could rewrite his personal history, whom do you think he would have married?"

He held his breath.

"Melody." Veronica's soft, almost childlike voice, tickled his ears.

A small twitch began in Isaac's left eye. His whole body stiffened more rigid than an iceberg, and he felt just as cold.

Everything came to a standstill while Isaac contemplated her answer. Melody. He hadn't even thought of her. Hadn't he loved Melody?

Not like I love Brooke.

Isaac felt broken. Life had gone on without him while he merely existed. It wasn't what God had planned or what Isaac had wanted. The time had come to let go of the guilt and move through the grieving process. His love for Brooke had helped him begin to heal.

"I'm sorry, Veronica, but Isaac said it would have been Brooke."

Isaac turned and faced Veronica. A single tear slipped down her brightly painted cheek. "I love you, Brooke."

She reached up and pulled off her wig. "I had to know." Her bottom lip quivered.

She had read his letter. She knew about his past. Yet, here she was, giving her heart to him. Trusting him. He took her hands in his.

Cheers and applause filled the small, darkened studio while balloons fell from overhead.

Isaac ignored everything around him. "Had to know?" he asked.

"If I was second place in your heart."

He kissed her furrowed brow then leaned his head against hers, ignoring everyone around them. "I needed to know, too," he said, his voice choked with love for her. "You'll always have first place in my heart."

"Well, I guess the show's over." Jolene giggled. "But I can honestly say that these two—Isaac and Brooke—are right for each other."

BEV HUSTON

Bev lives in British Columbia—where residents don't tan, they rust—with her husband, two children, sister, and two cats, who give new meaning to the word aloof. Bev began her writing career in 1994 when, out of frustration, she wrote a humorous column about call waiting service, which sold right away. She is a contributing editor for *The Christian Communicator* and spent four years as the inspirational reviewer for *Romantic Times Bookclub*. Please visit her Web site and tell her what you think of her work: www.bevhuston.com.

Joyful Noise

by Janet Spaeth

Dedication

For Maria Williams Kennedy:
Thank you for sharing your gift with our children.
And for Colin Kennedy, who makes our beloved Maria smile.
May your marriage be blessed with the songs of your heart!
We love you!

Make a joyful noise unto the LORD.
PSALM 100:1 KJV

Chapter 1

A men."

Joseph Montoya waited a moment before raising his head and opening his eyes. He always added an addendum to the minister's prayer, a personal postscript of matters that were strictly between him and his Creator. Today, the topic was his new project: himself.

He'd decided it was time to reevaluate his life, to see what needed to be done, and furthermore, how to go about fixing it. This was just the second day of his annual project, so he hadn't gotten too far into his introspection.

Focus. Right now, that was what he needed to do. The new accounting software package that had arrived in yesterday's mail kept pulling his attention from the matter of worship. He'd experiment with it later. With an effort, he pulled his thoughts back to the sanctuary of Blessed Family Church.

A general stirring to his left reminded him that the choir was preparing to sing. If, he thought, that's what it could be called. *Ouch.* There was one of the first prickles of his inward examination, and he quietly took a small spiral-bound notebook and pondered how to record this. *Pot calling the kettle black?* Certainly there was a more spiritual way to phrase it.

But the fact was, he wasn't in the choir because, while God had gifted him in many ways, He'd omitted musical ability entirely.

He glanced at the bulletin and winced at the choir's forthcoming selection.

Joseph enjoyed a rousing chorus of "Amazing Grace" as well as the next fellow, but it certainly helped to have the choir members agree in advance on what key they were singing it in.

That was a bit nasty, he acknowledged, and he certainly wasn't in any position to be judgmental. He shrugged mentally and picked up his pencil and wrote again, this time: *Humility.*

The organist pounded out the first few notes of the hymn, and Joseph settled back, preparing to cringe as Tyrone Melton, the resident tenor, cleared his throat. Tyrone fancied himself to be Tierra Verde's Pavarotti, but Joseph was sure that Pavarotti wouldn't appreciate the comparison.

Snideness. Maybe it wasn't a real word, but that inward twinge told Joseph he needed to watch for it, and he wrote it down anyway.

Something began to happen over in the choir area. He paused, his pencil poised over the little notebook, as he tried to identify what was different. Tyrone was there, his mouth open wide, but—

They were in tune. Or could it be that the other voices were softened by the new sound that had joined them? A soprano, as pure and clear as Blue Creek, the mountain stream that flowed behind Tierra Verde, carried the choir forward.

He sat up. What was this? Or, more importantly, who was this?

For the past twenty years, he'd watched the back of Mrs. Adams's head. Her hairstyle and color had never changed. She was thin and gaunt, her hair puffy and round. Once, long ago, one of the members of the Bachelor Club had called her the Human Cotton Swab, and the name had stuck. It was one of those boyish jokes that had been horrible—and true. She did look like a cotton swab from the back.

In those twenty years, Mrs. Adams had never missed a service. Sunday after Sunday, Joseph had watched the back of her head as the choir warbled its way through the musical selections.

Today, however, the hair was not white and fluffed. Instead he saw dark hair, with only a hint of curl. Had Mrs. Adams undergone some sort of fashion overhaul? He felt the world tremble a bit at the thought.

The bulletin, which he'd placed next to him, caught a stray breeze and began to drift off the pew. As he caught it, he noticed for the first time the words: VISITING CHOIR DIRECTOR.

Aah. That explained Mrs. Adams's hairstyle change—and her voice. He read eagerly:

> *Blessed Family is fortunate to have with us today*
> *Rosa Cruz, who is filling in as choir director while*
> *Angela Adams goes to Arizona to visit her new grand-*
> *child, Andy Adams. This will be quite an adventure for*
> *Mrs. Adams, as it will be her first trip on an airplane.*

Give the woman an A for awesome, Joseph thought. What was

really awesome, though—actually, he decided it was almost amazing—was that Rosa Cruz and her voice had come to Tierra Verde.

"Continuing our announcements. . ." The minister was speaking, and Joseph turned toward his voice. "We'd like to welcome Rosa Cruz, who's filling in for Mrs. Adams today. Rosa, would you please stand?"

She stood, and as she turned to face the congregation, Joseph's breath caught in his throat. If ever he had dreamed of an ideal woman, this would be her. Long black hair fell like a glistening cascade over her shoulders. Eyes as dark and deep as the canyon at night sparkled with life. Her smile was as friendly as a warm handshake between old friends.

As Rosa acknowledged the congregation, the minister added, "She has quite an incredible voice, as I'm sure you noticed. She recently graduated from the University of New Mexico with a degree in vocal education, and she's starting her own music studio right here in Tierra Verde. If you're interested in voice lessons, see her after the benediction. She's setting up shop in the old Ortiz building. . . ."

Joseph's attention drifted. Music lessons? That meant she was going to stay.

Maybe, just maybe, it was time to add another line in his self-study notebook: *Meet someone. Fall in love. Get married. Have babies. Live happily ever after.*

Rosa smiled at the congregation, but her heart was unsure.

Doubts, one after the other, assailed her. What had she done? Why had she come to Tierra Verde? She could have stayed in Albuquerque and worked for the music store where she had been employed all through school. Or she could have pursued the teaching leads. Some school district somewhere was surely looking for a music teacher.

No, she told herself firmly, she hadn't made a mistake.

This *was* the right thing to do.

Still. . . Her mind laid out the problem in a grid. Most church choirs were made of people who had the best voices in the congregation—or who thought they did. From the looks of this choir, talent wasn't flowing quite as profusely as she'd hoped. If she didn't get some students from the church, she might as well pack up her bags and look into a career teaching third-graders to make pear-shaped tones and to sing from their upper voices, not their lower voices.

Oh, she'd paid attention in the music education classes. She knew how effective marching out rhythms could be or how to make warming up a whole-body experience. The one thing they hadn't taught her in school was how to make a living with her gift.

At last the spotlight was off her, and she sank to her seat gratefully. *God, I know You have something in mind for me. Is this it? Could You—please excuse me if this is a bit cheeky—could You possibly let me know if this is it? I have these doubts, You see. . . .*

Through the robed shoulders of the choir, she saw in the congregation a man who was looking directly at her. His hairline was receding just a bit over a brow that was lined with early worry. But the eyes that watched her were kind and welcoming and friendly, and she knew that she would stay.

The young woman was surrounded by members of the congregation; some were studying a roster that was beside her on a small table. Joseph stood to one side, like the proverbial boy outside the candy shop window.

"Takes some nerve, if you ask me."

Of course, he hadn't asked Tyrone Melton anything, nor was he likely to. The man had an absolutely poisonous sense of himself.

"Last thing we need is another music teacher here in Tierra Verde."

Another music teacher? Since when had they had even one?

Tyrone continued his one-sided conversation. "Angela Adams is a splendid music educator." He sniffed. "She certainly doesn't need this kind of competition from anyone."

He knew he was going to regret it, but Joseph found himself asking the question anyway. "Mrs. Adams teaches music?"

Tyrone's answer said it all. "She teaches me."

If Joseph hadn't been quite so smitten, and if he hadn't been quite so angry with Tyrone, and if he'd had just a bit more sleep the night before, he might not have done it.

He strode over to the roster and signed his name with a flourish.

He, Joseph Montoya, the man whom God had slighted with completely imperfect pitch, he of the leaden pipes, had signed up for voice lessons.

Impulsive action—wow, there was a new one. He'd never been accused, ever, of being impulsive. *Quick anger. General crabbiness.*

The list was getting entirely too long. With a hasty pledge to God to finish the self-improvement project later, he left the church, trying not to think about what he had just done.

But he couldn't stop the image of Rosa Cruz from entering his mind, again and again and again.

Rosa curled up in front of her fireplace and wrapped her hands around the earthenware mug. The September evening had turned cold, and the fire made her small house cozy and—more importantly—warm. The old building leaked around the corners, so tendrils of cold crept in regularly. Here in the mountains, the nights were cold early.

An unexpected cold front had come through, and almost everyone in Tierra Verde, she'd heard, had turned their furnaces on. She had resisted, though, preferring to use her fireplace and blankets to keep warm. She wasn't quite ready for winter, not when September skies were still golden with bits of summer.

Yet, cold it had been, and she could feel the edge of it—the promise that summer was over, autumn was nearing, and soon winter would arrive.

The church hadn't been much better. Heat from the furnace didn't seem to reach the choir loft at all. She grinned as she remembered how eager the choir members were to get robed this morning. They were probably grateful for the extra layer.

She pulled the granny-square afghan off the back of the couch and wrapped it around her as she snuggled in. The roster was on the table beside her, and she picked it up and studied it with a combination of dread and relief.

It contained more names than she had initially expected. Most of her students were apparently under the age of ten. That was fine, she reminded herself. They'd be potentially taking lessons for nearly a decade.

Plus she liked working with children. Younger students challenged her to be inventive in the ways she taught them. They didn't really understand the concept of practice, so she had come up with some interesting ways to integrate singing into their lives. If she could catch those with talent early, they would learn how to preserve their voices from damage.

Two of the children were four-year-old twins, a boy and a girl. Already her mind leaped ahead to recitals and concerts and the fun they could have.

The last name on the list was bold. The writer had pressed so hard with the pencil that the crossbar on the T had gone right through the paper.

"Joseph Montoya."

So that was his name. She had watched him sign the roster after church. She took a sip of her tea and leaned back, letting her mind roll over his image. He wasn't movie-star gorgeous, but that was fine. He seemed mild, and tame, and safe.

Besides, it wasn't like she was going to marry the fellow or anything like that. She was just going to teach him to improve his voice. That was all.

Chapter 2

"Y ou did what?"

Joseph winced as Will's voice boomed from the telephone. "I signed up for voice lessons."

There. He'd said it. He knew he shouldn't have admitted it to anyone. In fact, it was such a dumb idea that he ought to do the only intelligent thing and call Rosa Cruz and cancel.

"Voice lessons, huh?" Laughter touched Will's voice. "So did you get a voice transplant?"

"Not funny."

"Well, come on, guy. You're legendary for, well, your, um— how can I say this without hurting my best friend's feelings— your complete and total lack of anything approaching even a smidgen of musical ability."

"Ouch."

"There has to be more to this than meets the eye—or the ear. What could ever convince Tin Ear Joseph to sign up for music lessons? Do you have something against this teacher?"

Joseph couldn't answer for fear that the truth would show in his voice. This was absurd, the way Rosa Cruz had made him do something this outlandish. Safe, a bit stodgy—that was him. Not crazy and impulsive.

Regain control of my life. There. That was a good entry. Once he got the reins back on his brain, he'd be just fine.

"Joseph? You still there? I was just kidding. I really was. I'm sure you'll be a wonderful singer. I didn't mean to insult you." Will's words poured over each other in a cascade of concern. "Did I hurt you? I'm sorry. I'm so sorry."

Joseph interrupted the flow of apology with a quick, "No, no, of course you didn't hurt me. I'd be the first to admit that I'm not exactly headed for the Metropolitan Opera Company—except as an audience member. I don't know what made me do it."

"Well, you have a severe case of psychological something-or-the-other if you're actually signing up to take lessons from someone who's nearly ninety."

"Who's ninety? Rosa's not ninety!"

"Who's Rosa? I'm talking about Mrs. Adams."

"I'm not taking lessons from her. My teacher is Rosa Cruz, who is closer to twenty-two than ninety. She's new in town, and when she sings, the angels weep with joy."

" 'The angels weep with joy,' do they?" Will cleared his throat. "Weep with joy, huh? Since when did you leave accountancy for poetry?"

"I—"

Sanity. That should be the biggest entry in his notebook. Given one big dose of sanity, he might actually be all right.

"You know," Will continued, "I think the last Bachelor Club holdout may end up walking the aisle after all."

Joseph flushed, gratified that his boyhood friend couldn't see his embarrassment. "They're just lessons, Will. That's all."

"So tell me about these *lessons*, pal. What's she like?"

Joseph cleared his throat. "I haven't talked to her yet."

"Aha. Gotcha. You haven't talked to this woman, but you've decided to take lessons from her? So what does she have besides pipes that make heaven get teary?"

Eyes as everlasting as a twilight song. Hair as soft and silky as a midnight summer breeze. A smile as radiant as the first morning's glow.

"I don't know." Joseph shut his eyes as a mixture of pain and happiness swept over him. "I don't know."

Rosa sat at her kitchen table, daylight pouring over the oaken surface, which was nearly covered with heaps of paper. Whatever had made her think that she could do this? She had to be the most disorganized person in the world.

No, she told herself, *you can do it. All you have to do is get your mind settled, and you'll be great. Right, God? You'll help me, I'm sure.* She knew this as certainly as the course of the sun over the earth. She had asked for God's help, and He'd give it. He always had. Always. Prayer worked.

She took a deep breath and slowly and carefully separated the chaos on the table into identifiable piles. These were the letters for the new students. All she had to do was put a letter in each envelope, address it, stamp it, check it off, and then she'd pop the whole batch into the mail.

Actually, it was quite amazing how many people had signed up. Mostly children and teenagers, as she might expect, but there was one adult.

She paused as she wrote his address on the envelope: *Joseph Montoya, 317 Seventh Street, Tierra Verde, New Mexico.* He must be—who was she kidding? She knew exactly who he was.

He'd stood out in the congregation. In the days when more people were coming to church dressed casually, he was like a throwback to an earlier time in his charcoal gray suit, his neatly pressed shirt, and his precisely knotted tie.

There had been something more, too. She'd sung along with the choir as she directed them—partially because the sopranos were a bit thin and reedy that morning, but more so because she couldn't stop herself. She loved to sing, and the song—an intriguing arrangement of "Amazing Grace"—was one she'd chosen because it was spectacular.

After the choir finished, she'd turned toward the congregation and seen his expression—eyes as warm as melted chocolate and a smile of appreciation lighting his face.

Kind of cute, wasn't he?

She shook her head and straightened her back. With renewed resolve, she laid the envelope bearing his name on the stack of the others. He was a student. About the last thing she needed was to get all gushy over a student. Enough was enough, and this was enough.

With great effort, she corralled her thoughts and got the letters ready to mail. She'd just pulled on her fleece jacket when a rhythmic rap on the door startled her. She paused and grinned before opening it. That *rat-a-tat, rat-a-tat* could only be Ella.

"You know that it's still September," she said to the woman with the flaming red hair as she opened the door, "and already you're tapping out 'Jingle Bells' on my door."

"You are too good," her visitor said, her eyes gleaming with the challenge. "I'll get something a bit more seasonal, just as soon as I think of a good autumn song."

"I have a few I could suggest," Rosa responded.

"No fair. You're a music person. I'm a chef person, and if Miss Perry didn't teach it to me in grade school, or if it's not on the oldies station, or if they don't sing it in church, I'm clueless. I like your coat. Did you get it in Albuquerque? You going out now?"

Rosa loved the way that Ella lived and spoke at the speed of sound.

"I have to mail these letters. Want to come along?"

"Sure."

Ella James had been Rosa's best friend when they were children growing up in Santa Fe, and it had been Ella's urging that had brought Rosa to Tierra Verde. If nothing else, Ella had reassured her, she could work at Ella's café, Turquoise Alley. It had just opened, and her stuffed sopapillas, small envelopes of dough filled with a seasoned mixture of meat and fruit, had made the Turquoise Alley a favorite stop in the mountains.

"Rodney's got the Alley under control tonight," Ella said as they walked on the cracked sidewalk toward the post office. A few random flakes of snow settled on their shoulders. "But of course I have my trusty cell phone, so if my hip suddenly bursts into song, that's why. This is posole night, by the way. I spent the afternoon making vats of it."

Rosa's mouth began to water. Posole. The hearty soup made of hominy was a treat, indeed. "I'm going to stop in and get some to go. I adore posole."

"You will do no such thing. You'll sit down at a table like a regular human being and eat your posole with me."

There was no arguing with Ella. Instead, Rosa mailed the letters to her new students, and the two of them headed for Turquoise Alley.

"Not that it's any of my business, but I'm going to ask anyway. What was that bundle you just mailed? Early Christmas cards? Bills from the past ten years? Chain letters?"

"Notices to my new students. I actually have a whole bunch of them. Of course, not everyone will stay, but it's encouraging."

"I know you'll do great here. Tierra Verde's children need someone like you."

"They're not all kids." *No! No!* Why had she said that? Ella was the kindest soul on earth, but she was also the snoopiest.

"Oh, really? Anyone I know? Mrs. Adams?" Ella went to Blessed Family but had been sick the day Rosa filled in as the choir director.

"Right. No, not Mrs. Adams."

"Tyrone Melton?"

Rosa shook her head. "Nope."

"Someone from the church?"

Rosa sighed. "Ella, you are my best friend in the whole wide world, but you are such a snoop."

She just wasn't ready to say anything about Joseph Montoya at the moment. It was silly, goofy, and just plain nuts, but there was something about those warm coffee-colored eyes. . . .

One of the best things about Ella was that she could abandon a topic and move on to another one without a blink. Immediately they were discussing whether Ella should look into serving outdoors in the summer, in a patio setting.

At last Rosa laughed. "Try as I may, I just can't imagine sitting outside to eat, at least not tonight."

Ella pulled the hood of her jacket up over her head. "I know what you mean. I can feel winter in the air, and I have to say, I'm kind of happy. I love the change of the seasons. But I know that by February I'll be beyond fed up with winter. It's like the houseguest you were delighted to see at first but has lingered a bit too long."

"Me, too. That's why I think I'll really like being here—winter driving. I won't have to worry about how I get around Tierra Verde. It's not like I need a car to get to work. The Ortiz building is just three blocks away from here and from the church. It'd take one fierce blizzard to keep me from hoofing it to either one."

The smell of warm posole drifted from Turquoise Alley even before Ella opened the door.

"Ella!" Diners smiled as they called out comments to her as the two women walked toward the kitchen. "The posole is great!"

"As usual!" another called.

"Getting cold again. Green chili stew soon?" asked yet another.

A solitary diner in the corner was hunched over a laptop computer and was making notes on a yellow pad. He looked up as Rosa neared his table. A smile of recognition passed between them, and he stood up quickly, nearly upending a glass of ice water.

Rosa reached for it at the same time he did, and their hands closed around the glass at the same time. For a moment they stood locked in place, their fingers wrapped around the glass, until Rosa found her voice. "We caught it."

"So we did."

She cleared her throat, which seemed to have gotten suddenly dry. "I wouldn't want your computer to get wet."

"That'd be a problem, for sure."

"It might break it."

"Maybe."

"Not good for it."

How to Become a Dynamic Conversationalist in Three Easy Lessons by Rosa Cruz. In this short work, Miss Cruz shares her knowledge of interpersonal communication. The three lessons are: 1. Speak with enthusiasm. 2. Use vibrant words. 3. Introduce a fascinating topic of conversation.

She was making a terrible mess of this. Joseph looked miserable, as if he were unable to find the words to rescue this interchange. She took a deep breath, offered a quick silent prayer for guidance, and tried again.

"I'm Rosa Cruz. Didn't I see you at Blessed Family Church?"

"You did. I'm Joseph Montoya." He looked relieved that the conversation had finally moved forward.

"And you signed up for lessons, too?"

"I did." He coughed and took a sip of the water. "About the lessons, I should—"

Ella waved to Rosa and pointed meaningfully to an empty table.

Rosa smiled at him. "Looks like my table's ready. About the lesson—I just mailed you a tentative schedule about five minutes ago. If you need to change your lesson time, give me a call. Okay?"

"I—"

The poor man seemed as if he wanted nothing more than to move out of this conversation, so Rosa smiled brightly at him. "I think I have you down for Thursday at seven thirty. See you then!"

She managed a cheerful wave and made her way to the table where Ella was waiting.

"Oh, do tell," Ella said as she sank onto the seat. "Joseph Montoya, huh? Don't tell me that someone has finally made Mr. Accountant sit up and take notice?"

"He was in church on Sunday."

"And?" Ella's question hung unanswered in the air.

"And nothing. I was just being cordial. That's all. Why—" Rosa began, but her question was forgotten when the waitress, carrying steaming crockery bowls of posole, arrived in front of the two women.

Ella began the grace and Rosa picked it up. Rosa had written it when she was seven and the two girls had been at church camp, and they'd said it together ever since: "For this bread, for this water, for this fellowship, we thank Thee, Father."

It was simple, but the words said it all, and they'd kept the tradition alive of praying the grace over every meal, even when they were apart.

"Go to choir?" Joseph held the envelope in limp fingers and stared out the window at the falling leaves silhouetted against the stars as they traced their way across the night sky. "Choir? Choir?"

Two days had passed since he'd spoken to Rosa in Turquoise Alley, and the letter she'd spoken of had finally arrived. His lesson was Thursday night at seven thirty, starting in a week.

His lesson! Had words ever spelled trouble as surely as those two?

But first, the letter said, he needed to join the choir. Rehearsal was Wednesday at seven thirty. Today was Wednesday. He groaned.

"God," Joseph said aloud, putting the letter down and closing his eyes in prayer, "is this true? Do You want me in the choir? I mean, You know what my voice is like. After all, You chose it for me. I'm not sure why You decided to have me not be able to even faintly carry a tune, but I can't, and You know it. Since this is all about You, do You want me in the choir? Do You?"

As if in answer, the grandfather clock in the hallway bonged seven times.

"All right. I'm getting my coat."

As he walked along the deserted sidewalk, he mulled over his predicament. What was he going to do?

He needed to make an emergency entry in his notebook, and he pulled it out of his pocket. *Predicaments: Avoid them.*

By the time he arrived at the church, he was no closer to an answer.

Mrs. Adams looked at him with surprise. "Joseph! Is there a trustees meeting tonight?"

"No." He felt himself flush. "I'm here for choir."

"Choir? You—oh, well, certainly. I don't have an extra folder, but you can share with Tyrone."

He sank into the chair next to Tyrone Melton, who grinned wolfishly at him and said, "Has the earth come to an end? Has the sun ground to a halt in its tracks? Have the stars fallen from the sky?"

Joseph took out his mental self-improvement list and added *Patience*, even as he smiled at Tyrone.

This whole thing was like one of those bad dreams, where things just got worse and worse. Not only did he get himself signed up for singing lessons, which he'd have to get himself unsigned-up for, pronto, he'd managed now to somehow be sitting in the choir loft—next to Tyrone the Terrible Tenor.

Well, he assured himself, nothing could be worse. Nothing.

Rosa waved at him and said to Mrs. Adams, "Joseph is going to be taking voice lessons from me."

"Really?" Mrs. Adams replied. "We'll have to get him to do some special music for us, then. A solo?"

Oh, yeah, he thought, *that would be special music, for sure.*

Fortunately, someone's watch buzzed, and Mrs. Adams realized it was time to start choir.

Joseph did the best he could. He mouthed the words whenever possible, but occasionally his love of God got the best of him and a note or two escaped.

He ignored the glares that Tyrone shot his way and tried to look innocent whenever Mrs. Adams glanced questioningly his way.

How odd could his life get? Joseph Montoya was in the choir.

Chapter 3

Joseph faced his reflection in the mirror and grimaced. No matter what he did, that one piece of hair insisted on going straight up. His mother had called it a cowlick, and he had to admit, it did look like he'd come into close contact with a cow's tongue.

He'd given up worrying about how he looked—after all, there was only so much he could do, considering the raw materials the Lord had provided him with—but tonight he would have appreciated an improvement of some sort. *Tonight,* he thought as he tugged on his tie, *tonight I am having my first music lesson with the lovely Rosa Cruz.*

Music lesson. He laughed. He'd last maybe five minutes with her before she found out that her student had absolutely no talent at all. The kindest thing to do was to go in to the studio, confess to her that he didn't know a C-sharp from a Z-flat, and bow out gracefully.

Yes, that was exactly what he was going to do.

But he was going to have to deal with this odd feeling in his stomach whenever he saw her. He wasn't the most social person in the world, but there was something about her that made him incapable of coherent speech. Like the night at the Turquoise Alley—he must have come across as an inept loner, capable only of short sentences devoid of meaning. *Charming. Absolutely charming.*

Develop social graces. Pronto.

He glared at his hair one last time. Maybe if he got the nail scissors and cut the offending lock off—

The phone jarred him from his thoughts. It was Isaac this time, one of the other members of the Bachelor Club.

"Hey, Joseph, what's this I hear about you having a girlfriend?"

"News to me."

"Will told me that you've met up with a cute music teacher."

Joseph resisted the urge to whack the telephone on the table and tried instead for a diversion. "Will thinks she's cute?"

"Well, he thinks that you think—oh, never mind. But could I have heard him right? He says you're going to take music lessons from her!"

"Well, as a matter of fact—"

"Hey, I think that's great! Everybody should do something for self-improvement. Why not?"

"Isaac, this is me. Joseph. Remember? Tin Ear Montoya?"

"So what? If you were the best singer in the world, why would you need lessons? When's your lesson?"

"Ten minutes. But I'm not going to—"

"Oh, then, pal, I'd better let you vamoose. Talk to you later!"

With a click, the call from Isaac was disconnected.

Joseph stood just a moment, phone in hand, debating what to do.

Develop quick-thinking skills. Develop any thinking skills.

He opened the door and walked outside.

Rosa straightened the books on the shelf beside the piano. Most of them were volumes of music, and they represented over a decade of devoted musical studies.

She'd ordered some new books for the littlest students, and their colorful covers were quite a change from the drab ones she'd used as a child. She was quite pleased with how well they were working out. The students' faces lit up with excitement when they realized that they'd be singing some familiar songs as well as some new ones.

But her next student wouldn't be singing about bunnies that hopped and elephants that waltzed. No, Joseph Montoya was a bit of a challenge to her. Until she knew where his musical interests were, she wouldn't assign him a book.

She knew little about his musical background. He'd been in choir on Wednesday, but the piece they were working on was quite convoluted, and the choir as a whole struggled its way through. He seemed to have a distinct assemblage voice— one which blended in so well with others that it was difficult to pick it out. At least she hadn't been able to discern which was his.

He was a hard one to read. Was he a classical singer? A

smooth jazz devotee? Certainly he wasn't a rock-and-roll singer! Or a rapper!

She grinned at the thought of Joseph doing modern music. Somehow he didn't seem like that kind of fellow.

Easy listening, perhaps? She pulled one of her favorite books, *Songs from Memory Lane*, off the shelf. It was filled with the old standards and a few nice arrangements of some hymns.

She glanced through the contents, trying to select just the right song to start him off with. Popular music and show tunes were a bit risky this early on in the lessons because they relied quite a bit on the singer's range and skill.

"Amazing Grace." *Aah!* This was her favorite hymn, and automatically she began humming it. It was perfect for Joseph Montoya's first lesson. Anyone could sing it.

Joseph raised his hand to the door of Rosa's studio in a tentative knock. From inside, she called, "Come in!" He smoothed his hair self-consciously. The wind had picked up on the way over, and whatever progress he had made with the cowlick was lost. With sweaty fingers, he turned the doorknob.

The door opened slowly, and he paused, taking in the room that undoubtedly signaled his doom. The walls were newly painted a blue as soft as the New Mexico sky, and in the whitewashed fireplace, a small fire crackled in welcome. A tall bookcase held row after row of books.

On one wall, large turquoise letters proclaimed, *Make a joyful noise unto the Lord.*

He couldn't take reassurance from the biblical words. *Joyful noise, indeed.* Just wait until Rosa heard his caterwauling.

"Come on in," Rosa said. "Joseph, right? Or do you prefer to be called Joe?"

"Joseph." The single word came out in a squeak. His hand flew to his throat. What was happening to his voice?

"Is something wrong? Are you ill?" Her forehead furrowed with concern. "If you have a cold or a sore throat, you shouldn't sing. It might damage your vocal chords."

Damage his vocal chords? He restrained a slightly hysterical laugh. What? And ruin his budding career as an operatic tenor?

"I—" He coughed. "I—" The word came out as a scratchy syllable.

"You *are* sick, you poor thing." Rosa touched his hand, and Joseph's breath caught in his chest. Not only couldn't he speak, he couldn't breathe, either, not when her small hand touched his.

"I'll be—" He cleared his throat. "I'll be okay."

"Are you sure?"

He nodded. "Yes. We can—go ahead."

There was nothing to do, he reasoned, except to proceed and let her learn—let her hear—the awful truth.

"Well, all right. But let me know if your throat begins to bother you, okay?"

She sat at the piano, her pale yellow skirt, as bright as a spring daffodil, draped over the bench. "Let's warm up. Are you all right?"

"Yes." The word was almost a whisper.

"Let's start with the exercise we did at choir. Me-may-maw-mow-moo is a good one. It not only warms up your vocal chords, it also stretches out your lips and gets them ready to sing. Listen to me first and then you sing it, okay?"

She began to sing, and he lost himself in her voice. Had such nonsense syllables ever sounded so pleasant, so melodic? The phrase inched up the scale, and to his ears, the notes sounded like the finest aria.

He realized at last that she was looking at him intently, a smile playing around her upturned lips. "Join in? Please?"

"Sorry."

The moment of truth had arrived. He opened his mouth and—nothing came out. Not a word. Not a syllable. Not even a sound.

"That's okay," Rosa said reassuringly. "Not a problem. You're a bit nervous. How about if you sing with me?" She started again the me-may-maw-mow-moos, motioning encouragingly for him to join in, but he shook his head.

Can't. The word didn't even make it past his lips. Not only couldn't he sing, he couldn't speak.

"Is it your voice?" she asked with sympathy.

Why, yes it is, he thought. He nodded numbly.

"It's the time of year," she said. "You walked over here, didn't you?"

"Yes." The word came out as a rasp.

"That's it, then." She smiled at him. "It's going from the cold outside into the warmth of the studio. Plus that dreadful wind!" She gestured toward the fireplace. "And I didn't help anything at all by having a fire going. No wonder your poor voice gave out."

Poor voice? If she only knew!

"Let's finish up then with my giving you a song to work on, okay? Do you know 'Amazing Grace'?" She didn't wait for his answer but continued, "Of course you do. Why don't we go through that one next time? Two weeks from today okay with you?"

She stood up and walked him to the door. "Don't talk, at least not tonight. Don't overwork your voice, promise?"

He dipped his head in agreement.

"Take care of yourself, Joseph! We don't want anything to happen to those precious vocal chords!"

Laughter threatened to engulf him, so he coughed lightly into his sleeve to cover the sound. "I'd better go," he said, his voice raspy as he fought the urge to give in and snort with amusement. Precious vocal chords, indeed!

"Have some tea and honey when you get home, all right?" she asked as he opened the door. "And cuddle under a blanket and read a nice mystery novel. It's going to be a cold walk tonight and you need some rest. I'd give you a ride if I didn't have another student coming in."

"I'll be fine," he assured her, his words scratching their way out.

He left the studio, aware of her gaze following him, her eyes gentle with concern, and his hand automatically strayed to his throat. It *did* hurt. He swallowed experimentally and frowned. He had quite a full load of work on his desk to get to. That new accounting software wasn't working quite right yet, and he had taken on a new client, to boot. He couldn't afford to be sick.

Watch health, he noted mentally. *Take vitamins. Get more sleep. Eat broccoli and drink orange juice.* His self-improvement list was getting outrageously long.

The temperature had dropped considerably while he'd been in the studio, and his breath puffed out in white clouds as he walked toward his house. He'd gotten three blocks when he realized he was still clutching the music she'd handed him, "Amazing Grace," which he was supposed to be ready to sing—in two weeks.

At his next lesson.

God, he prayed as he slowed his stride through the frosty air, *I think I'm getting into this over my head. What should I do? What should I do?*

Was it terrible, really? He was putting his heart at risk, something he'd never done. Rosa had given him absolutely no indication that she was feeling the same way.

You don't see it, Montoya? You really don't? What do you want—a trail of rose petals through the snow right to her door?

Joseph realized he'd stopped moving and was standing in the middle of the sidewalk. His right hand was raised, and he grimaced. He'd been gesturing as he carried on his silent conversation. At least he hoped it had been silent. It was a good thing that at this time of night, the streets were deserted, so no one had seen him in his animated discussion with himself—and with God.

Clearly he was sicker than he thought. Delirious, in fact. It was the only explanation. Why else would he, a normally sane accountant, feel the sudden urge to burst into song in the middle of Third Street?

Chapter 4

R osa frowned into her caramel mocha. "I don't know, Ella," she confided. They were seated in the plaza outside Turquoise Alley. Colorful leaves scudded around their feet as early autumn took over for summer. "Maybe I was wrong about him. He acted almost like he couldn't get out of there fast enough last night. I was ready to discuss his musical background with him, but he—well, it's odd. He was antsy to leave as soon as he got there."

"You said he was sick, though. Maybe that was it."

"Sick? I don't know. If he'd been sick, why did he come? I think he had buyer's remorse—or whatever it would be for private lessons. Student's remorse?" Rosa jabbed at the whipped cream topping her drink. "I'm afraid he doesn't want to take lessons from me."

"That doesn't make sense," Ella said practically. "Think about it. If he changed his mind, wouldn't he call you? Why would you think that he'd show up if he didn't have any intention of having a lesson?"

"Maybe he has an incredible voice and he's realized now

that I don't have anything to offer him."

"I don't know anything about his singing ability, but if he really were all that extraordinary, wouldn't he be singing? Wouldn't we know? After all, Tierra Verde isn't exactly New York City. I've always thought that there were precious few secrets here, but if Joseph Montoya is hiding a world-class tenor, I'll have to rethink that."

Tierra Verde certainly had secrets, Rosa thought. The reaction of the choir members when Joseph had shown up for practice told her that there was something going on behind the scenes. A quick murmur had gone through the members like an underground stream, but no one had volunteered any information, and she hadn't asked.

"I just have the feeling that I'm not being told everything," she said. "Nothing I can put my finger on, though."

Ella grinned at her. "Want me to snoop?" she asked, leaning conspiratorially across the table.

"No!" Rosa answered with a horrified whisper. She could imagine what Ella would say—or, more likely, she couldn't imagine. Ella had no problems sharing whatever was on her mind, whereas Rosa always thought twice, or three times, or four times before speaking.

"I could find out for you. If Joseph has a mysterious past, I'll dig it up. Let me play Sherlock Holmes." Ella's gray eyes sparkled mischievously.

"No!"

"You sure?"

"Yes, I'm sure. I may be overreacting, anyway." Rosa smiled at Ella with a conviction she didn't truly feel. "After all, my intuition doesn't have a stellar history. There's the matter of a fiancé who had another life I didn't even suspect."

Ella covered Rosa's hand with her own. "Honey, don't go there. Andrew Russell was a class-A, top-of-the-line jerk, and you deserve much better than someone like that."

Rosa could only nod.

"You're not still holding on to that, are you? Rosa, you know he was a real loser. You're lucky to have gotten out of that relationship, if you could even call it that."

"I know. And it's not that." She managed a shaky smile at her best friend. "I've put him out of my heart entirely. Really, I have," she added when Ella looked unconvinced. "I thank the Lord, literally, every night for sparing me from that marriage."

She shuddered. If she hadn't found out before the wedding how dreadful Andrew had been. . .

"Aah," Ella said knowingly. "Ah. Ah."

"Choo?"

"You're funny, you know that? I just figured this out."

"Figured what out?"

"You have a thing for Joseph Montoya. That's what this is all about."

"I do not!"

Even as she protested, Rosa's attention began to waver. Two people were standing just outside the door of Turquoise Alley. They had their backs to her, but there was something quite familiar about the one on the right. She didn't know a lot about fashion, especially men's fashion, but she could tell that his long overcoat, cut from a deep charcoal gray woolen cloth, was expensive. It was the kind of coat that a lawyer might wear.

Or an accountant.

He turned his head and laughed at something his companion said. It was Joseph.

"Earth to Rosa. Come in, please. Hello?" Ella shook Rosa's hand lightly.

"It's him. Joseph," Rosa whispered. Emotions collided with frantic velocity. She wanted to talk to him. Didn't want to talk to him. Needed to talk to him. Couldn't talk to him.

Ella swiveled in her chair and waved vigorously at the two. "Oh, look. That's Adam Chambers with your Joseph."

"He's not *my* Joseph." Rosa knew she was blushing. The hot wave rose up her neck and flooded her cheeks.

Ella snorted and motioned the two men in and introduced Adam to Rosa. "I've seen you in church," Adam said. "You're a definite asset to our choir." As he shook her hand, his gaze seemed to sharpen, as if he were trying to decipher something hidden.

At last he turned to Joseph, nodded briefly, and excused himself. "I'd love to stay and have one of your wonderful berry empanadas but I promised my blushing bride I'd take her to Santa Fe today to do some shopping." He winked at his friend and left.

She was going to comment on how mysterious Adam had been, but as she started to speak, she realized that Joseph was flushing.

"Is your throat better?" she asked, feeling just a bit horrible for the thoughts swarming in her mind. She quickly asked God's forgiveness for doubting Joseph's story last night—if indeed she needed it. The Bible said something about being as wise as serpents, and while she wasn't crazy about the image, she understood it.

Protect your heart, she heard a small voice say. It belonged, she knew, to that tender young woman who had been so desperately hurt by the broken engagement.

But I don't have to guard myself around everyone, she argued back. *Some men are nice. Some men are real. Some men are honest.*

"I'm much better," Joseph said to her. His voice was raspy and strained. "By the time I got home last night, I felt like I'd swallowed a hairbrush."

"And today?"

"Only a toothbrush."

They grinned at each other. If her heart—that protected organ—could have sprouted wings and flown around in her chest, it would have.

He was sick! Hooray!

Almost immediately her conscience kicked in with a reminder: Was it right for her to be so wildly happy that her student was ill?

She didn't take the time to sort out the moral dilemma. Both she and God knew what she meant.

And hope, that small white bird that dwelled in her spirit, soared.

Joseph glared at the clothes laid out on his bed. This was wrong. He was an accountant, not some fashionista. Or clotheshorse. Whichever.

But the fact was that he had no idea what to wear. Casual? He wasn't a T-shirt kind of guy, so his concept of dressing down meant a pair of jeans and a polo shirt. Or should he wear what he wore to work and to church—a suit, or at least a pressed cotton shirt with dress slacks?

He mentally raced through his memory banks, trying to remember what the others had worn to choir rehearsal. He couldn't remember a thing except how lovely Rosa had looked. She'd been wearing something whitish, sort of beige—the color of vanilla ice cream, a sweater maybe. Oh, he was pitiful. He had no eye for clothing at all.

None of his reflections were going to get him any closer to deciding what to wear, he realized. If he didn't decide soon, he'd end up in his bathrobe, right there among the tenors.

He finally chose the jeans and polo shirt and tossed a navy blue sweater over the top. One last glance in the mirror told him he was presentable, even if a fashionable gentlemen's magazine wouldn't come bashing down his door for an interview.

He arrived a few minutes late. At least he didn't have to make informal chitchat with the others while waiting for Mrs. Adams to start. He entered the room just as they were beginning the warm-ups.

"Me-may— Oh, hello, Joseph. Good to see you again." He couldn't ignore the surprise in Mrs. Adams's voice, but he nodded as if his presence there were the most natural thing in the world. "Grab one of those black folders and, yes, Tyrone, he'll sit next to you in the tenor section. Joseph, you are a tenor, aren't you?"

"Uh, sure." He mumbled the response as he took one of

the music folders and carried it to the empty chair by Tyrone.

He attempted not to look at Rosa, but it was like trying to avert his eyes from the most glorious sunrise, the most stunning meteor shower, the rarest rose. His eyes turned of their own volition toward her. Her ebony hair was caught back in some kind of clasp, and tendrils escaped like tiny ringlets around her perfect face. She smiled at him, her lips faintly rubied with a light gloss.

Sing? How could he help it? If ever there were a moment when the impossible was possible, this was it. He opened his mouth and sang.

Chapter 5

This was possibly the worst sound he'd ever produced. It was a cross between a donkey's bray and the caw of ravens.

Tyrone glanced at him, quickly, in questioning surprise. Mrs. Adams's head snapped toward him, startled. And Rosa—he didn't dare look at her to see her response.

Joseph coughed, tapped his throat, and mouthed, "Water." He slipped out of the choir room and sped to the privacy of the outer hallway. By the water fountain, he rested his head against the cool plaster wall and willed himself to die.

This was terrible. He'd surely embarrassed himself beyond any hope. Rosa would know that he was a fraud, a pretender, a loser.

"Joseph?" Rosa's voice was tentative.

He didn't trust himself to answer, afraid his voice would betray him again.

"Are you all right?" she persisted. "It takes awhile to get over a bad sore throat. Maybe you started back singing too soon."

He had to tell her the truth. He faced her, ready to end the charade and tell her that he had no musical talent. His heart hammered and his breath caught in his throat, but he forged onward. He had to do this. He opened his mouth, ready to be straightforward, and once again his voice was traitorous. "Would you like to go out to dinner?"

She paused, a faint smile playing around her lips as she studied him, and he knew he'd been foolish to even think that someone as beautiful and as talented as she was would even dream of dating someone like him. What had he been thinking?

"I'd love to go," she said after what seemed to be nearly an hour but he knew must have been only seconds. "When?"

What now, Montoya? Think quickly! When? Where? Dinner! With Rosa Cruz!

"We can work around your teaching schedule," he said, and almost cheered at how smooth he sounded. "We can go into Santa Fe if you'd like, or we can stay here and eat at Turquoise Alley."

"I have Friday nights free."

"Friday night is great." He tried to breathe naturally. He was going to dinner with Rosa! "This Friday, right?"

"Unless you have something else planned."

"Nothing," he hastily interjected. He could have had a meeting with the president of the United States scheduled for Friday, and he would have thrown it by the wayside for dinner with Rosa. But, as with every Friday night, his calendar was wide open.

"You know what I'd like to do?" she asked. "That is, if you don't mind me just butting in here. I'd like to go to dinner at the Alley and then take a nice, long walk. Could we do that? I'm still new to Tierra Verde, and I have to admit I'm a bit chicken about going out by myself at night."

"Sounds great," he said. "I'll pick you up around six. Where do you live?"

"I'm across the street from the studio in that orange-painted adobe. Do you know it?"

He laughed. "I sure do. I can still remember when they painted it orange. Caused quite a stir here in Tierra Verde, let me tell you."

"I wonder why they chose orange. It's not exactly a traditional color."

"It was to Miguel Sanchez."

She tilted her head in an unspoken question.

He smiled at her. "Miguel's wife was going to California to visit her parents for a week, and Miguel decided to paint the house as a surprise. Was she ever surprised to come home and find it orange!"

"But why orange?"

He leaned in and whispered, "Never send a color-blind man to buy house paint."

Rosa sat at the kitchen table, smoothed a place mat, stood up, went into the living room, sat down, stood up, returned to the kitchen, and stared out the window. "Settle down, kiddo," she chided herself aloud. "Breathe deep. Think calm thoughts. Pray."

She folded her hands together and shut her eyes. "Dearest

Lord, here I am again, asking for Your help. Tonight is, well, it's very important to me. I want it to go well. I really do. You see, I really like Joseph. I barely know him, but—God, I want to know him better. A lot better."

Her words ended, but she stood in the kitchen, letting the peace of prayer wash over her like a cooling stream. The power of it was so strong that when her doorbell rang, she went to greet him, her heart fluttering only slightly.

He was wearing a red sweater that set off his dark hair and eyes. He wasn't fashion-model gorgeous, but she had to admit again that God had done spectacular work with this man.

She let him help her with her jacket. Andrew, her ex-fiancé, had never done that, but manners had never been his strong suit. Joseph was certainly quite different.

"I thought we'd walk to Turquoise Alley," he said, "if that's all right with you. It's a glorious night, and we might as well take advantage of it."

What he said was true. The sky was clear of clouds, and in the early evening sky, the first stars were twinkling. A faint breeze lifted her hair from her face, and she could smell the promise of snow coming off the mountain.

They didn't speak much as they walked the three blocks to the Alley, and Rosa reveled in the comfort of having his strong presence beside her. The sidewalk was narrow, and occasionally his arm brushed against hers. The image of them walking together, hand in hand, popped into her mind, and she smiled.

"Penny for your thoughts," he said.

"Haven't you heard of inflation?" she teased. "They're worth at least a nickel now."

"Pricey but probably worth it." He dug in his pocket and examined the change he found there. "No nickel, but here's four pennies. Can I owe you one?"

"I suppose I can trust you." She paused as she tried to formulate what she was going to say. "Actually, I was thinking about the weather and how nice it is to be walking with you." There. That wasn't an untruth. It was just a vague truth.

"It is a wonderful evening," he said, "made better by your company."

If roses had fallen from the sky at that moment, she wouldn't—she couldn't—have been happier. His simple compliment was perfect.

"Turquoise Alley is crowded tonight," he said as they turned down the narrow path to the restaurant.

"Date night," she responded automatically, and he laughed. "It sure is."

Amber light spilled from the luminarias that lined the sidewalk. She knew that Ella had gone round and round with the city council about using the traditional candles in paper bags, and they'd finally compromised with sturdy fireproof canvas for the bags and small outdoor lights to substitute for the candles. The glow they cast made the alleyway come alive with a romantic charm.

A group was leaving the restaurant, and as they opened the door, guitar music drifted outside. "I think that's Benny Alvarez," Joseph said. "Have you heard him play yet?"

"No, but I think I'm going to like it."

"His style is a blend of flamenco and smooth jazz. Very inventive, very exciting."

"You must know a lot about him," she said.

He nodded as he opened the door for her. "Benny teaches music in the schools here. Everybody in Tierra Verde knows him."

All of the tables were filled, and a delicious aroma floated from the kitchen in the back. "Aah," Rosa said, taking a deep breath. "Tamales. They must be the special tonight. I love tamales, especially—"

Ella glided from the kitchen, a whirl of enthusiastic colors in her patchwork dress. "Rosa! Joseph!" she called as she came toward them, her arms outstretched. "I've been waiting for you. I have your table all ready."

Joseph frowned. "Okay, I'm confused. We have a table? I thought that the Alley was a no-reservations restaurant."

"Ella is my best friend," Rosa explained to him. "She has been since we were kids. I told her we were coming, and Ella being Ella, she's done something totally wonderful and wildly out of proportion, I'm sure." She smiled, but inside her stomach rolled.

Ella was, without a doubt, the finest friend Rosa had ever had. She was loyal and responsible and one of the best Christian women Rosa had ever known. But she had one flaw. Just one, but it was a big one.

She could never pass up the chance to help Rosa. Sometimes her help was valuable, like getting Rosa set up with a place to live and work in Tierra Verde when she needed to get out of Albuquerque before her heart withered away entirely.

Plus she lived life the way she dressed—in broad strokes of artistic panache. It would be just like her to have the olives on the nachos arranged in a heart shape and their names spelled out with a big plus sign between them, or even worse, something with a piñata. Ella loved piñatas.

"Come, come with me." Ella motioned them toward the back. "I have you set up back here."

She lifted a thick velvet curtain—its color the exact pink of sweetheart roses in full bloom—to reveal a small table in an alcove already set for two.

Rosa took a quick inventory of the area. So far, so good. Nothing seemed out of place.

Ella handed them both menus and pulled out their chairs for them.

"I didn't know this room existed," Rosa said.

Ella grinned. "It doesn't. You're seated where the silverware carts usually go. We're a bit crunched in the back now, but it's worth it. By the way, tonight's special is tamales with the usual sides."

"Sounds good to me," Joseph said, returning the menu. "With lemonade to drink. Rosa? What would you like?"

"Same for me. I'll never pass up tamales, right, Ella?"

"Right. Joseph, you'll have to get her to tell you the tamales story. I'll be back in a flash with your food."

In a rainbow swirl, Ella was gone.

Joseph tilted his head questioningly at Rosa. "Tamales? What story?"

Rosa laughed. "Ella and I were, oh, maybe four or five at the time. My grandmother made the most wonderful tamales ever, and Ella and I loved them. My grandmother, Abuelita, is tiny—my grandfather used to say that she was the size of a large house cat, which made no sense to me at the time."

He grinned.

"One day Abuelita made tamales, a lot of tamales. She was going to take them all to the church for a dinner, and she went into the bathroom to get ready to go. She told us to leave the tamales alone and set us out in the living room with our dolls, but Ella and I couldn't stand it. They smelled so yummy and we were so hungry—well, you can imagine. Ella and I opened one jar and ate them. Then we opened another jar and ate them. And another, until we literally couldn't eat any more."

He smiled. "And?" he prompted.

"Then we heard Abuelita come out of the bathroom and go into her bedroom to get dressed. We realized that we were going to be in trouble, big trouble. Abuelita may be small, but she has a mighty temper."

"What did you do?"

"We decided we needed to fill the jars back up. Now, remember, we were four. We figured we needed to make tamales."

He began to grin. "So what did you do?"

"I tried to remember what went into them. Some masa and water; I knew that. Luckily—or not—I was able to reach the bag. I had Ella start on that while I made the sauce. I knew there was some brownish-red powder that she used, so I got a chair from the dining room table and got some brownish-red stuff from the cupboard."

"What was it?"

"I knew it was supposed to be ground chilies—you have to give me some credit—but I couldn't read yet. I didn't let a little thing like that bother me. I was cooking. Anyway, fast-forward a few minutes to Abuelita coming back into her just-cleaned kitchen, which now looked like an explosion of gummy, floury stuff and gooey red stuff."

"Was she mad at you?"

"Furious at first. We told her what we'd done, and we said we were sorry. Then Ella assured her that it was okay. We'd done what she'd always told us to do if we messed up: ask forgiveness and try to fix it. We ate the tamales and to set things right, we'd made more. We were sure she'd understand."

"And?"

"Abuelita opened a jar and tasted one of our tamales. Suddenly her fury just vanished and she sat down and roared with laughter. I'd never seen her laugh that hard. We hadn't used chili in the tamales. We'd used cinnamon."

He grimaced. "So what did she do?"

"Bless her heart, that woman tied aprons on all of us and taught us how to make tamales." She pointed to the menu. "In fact, the Abuelita's Tamales on the menu are made using her recipe." She grinned. "Not ours."

"I hope so! I like cinnamon but not in my tamales. So you two grew up together in Albuquerque?"

"Santa Fe. How about you?"

"I'm from here."

"Do you want to stay here?"

"Actually, I do. Tierra Verde is perfect for me. I did leave to go to college to get my degree, but I was glad to come back here. It's home."

"I like it, too," she said. "It's peaceful here."

Ella returned with two large platters containing their meals.

"Here you go. Abuelita's tamales. Enjoy!" And with that, she pirouetted out.

Joseph glanced at his plate and then looked at Rosa. "I always say grace."

A bit of Rosa's heart moved. She could feel it. Right here in Turquoise Alley, she was falling in love.

Andrew Russell hadn't been a Christian, but she'd overlooked that, thinking it wasn't all that important in the grand scheme. But it was.

Joseph clearly wasn't a Sunday-only Christian. Unless she was reading him entirely wrong, his belief ran true and straight.

"Let's pray out loud. Would you like to, or should I?" She smiled. "Ella and I always say a grace I wrote at church camp when I was seven. It's not eloquent or deep, but it's heartfelt."

"By all means, let's do that."

She bowed her head and prayed, "For this bread, for this water, for this fellowship, we thank Thee, Father. Amen."

"Amen." His lips curved up softly. "Thank you for sharing that with me. It's—"

The curtain moved, and the guitarist stepped into the room. He stood over the table, strummed a few notes, and then began to sing softly.

Rosa's breath caught in her throat. She didn't know whether to hug or throttle Ella, who was the evident mastermind behind the musician's presence and his choice of song. The guitarist was extraordinary, his playing and singing flawless.

At the end of the song, he slipped out as silently as he'd entered.

"You have tears in your eyes," Joseph said.

"Yes. That's my favorite song. 'Beautiful Dreamer.' It's an old classic, and I love to hear it performed well."

"Benny did a good job, I think."

"Absolutely. I've never heard it interpreted that way. You're lucky to have him teaching in the schools here."

They spent the rest of the meal getting to know each other a bit better. He told her about growing up in Tierra Verde, about the four boys who had formed a close friendship in the Fix-It Shop.

She took a bite of her tamale. "Oh, this is really good. Yum. I think that's neat that you four stayed friends this long. Did you guys have a club or something?"

He cleared his throat. "Well, yes, we did."

"Ella and I did, too. Just the two of us. We could never settle on a name, though. We were the Blutterfies, which was what my grandpa called us, first, I think. Let's see, who else were we? Oh, the Golden Apple Polishers when we decided to do secret good deeds. That lasted about a week. And when we were into movie stars, we were the Stars of the World. That was Ella's choice. She always thought on a grand scale. What about you four? Did you have a name?"

He coughed into his napkin and said something.

"I hope you're not getting sick again." She touched his hand. "Are you okay?"

"I'm fine."

"Good." She took another bite of the tamale. "I didn't catch the name of the club you four belonged to."

He didn't answer right away. But when he looked up, his dark eyes were dancing with laughter. "The Bachelor Club."

Chapter 6

The Bachelor Club? Are you serious?" Her eyes reflected her laughter.

Now, two decades later, the club and the promise seemed incredibly silly, and he was embarrassed to discuss it, especially now, on their first date. He sipped his lemonade. "There were four boys in it—Will, Isaac, Adam, and me. We were really young, and it seemed like a good idea at the time."

"Like the tamales," she said. "Plus, at the time, you were all young bachelors, so it fit. I think it's cute."

Ella floated in at that moment, and he was deeply grateful for the diversion. "How were the tamales? Do you have room for dessert?"

Both Joseph and Rosa groaned, but Ella persisted. "Oh, it's wonderful. It's a cherry cobbler that is a perfect ending for your meals."

"I don't have enough room," Rosa said, and Joseph nodded in agreement.

Ella waved away their objections. "I'll bring one serving and two forks."

"The woman is going to make me into a blimp," Rosa moaned. "She'd be happiest if I were shaped like a big pumpkin. I don't know why. Probably payback for the tamales thing."

He couldn't picture her as anything but the trim young woman she was. He studied her as she chattered on about Ella, and he tried to imagine what she'd look like as she aged.

Her face would soften, definitely, and she might fill out a bit. Her hair, so inky black now, would probably be streaked with white. A few lines in her face would only add to the character he saw there. Her deep brown eyes—age couldn't touch them. They'd still be warm and welcoming, the perfect thing to come home to after a hard day at the office.

"Right?" Rosa was watching him, obviously waiting for a response from him.

"Um, sure."

She laughed, and the sound danced through the air. "You didn't hear a word I said. You were out in la-la land, weren't you?"

He grinned. "Just visiting there." He needed to make another entry in his self-improvement list: *Don't daydream on a date.*

"It's been a long week for both of us," she said as she put her napkin on the table beside her plate. "Maybe we should go. I have students coming in tomorrow morning. My chickadees."

"Chickadees?"

"The little ones. My first student of the day is five. Oh, make that five-and-a-half. She corrected me on that when I saw her at the park this week."

Ella reappeared and waved away Joseph's request for the bill. "I'll put it on your tab."

"I don't have a tab here."

"You do now."

Rosa leaned over the table and said to him in a stage whisper, "See? You have to watch this one. She's cagey. You start a tab, you'll be in here more."

The words were out of his mouth before he could rethink them: "That's fine, as long as you're with me."

She stopped, her rosebud mouth open a bit in obvious surprise. "Yes. Yes."

Rosa sat in her living room, her legs up on the hassock. She was wearing her bear-paw slippers, a Christmas gift from Ella, and they made her feet look twice their normal size.

"So what do you think?" she asked them. "Does he like me? I mean, really like me, not like-like, but like-like-like."

She swung her feet off the stool and stood up. "I'm pitiful. Just pitiful. I'm talking to slippers, and they're making more sense than I am."

The kitchen in her little house was unheated, and she hurried through making tea and bringing it back into the living room. She'd have her tea and then go to bed on the off chance she could sleep.

She cradled the warm cup in her hands as she waited for it to cool off. It probably wasn't a good idea to have tea and then try to sleep, but at the moment, she couldn't even muster up a yawn.

"If only I could be this wide-awake at seven in the morning," she said to her toes.

If she was going to talk, she decided, she would have much better luck doing so with God. She put the cup on the table beside her chair and leaned back, her eyes shut.

He's a good person, God. He really is. I think I'd like to. . . She opened her eyes, unsure of what to say. She glared at the felt claws on the furry slippers and then shut her eyes again. *Okay, I don't know what I want, but I do know that what I want might not be what You want or what You want me to want.*

She tried to sort it out, but even though her mind was racing, her limbs relaxed and her eyelids grew heavy, and she was so comfortable in the chair. . . .

Joseph sat at his table, his electronic planner in front of him. Again he counted: Saturday, Sunday, Monday, Tuesday. Four more days until he was scheduled for another voice lesson.

They'd rescheduled his time slot to accommodate another student on Thursday but otherwise hadn't discussed his lessons the entire evening. At some point, he was going to have to stop the lessons. He'd heard that afternoon that she now had a waiting list for lessons. She needed to have that time to teach someone who was talented, not a fellow whose voice rang as true as a rusty pump.

He'd have to tell her. He would. This Tuesday he'd definitely say something.

But right now, he wanted to think about the evening they'd shared. Moments reappeared in his memory like bright photographs. Her laughter as she told the story of the tamales. . . Her honest words of prayer. . . The way her eyes had shone with unshed tears when Benny had performed "Beautiful Dreamer."

There had been many times in his life when he had wished for vocal talent, but never more than this moment. How he would love to sing that song for her.

He tried it, softly. But it was no good. His voice wavered and cracked over the melody.

He put his head on the table and prayed. There weren't words to his prayer. It was simply the sighing plea of his heart.

Rosa straightened the music on the rack and checked her watch. It was exactly forty-seven seconds later than the last time she'd checked.

Joseph was now three minutes late for his lesson. It wasn't a big deal to have a student running behind—it happened all the time—but tonight was important. She was going to talk to him about the recital in June.

Oh, who was she kidding? She wanted to see him, just wanted to see him. He'd called once since their dinner, but she hadn't been home and he hadn't left a message. The only way she'd known he called was from the caller ID log.

She checked her watch again. Now he was four minutes late. All sorts of reasons began to race through her mind. He had changed his mind about the lessons. He had changed his mind about her. He had been in an accident. He was—

Knocking on the door.

She opened it and let him in. His hair and shoulders were damp. "It's raining," he said.

"And here I thought you were playing in the sprinklers."

He didn't take off his coat. He simply stood by the door in a terrible silence. A droplet of water clung to his hair over his forehead, and she watched, transfixed, as it broke loose and made its way down his forehead to the end of his nose, where it hung for a moment until he wiped it away.

"Take off your coat and stay awhile?" she said, her stomach churning. Nothing about this looked good. Not a bit.

He shook his head. "I—we—no, I, well. . ."

He wouldn't meet her eyes, and the turmoil inside her upgraded itself to a small storm.

"Joseph, is there something wrong? Do you want your lesson tonight?"

He seemed to have made up his mind about whatever was bothering him, because he took off his coat and hung it on the wooden peg by the door.

"Good. Now, are you ready to sing?" With an effort, she made her voice sound upbeat. "Let's start with a warm-up. We'll run through some scales, get the old vocal chords loosened up, and then you can show me what your voice is like now, what kind of range you have, and where you can go from here."

"Rosa," he interrupted, "I'll tell you all that. You don't need to—"

A shrill sound interrupted him.

"Mr. Montoya," Rosa said lightly, "your overcoat is ringing."

He hurried to the coatrack and pulled the cell phone out of his pocket. He jabbed at the tiny buttons. "I thought I turned this thing off before I came in." He shook the tiny phone. "There has to be some way to make it stop," he muttered, but it kept ringing. "Sorry, Rosa. It's new, and I haven't quite got it figured out yet. Maybe I should take this call," he said.

She nodded, her stomach rolling around somewhere down by her knees. She wanted to suggest that he let it ring, and the caller would soon hang up, but he seemed anxious to leave. Reasons why spun through her mind like the wind-tossed leaves outside her studio.

The phone continued to ring, and he spoke over the trill. "I'll see you at choir, and would you go out with me again this weekend?"

She nodded mutely as he left the studio, and her stomach resumed its rightful place.

Well, God, that's interesting. I have no idea what just happened, but I'm trusting that You're keeping track here.

She picked up the handout she'd intended to give him about the recital and laid it aside. She could give it to him at choir rehearsal, or she could wait and give it to him this weekend when they went out again.

First dates, she realized, were good but not as satisfying as second dates. As she prepared for the next student, she realized she was smiling like a schoolgirl.

She was smitten.

He leaned against the wall outside the studio and spoke into his tiny cell phone. The rain had paused, and the evening smelled washed clean. "Will, your timing is either horrible or impeccable."

"What'd I do?"

"I was in the studio with Rosa. I'd decided to tell her that I should never have signed up for lessons in the first place, that I can't sing, can't hum, can't even whistle."

"You could have turned your phone off."

"I know I should have."

"No, I said, you *could* have turned your phone off."

"Sure, I know that."

"Joseph, listen to me. You could have turned your phone off. You usually do. You didn't this time." Will spoke slowly and clearly. "Get it? You didn't turn your phone off."

"It's a new phone," Joseph protested. "That's why. I thought I had it turned off, but I guess I didn't."

"Was it? You're Mr. Precision. Your pencils are always sharp. You always park exactly in the middle of the space. Your ties are color-coded, and your shoes are lined up in precise order."

Joseph looked back at the studio's closed door. "I always turn my cell phone off."

"Yup. Face it, my friend, you're falling for this chick. I think pretty soon the Bachelor Club is going to have to rename itself."

"To what?"

"The Husband Club."

Chapter 7

Joseph snorted. "Aren't you jumping the gun just a bit, Will? Rosa is a terrific woman, but we've only gone out once."

"You had two lessons, remember."

"Not exactly." Joseph flushed a bit at the memory of both times when things didn't go at all as he'd planned.

"I thought tonight was your second lesson."

"It was, sort of. I didn't get very far with it."

"So when do you see her again?"

Joseph sighed. "Will, just because you and Charisma are happily hitched doesn't mean that we all have to pair up."

"Pal, I just want you to be as happy as I am." Will sounded sincere and just a bit worried.

"I am happy. I am. I really am."

But even as he said it, he wondered: Was he trying to reassure Will—or himself?

The choir members milled around, waiting for Mrs. Adams to

get started. Rosa stood by the table with the folders and straightened them for the seventh time. Where was Joseph?

Someone touched her elbow and she relaxed. He had come. When she turned around, the face she saw was not Joseph's but Trevor Melton's. His usual smirk was replaced by a petulant frown.

"I hear that Joseph Montoya is taking voice lessons from you. Is that true?"

If there was one person who could make her blood boil, it was Trevor Melton. She couldn't tolerate his self-satisfied manner.

Excuse me, God, she prayed silently. *I know that there is something special and glorious in each of Your creatures, and sometimes You want us to look hard to find it. I'm afraid, though, that I'm going to have to dig deeper than is comfortable for me with Trevor.*

She tried for what she hoped was a friendly smile. This was, after all, the church. As far as being pleasant, she could make the attempt. "Hi, Trevor."

"Well, is he?" he demanded.

She wanted to ask him what difference it made, but she couldn't figure out how to build the question. It didn't matter. Trevor launched into a diatribe. "You're wasting your time, you know. You can't teach him anything. We're talking about Joseph Montoya, after all. He's—"

Mrs. Adams, mercifully, chose that moment to tap on her music stand. "Places, people, places! We have a lot to cover tonight. Trevor, here's the tenor solo part. There's one part—"

She didn't hear the rest of what the choir director said. Her attention was drawn to a figure silhouetted in the doorway. It was Joseph. Had he heard what Trevor said? Part of her said he couldn't have missed it. Trevor's voice was, if not quite stable on the high notes, extremely carrying. But perhaps Joseph had just arrived and had missed it.

Mrs. Adams tapped again on the music stand. "People, people, please. We'll get through this much faster if you'll all take your seats."

Joseph entered the room and walked quietly to the table, picked up a folder, and took his seat with the other men. Trevor's haughty glance didn't seem to faze him. Instead, Joseph opened the folder and studied the sheet music that was tucked inside.

The little choir rehearsal room suddenly seemed too small and too hot. Rosa wanted, more than anything, just to flee the stifling atmosphere. It was like the oppressive heat before a major storm. Too quiet. Too still. Too terrible. Trevor had something on his mind.

"All right, everyone," Mrs. Adams announced from the front. "Let's get started. Now, sing out. Big voices!"

Rosa tried to listen for Joseph's voice as the choir boomed its way through the selection, but Trevor drowned out most of the men's voices. She'd never heard him sing so loudly.

She stole a peep at Joseph. He held his book up and sang along. She could see him singing, and she wasn't hearing anything horrible.

Then, suddenly, Trevor stopped. The other choir members, surprised, warbled unsurely for a few bars before stopping, too.

"Why, Trevor, whatever is the problem?" Mrs. Adams asked. "Are you all right?"

He looked cross, like a child who had missed his nap and was now cranky. "It's—oh, never mind."

Rosa studied him covertly as she sang along, her mind only partially on the music. What had he hoped to do by stopping suddenly? Apparently his plan hadn't worked out at all well, judging from the look on his face.

Could he have been. . . ? She stopped, unwilling to let her thoughts finish, but they did anyway. He was trying to trip Joseph up.

Whatever his intent, it hadn't worked, and Rosa couldn't resist a little smile of triumph.

As the rehearsal disbanded, she hurried out of the church, anxious to leave the tension behind. The moon was full, and the trees were touched with a light coating of frost. The air was cool but sharp with the scent of autumn. Somewhere someone was burning leaves, and the rich aroma bespoke of autumns past and autumns yet to come. How could anyone not believe in God when there were moments like this?

Almost immediately her stress evaporated. God was here. He was in charge. Whatever crazy stuff went on, He was watching, caring, loving.

"Rosa! Wait up!" Joseph ran to meet her. "I'll walk with you, if that's okay."

"I'd love your company, but I'm almost home. Actually, my house is right there. The orange adobe, remember?"

"I just wanted to ask you again about this weekend. The Grand Theater is having a Judy Garland festival. Are you in the mood for *Meet Me in St. Louis* on the big screen?"

"Oh, I'd love to go! The music in that film is wonderful!

What time, when, where, and all that?"

"Saturday, I'll pick you up at six forty-five so we can get good seats and a bucket of popcorn."

They stood for a moment, illuminated by the moonlight, before he said, "All right. I'll see you then."

He paused then moved toward her.

She couldn't breathe. Was he going to kiss her? Right here on Linden Avenue? But instead, he patted her arm a bit awkwardly and left.

And her heart sank.

Inside the darkened theater, Joseph tried to concentrate on the film, but it paled next to the woman sitting next to him. Over the smell of nearly seven decades of popcorn came the fresh, clean scent of Rosa's hair.

The seats were small, and their shoulders touched. When Judy Garland began to sing "Have Yourself a Merry Little Christmas," Rosa leaned against him and sniffled. Putting his arm around her was the most natural thing in the world, and she moved easily into the bow of his arm. He tightened his hold, and she relaxed, staying there until the final credits began to roll.

"I love this movie," she said as they stood up to leave.

"Me, too," he responded, although they might as well have been showing a Porky Pig cartoon, as much attention as he'd paid. All he could think of as they left was how beautiful she was, her long black curls disarranged a bit by his shy embrace.

Around them, other couples were chatting amiably as they left the theater, their arms often looped together in a friendly camaraderie. He sought words and came up with: "Wow, that was really good."

Joseph's fingers itched to get to his self-improvement notebook. *Boost conversational skills to a decent level.* He wished he could banter like the others in the theater did, easily and fluidly, but he couldn't. Snappy dialogue would come to him—about an hour later.

He needn't have worried. Rosa took over the conversational reins and talked about the movie's sound track, requiring only an occasional nod from him.

Their ramblings took them to the vicinity of Turquoise Alley, but she shook her head at his offer of a late-night mocha. "Let's walk down by Blue Creek," she suggested. "We can look for signs of winter."

He was about to point out that they couldn't see much at night, even with the filtered moonlight, but for once his heart overruled his brain. As they walked toward the stream, the buildings faded into the trees until they were completely surrounded by scrubby piñons and juniper.

Rosa stopped so suddenly that he almost ran right into her. "Shh." She held her finger up to her lips. "Can you hear it?"

"The creek?" he asked, but she shook her head.

"No. Listen. Do you hear it?"

He tried. He really tried, but he didn't make out a thing. "We're too far from town," he said practically, "not that Tierra Verde is ever very noisy. And the trees block out what little sound there is. Plus we're in a little dip—"

She touched his lips with her fingers. "Shh. Listen."

The faint burble of Blue Creek, the creak of a juniper in the light breeze, the rustle of fallen leaves—he heard them now.

"Silence," she said, "is rarely silent. Even in music, there's the anticipation of sound. You were listening for something so hard that you couldn't hear what was there."

His heart was no longer silent. He reached for her hand, and together they stood under the night sky, listening to nothing, hearing everything, and Joseph knew he was falling in love.

Chapter 8

*L*ife moves at a dizzying speed, Rosa thought as she woke up to a snow-covered Tierra Verde. When she had first moved to town, the last vestiges of summer were still touching the land with golden warmth. How things had changed.

How her heart had changed. She'd come to Tierra Verde with the plan to mend her broken heart, only to find out that it had never been broken. Her pride—well, that was another matter. Now, having spent many evenings with Joseph, she saw that she had never loved Andrew Russell—and it was just as well.

She left the frosty window and poured herself another cup of tea. Every cell in her body seemed to be smiling. She and Joseph had gone out weekly now for seven weeks. It wasn't exactly a lifetime but was enough for her to know that God had never intended for her to be with Andrew, that He was saving her for Joseph.

She looked at the Albuquerque paper again. From the engagements section, Andrew and a woman she didn't recognize flashed dentist-perfect smiles from a blurry photograph.

She didn't feel at all saddened. In fact, she felt nothing but joy and good wishes for them.

She had Joseph.

There was only one problem she couldn't quite resolve. His singing.

He'd had two lessons—the third one had been canceled when he'd gone out of town to a conference—and although he loyally came to choir every Wednesday night, she still hadn't heard him sing.

The Christmas concert was still several weeks away, but would he be ready in time for it? She'd counted, and he had only three more lessons between now and the concert.

Was that enough time?

That wasn't all, though. Every once in a while in choir, a sound—she couldn't really call it a note—emerged from the tenors' area. It was an odd sound, a cross between a goose's honk and a rusty well handle. At first she'd attributed it to the antique furnace below them. It certainly produced its share of unusual groans and squeaks. But now she had a growing suspicion that the noises were coming from her beloved Joseph's throat.

It would explain quite a bit: why the others in the choir were surprised when he began coming to rehearsals. . . Why they were even more astonished that he was taking singing lessons. . . Why Joseph had never sung for her, even in his lessons.

But if he couldn't sing, why would he sign up for lessons and then not sing? Was there any logic to this at all?

I'm giving this to You, Lord. I can't figure it out.

Joseph had to have a good reason for what he did. He was an honest man. She'd just bide her time, and he'd explain it all to her. She knew he would. But it sure would be nice if God would give him a little nudge. The Christmas concert was coming quickly.

Joseph glared at the cowlick, which refused to stay down. Maybe he should give in and get one of those punk hairstyles that stuck out all over his head in stiff spikes. Just his luck, though, the cowlick would decide to curl or do something else odd.

He had a lesson in—he glanced at his watch—twelve minutes. Twelve minutes until he saw Rosa again. Twelve minutes until he would stand close to her. Twelve minutes until he made a fool of himself.

The piece of paper on the kitchen table bore the evidence of his ruminations—a flow chart, complete with circles and arrows. He'd tried to figure out what was the emotionally safest way to proceed, only to realize that, in love, there was no emotionally safe way. It was all risky. And all worth it.

His eyes fell on the pottery cross on the wall in the hallway. *I'm beginning to understand,* he thought. *Love asks a lot of us, doesn't it, God? It sure asked a lot of You.*

And yet You gave and gave and gave, and You continue to give.

It was time Joseph faced up to love.

With renewed resolve, he pulled a knitted cap over the wayward cowlick, buttoned up his overcoat, tugged on his gloves, and headed out the door.

The snow, which had been falling all day, was getting increasingly heavier, and by the time he reached Rosa's studio, his dark coat was frosted with white.

"Aah, my own snowman!" Rosa greeted him as he came in. "And here I'd thought that Frosty coming to life was just a holiday story."

Her long hair was caught up in some kind of a bun, but bits of it had escaped and curled down her neck. She wore an oversized blue sweater that engulfed her. On her feet were the most amazing slippers he'd ever seen. They were huge and furry. Bear paws.

He smiled. He got it. Bear feet. Bare feet.

"Like my slippers?" she asked, sticking one out in front of her and almost losing her balance. "I brought them with me since the heel came off my boot and I had to wear my sneakers here and—"

She continued to talk animatedly about her shoe mishaps, but he couldn't focus. This woman, her pencil shoved, apparently forgotten, in that straggling bun, was the most beautiful creature he'd ever seen.

He reined in his thoughts sternly. First, he had to take care of the matter of the lessons. "Rosa, I need to say something." He took a deep breath. "About my lessons."

"And I need to talk to you, too," she said.

"Me first." He took her hand and led her to the small love seat in front of the fireplace. "Let's sit. Rosa, I can't—"

"Sing. I know you can't."

"You do? How?"

"I've wondered. I've listened." She squeezed his hand. "And it's all right."

"No, it isn't." He swallowed. *Guide my words, dear Lord.* "I wasn't honest with you. I didn't take lessons to learn to sing. I know you're a Christian, but anyone trying to teach me to sing would need truckloads of prayer and a few miracles airlifted in."

Her eyes glimmered with concern. "Why did you take lessons, then?"

He pulled out his notebook and opened it, showing her page after page of tiny, precise lettering. "This is my self-improvement project," he said. He turned to an early entry. "Look: *Impulsive action.* I wrote that one the day I met you, when I signed up for lessons."

"But I don't really understand why you did that."

He pointed to the next two entries. *Quick anger. General crabbiness.*

"You?" She frowned. "You? I don't think so, Joseph. Why, you're just about the nicest guy—no, you *are* the nicest guy I've ever met."

"I did it because I lost my heart—and apparently, my mind—to you that day. Rosa, I can't sing, but I can love. I can love you for the rest of my life."

She nodded, tears spilling down her cheeks. "I love you, Joseph Montoya. I love you."

The church was draped with greenery, and below them the furnace clanked in its own rhythm.

The Christmas recital was under way. Joseph stood at the back of the church, the stack of printed programs nearly depleted. He clapped enthusiastically as child after child sang carols and hymns; and at the end of the recital, when Rosa went to the front of the church, he beamed happily.

The children swarmed about her, and she smiled at him over their heads.

As soon as the last singer left, happily sated with the cookies she'd provided in the meeting room, they stood in the empty church.

"It's been quite a day," she said.

"It sure has." His fingers sought and found a small box in his pocket. "Walk you home?"

The late afternoon sun filtered through the bare trees. A few random flakes floated downward, remnants of the snow that had fallen while they'd been in the church.

They walked together, hand in hand, their steps in rhythm with each other. Neither of them spoke, and Joseph was reluctant to do anything that would interrupt the afterglow of the concert.

Finally, they paused as they neared Turquoise Alley. "Want to pop in for a spiced cider?" he asked, and he breathed a sigh of relief when she shook her head.

"Let's just walk for a while. Look behind us, Joseph. See our footprints?"

The two sets of footsteps were marked in the snow, one large, one small.

"It's like we're the only ones here," she said, her face turned up to his. "Just you and me."

Oh, how he loved her.

They turned to the spot by Blue Creek where they had gone after the movie. The sidewalk ended, and they traipsed across the snow-covered grass to the spot where they'd been before. The setting sun cast blue shadows across the glittering boulders, and the piñons and junipers were dressed in their snowy best.

He'd chosen to propose here because this was the spot where Rosa had told him about hearing and listening. Now he listened to his heart, and he heard what it was telling him.

Rosa stood, her hands stuck in the pockets of her coat, and smiled at him. "The snow looks like it's wearing diamonds."

Now was the time. *Dearest Lord, give me the words.*

He'd had this all planned out, although this time he'd passed on making a flow chart and instead had written the words in his mind, and he'd gone over them again and again until they were perfect.

The only hitch was the pockets. He needed her hand. His script hadn't included her putting her hands in her pockets.

He held out his own hand, and she automatically put hers on it.

Another hitch—she was wearing mittens and he was wearing gloves. There was nothing to do but abandon his Grand Plan and wing it.

"Rosa," he said, their mittened and gloved hands together, "I love you. I don't know what else to say but that. I love you. I want to spend my life with you. Will you marry me?"

"Yes, yes, oh yes!" They embraced, and as they did so, a package nudged his hip. The ring!

He pulled out the small box and opened it. "Do you like it?"

"Oh, Joseph, it's beautiful!"

His gloved fingers were clumsy with the tiny box, and he could imagine the delicate ring slipping from his grip and falling into the snow. He pulled his gloves off with his teeth—this was not going at all the way he'd planned—and took the ring out of the jeweler's box.

Rosa took off her mitten and stuffed it in her pocket. As he put the ring on her slender finger, he felt something warm fall on his hand. It was a tear. She was crying. And smiling. And laughing.

"The snow has diamonds to wear," she said softly, "and now I do, too."

One year later

Joseph stood in the tiny room beside the sanctuary, his self-improvement notebook open in his hands. He ran his fingers over the words he'd written the day he met Rosa. Even today, on his wedding day, he knew they summed up everything he'd ever needed to know. He closed his eyes and silently, wordlessly, thanked God for bringing Rosa into his life.

"It's time!" Isaac poked his head in the doorway. "Let's get this wedding on the road! Or on the aisle—down the aisle. Let's get you hitched!"

Joseph looked at the words one last time, and as he put the small book back into his pocket, he saw her through the open door. She was standing at the back of the church, and in her white dress and veil, she looked as if she'd stepped right out of a dream—a dream he'd always had.

Meet someone. Fall in love. Get married. Have babies. Live happily ever after.

JANET SPAETH

For as long as she can remember, Janet Spaeth has loved to read, and romances were always a favorite. Today she is delighted to be able to write romances based upon the greatest Love Story of all, that of our Lord for us.

When she isn't writing, Janet spends her time reading a romance or a cozy mystery, baking chocolate chip cookies, or spending precious hours with her family.

Candy Cane Calaboose, **Heartsong Presents**
Angel's Roost, **Heartsong Presents**
Rose Kelly, **Heartsong Presents,** coming in November 2005
Novellas: "Only Believe" in *Harvest Home*, "Christmas Cake" in *Christmas Threads*, "Marry for Love" in *Scraps of Love*, "This Prairie" in *Attic Treasures*, and "Joyful Noise" in *Bachelors Club*—all Barbour anthologies.

Epilogue

by Janet Spaeth

Epilogue

Forks clinked against water glasses in an increasing demand until the din was almost unbearable. She knew what they wanted. Rosa leaned closer to her new husband for another kiss. She didn't mind. This was a day made for kisses.

She couldn't stop smiling. This was truly the happiest day of her life, and judging from the expression on Joseph's face, she knew he shared her joy. *Thank You*, she prayed silently. *Thank You*.

"Mrs. Montoya?"

At first the words didn't register, and then she realized, *That's me! I'm Mrs. Montoya!*

Ella beamed at her. "Yup, kiddo, that's you. So what do you think of the new Mrs. Montoya, Joseph?"

"Tap on that glass again and I'll show you." He threw his arms around Rosa and kissed her soundly. "There!"

"I'm going to walk through life with a goblet and a fork," Rosa teased when the dramatic kiss ended. "Whenever I want a kiss from my husband, I'll know what to do."

"You want a kiss, all you have to do is ask," Joseph said.

"I hope! Hey, Ella, are you having a good time?"

"Actually, yes, I am. Now that everybody's been served, I can kick back a bit and enjoy the rest of the reception."

"The tamales were wonderful," Rosa said. "You did a super job with them."

Ella winked. "You really think Abuelita let me make them? I got kicked out of my own kitchen. Nobody, she informed me, was going to make the tamales at her granddaughter's wedding except for her. Each and every one of them was made by her teeny-tiny hands."

"I have to talk to her before I leave and tell her thanks." Rosa glanced around. "I don't see her. Where is she?"

Ella motioned with her head toward the far corner. There, in a pink-and-yellow-striped chair, slept Abuelita.

The reception had been wonderful. Joseph's parents had flown in from California, and his mother was positively glowing with happiness as she chatted with Rosa's mother. At a side table, their fathers were deep in conversation, probably talking about the Lobos' chances this football season. Both fathers were great fans of the University of New Mexico's football team. It was clear that the families, even the in-laws, were going to get along famously.

"You staying warm enough?" The question came from Willard, who was almost unrecognizable in his wedding best. Rosa was used to seeing him in his ever-present overalls, and she almost expected to see a wrench peeking out of the pocket of his suit.

"It's perfect in here," she said. He was such a dear. "Now, go on and enjoy the reception!"

She smiled as he walked away, his rolling gait a visible sign of years of toil. He'd really saved the day.

The church's furnace, which had been functioning sporadically the past couple of winters, had decided to quit entirely the night before. Willard had come to the rescue. Just two hours before the wedding, she'd been shivering in the little anteroom where the last-minute preparations were going on, and she'd heard him downstairs, coaxing the furnace into operation, explaining that this was "his Joseph's" wedding day. At the very last minute, the furnace roared into operation, and the church was comfortably heated by the time the wedding started.

Will came over to the table. "Can you two meet us downstairs after this shindig?"

"Sure," Joseph said. "What's up?"

"Last meeting of the Bachelor Club." Will grinned at Rosa. "Spouses are invited to this one."

"Not to hurry you along or anything," Ella continued, "but it's getting to be time to fling that bouquet at the single women here. Aim carefully, okay?"

"You got someone in mind?" Rosa asked innocently as she stood up.

"Well, let's say you have a best friend who just happens to be single."

Rosa touched Joseph's arm. "I'll be back in a minute. I need to throw something at Ella."

True to her word, she lobbed the bouquet straight at her friend, who caught it easily. "There," she said afterward as Ella returned the bouquet to her, "you're next to get married. The flowers don't lie. Now you just have to find a fellow."

To her amazement, Ella blushed. "Maybe I have."

Rosa watched in absolute astonishment as Ella crossed the room and sat down next to Tyrone Melton. Ella blinked rapidly, and Rosa thought she must have had something in her eye. And then, when Tyrone's hand stole across to cover Ella's, Rosa realized with shock that Ella was flirting with him!

Can I have your attention, please?" Isaac stood on his chair. "We have some business to conduct here. Willard, could you do the honors?"

Willard joined him. Behind him, the antique furnace clanked noisily. Rosa suppressed a smile at the amount of duct tape wrapped around the bottom of it. "Excuse me if I don't stand on the chair," he said, and the others laughed softly. "Okay, let's see, first, thanks everyone for coming. Abuelita, Mr. and Mrs. Cruz, and Mr. and Mrs. Montoya, we're glad to have you here to witness this. Ella, come on in. You're welcome, too. Now, can I have Adam and Amy, Will and Charisma, and Isaac and Brooke join me?"

He waited a moment for them to assemble, and the group stood facing the newlyweds, each one solemnly holding a paper bag. "Joseph, it is our sincere pleasure to kick you out of the Bachelor Club!"

On cue, the other members and their wives reached into their bags and threw handfuls of confetti at Joseph and Rosa.

"And now, there's the little matter of some accumulated allowances here. By the way," Willard added as he faced Joseph's and Rosa's parents, "I don't want you to think that this was a gambling proposition. It never was. The original agreement was that the money the boys put into the Bachelor Club would be held until the last bachelor turned thirty, right, boys?"

"Yes, sir," the four men chorused.

"Old Ben Franklin said, 'A penny saved is a penny earned.'" Willard reached into his pocket and pulled out a slim black ledger. "I've been saving your pennies since you were all little tykes, and those coins have been in the safe hands of Tierra Verde Bank and Trust, quietly collecting interest for all these years." He opened the book and whistled. "And quite a pretty little sum it is."

"So who gets it?" Adam asked. "Joseph, because he held out the longest?" Amy elbowed him teasingly in the ribs, and he pretended to wince.

Willard shook his head. "Nope. Your agreement didn't allow for the possibility that none of you would *hold out* that long," he said, winking at the now-defunct Bachelor Club. "So as the unofficial Bachelor Club treasurer, I decided a long time ago that the money was to be equally split four ways when the last bachelor turned thirty *or* when the last Bachelor Club member married. It says so right here on the document from the bank." He showed them a yellowed document that was tucked inside the ledger. "As of today you each are entitled to a twenty-five percent share of the account." He handed the ledger to Joseph. "Now it's yours. All of yours."

The four men looked at each other with a mixture of surprise and confusion.

"Emergency meeting of the Bachelor Club charter members

in the corner!" Isaac announced.

The group conferred quickly with loud whispers in the corner and then returned. "Uncle Willard, you've always been there for us," Adam said. "And we can never pay you back for all you've done."

"But we want to do this for you. Please take this as a symbol of our love for you," Joseph continued, placing the ledger back into Willard's hand.

"Spend it however you like," Isaac said. "It's yours."

"Thanks, Dad." Will choked up as he spoke.

Willard sank into a chair. "I can't believe this. I can't believe this. The Lord is so good." A lone tear started down his face, and he wiped it away with his gnarled hand. "But I can't take it. I have all I need."

"Isn't there some special tool you'd like?" Adam asked. "Maybe some battery-powered hammer?"

Willard shook his head. "Even if there were such a thing, you goof, I'm more an arm-powered hammerer."

"A new car would be nice," Will said.

"The old truck gets me places just fine."

"A new wardrobe?" Ella spoke from the corner, where she was leaning on Tyrone's arm.

Willard grinned. "Something wrong with my overalls?"

"How about a nice long vacation in Hawaii, away from pesky furnaces?" Brooke suggested.

Willard studied the ledger. "No, not even that. Why would I ever want to leave Tierra Verde? It's like God dropped a little piece of heaven onto earth and let me live here. He has been so good to me."

Behind them, the recalcitrant furnace heaved one more time and clanked its last.

"Just in time," Isaac joked. "It stayed working just long enough to get you two married, and now it's done."

"That's it!" Willard snapped his fingers. "That's it! Boys, if it's all right with you, I'm going to put this money toward a new furnace for the church."

"Are you sure?" Amy touched his arm, her lovely face concerned. "This money is for you."

"I'm sure," he declared as he put the ledger back into his pocket. "If I do the work myself, we can get this church heated up nicely by next Sunday."

"Dad," Will began, but Willard interrupted him.

"Do you all realize that I'm being selfish here? For the past two winters, I've missed the first half of church when it gets cold, since I've had to be down here, tinkering with this monster." He lightly kicked the furnace. "Plus, when I think of how many pairs of my good pants have holes in them from kneeling in front of this thing while trying to make it work—well, I'd rather be wearing them out by being on my knees in prayer."

Abuelita chuckled. "And the Bachelor Club comes to a glorious end. Amen!"

Rosa and Joseph got into the waiting limousine, ready to head off for their honeymoon in Taos. She snuggled in the welcoming crook of Joseph's arm as he murmured, "Mrs. Montoya, I love you."

"Can I have another kiss?" she asked, lifting her lips.

"Haven't you had enough kissing for one day?" he teased.

"Nope. Kiss me again."

And he obliged.

A Letter to Our Readers

Dear Readers:

In order that we might better contribute to your reading enjoyment, we would appreciate your taking a few minutes to respond to the following questions. When completed, please return to the following: Fiction Editor, Barbour Publishing, Inc., P.O. Box 719, Uhrichsville, OH 44683.

1. Did you enjoy reading *The Bachelor Club*?
   ❏ Very much—I would like to see more books like this.
   ❏ Moderately—I would have enjoyed it more if _____
   _____
   _____

2. What influenced your decision to purchase this book?
   (Check those that apply.)
   ❏ Cover   ❏ Back cover copy   ❏ Title   ❏ Price
   ❏ Friends   ❏ Publicity   ❏ Other

3. Which story was your favorite?
   ❏ *The Rescue*   ❏ *Right for Each Other*
   ❏ *Stealing Home*   ❏ *Joyful Noise*

4. Please check your age range:
   ❏ Under 18   ❏ 18–24   ❏ 25–34
   ❏ 35–45   ❏ 46–55   ❏ Over 55

5. How many hours per week do you read? _____

Name _____

Occupation _____

Address _____

City _____ State _____ Zip _____

E-mail _____

HEARTSONG
PRESENTS

If you love Christian romance...

$10.⁹⁹

You'll love Heartsong Presents'
inspiring and faith-filled romances by
today's very best Christian authors...DiAnn
Mills, Wanda E. Brunstetter, Yvonne Lehman, to
mention a few!

When you join Heartsong Presents, you'll enjoy
4 brand-new mass market, 176–page books – two
contemporary and two historical – that will build you up in
your faith when you discover God's role in every relationship
you read about!

Mass Market 176 Pages

Imagine...four new romances every
four weeks – with men and women like you
who long to meet the one God has chosen
as the love of their lives...all for the low
price of $10.99 postpaid.

To join, simply visit www.heartsong
presents.com or complete the coupon
below and mail it to the address provided.

- -

YES! Sign me up for Heartsong!

NEW MEMBERSHIPS WILL BE SHIPPED IMMEDIATELY!
Send no money now. We'll bill you only $10.99 post-
paid with your first shipment of four books. Or for faster
action, call 1-740-922-7280.

NAME _____

ADDRESS _____

CITY _____ STATE_____ ZIP_____

MAIL TO: HEARTSONG PRESENTS, P.O. Box 721, Uhrichsville, Ohio 44683
or sign–up at **WWW.HEARTSONGPRESENTS.COM**

ADPG05